If Only

CAROLE GEITHNER

SCHOLASTIC PRESS / NEW YORK

Copyright © 2012 by Carole Geithner

Library of Congress Cataloging-in-Publication Data
Geithner, Carole.
If only / Carole Geithner. — 1st ed.
p. cm.
Summary: From the beginning of eighth grade to the start of ninth, Maryland thirteen-year-old Corinna grieves for her mother, who died of cancer, and struggles to cope with changes to all aspects of her life brought on by her loss.
[1. Grief — Fiction. 2. Interpersonal relations — Fiction. 3. Middle schools — Fiction. 4. Schools — Fiction. 5. Bethesda (Md.) — Fiction.] I. Title.
PZ7.G274If 2011
[Fic] — dc22   2010026527

ISBN 978-0-545-23499-3

10 9 8 7 6 5 4 3 2 1   12 13 14 15 16

Printed in the U.S.A. 23
First edition, March 2012

The text was set in Janson Text. Book design by Kristina Iulo
Permission has been obtained for use of "Transformation" by Molly Fumia in IF ONLY
by Carole Geithner

Credit line: Excerpted from the book SAFE PASSAGES by Molly Fumia. Copyright © 1992, 2003 by Molly Fumia, with permission form Red Wheel/Weiser, LLC.

www.redwheelweiser.com, 1-800-423-7087.

For Tim, love of my life,

Elise and Ben, my joys,

and in memory of Portia

Contents

Fall

Winter

Colors of Me

If seasons were tubes of paint, last fall would have been deep, dark black. Winter was also dark, but more like a foggy gray with lots of huge black blobs mixed in. Spring had some blue, but blue comes in lots of shades, from almost blackish blue to bright sky blue. And then there was summer. Summer had more colors than the other seasons, with hints of purples, but like one of my many soccer bruises, it could look pretty hideous with its swirling blend of black, blues, and tinges of sickly yellow. Grief is hard. Really hard. And you can't put the cap back on when you want to, like you can with a tube of paint.

A Gift

"I brought you something you can use when you're feeling like you . . . might . . . explode."

My mom's best friend, Deborah Rollins, passes me a rectangular package wrapped in bug paper. It's covered with crawling ants. What a weird way to express support. *"Here, have some bugs. I hope they make your skin crawl."*

"Oh . . . thanks," I stammer, as we stand at the front door of my house on what has to be the hottest day in August.

"Go ahead. Open it," Deborah says a little too cheerfully. Her eyes and mouth are smiling, but her body is stiff, like she really doesn't want to be here. My body is stiff, too, like one of those cardboard dolls little girls dress in paper clothes. I wasn't expecting her visit, and I don't know if I am supposed to invite her in. I don't really want to.

I slowly open the paper, feeling a bit like I need to protect the delicate paper ants.

"It's . . . cute," I force myself to say.

Deborah's gift is a pink furry book. I flip it open and see white. Blank white pages.

"It's for writing. Writing your feelings and, well, you know, things like that," Deborah explains.

"You mean like a journal?"

"Exactly. I think journals and diaries are great, don't you? Remember how Anne Frank wrote in a diary during the Holocaust?"

"Yeah. We read that in seventh grade."

"She was about your age," Deborah points out.

"I know."

Deborah wipes the sweat on her forehead, then asks me, "Well, don't you think it helped her deal with a bad situation?"

"Anne Frank didn't survive."

"Yes, but . . . but your situation's different, Corinna. *You're* going to survive."

My throat gets really tight after she says this, and my brain tells me: *Get out of here right now.*

"Thanks," I manage to squeeze through the narrow opening in my airway. I don't even bother to say good-bye. I turn away from the front door, walk up the stairs, and escape into the safety of my room, leaving Deborah standing there. Maki, my dog, follows me. I slam my bedroom door shut before tossing the journal on the floor and throwing myself down on my bed. What was Deborah thinking, giving me a totally tacky fake-fur journal? She must not know anything about what teenagers like. I seriously hope she doesn't follow me up here.

School is starting in two days. How am I going to make it through a whole day of school, much less a week or a year?

I wait until I hear the front door click shut and then decide to go for a bike ride on the Crescent Trail. It's so hot that Maki is panting even in the air-conditioning, so I let him stay home. The boiling August heat isn't going to stop me, though.

The wind blowing on my sweaty face feels good as I pedal hard and fast on my blue mountain bike, the one I got for my last birthday. I practically wipe out on the speed bumps just before the bike path, that's how much of a hurry I'm in. I want to be a *normal* biker going to downtown Bethesda. A *normal* girl.

"Watch out!" a lady yells. She's pushing a baby stroller.

Then I almost hit a Rollerblader.

My legs are exhausted and my entire body is dripping with sweat as I enter the refrigerator-cold of the gigantic bookstore on Bethesda Avenue. At first, I just catch my breath and enjoy the air-conditioning. Then I make my way to the back of the store, where they keep the racks of books and journals. I take my time as I look, but I always return to a brown suede one on the top shelf. When I hold it in my hands, it feels soft, almost like skin. Well, I guess it *is* skin, from a *cow*. Brown suede is much better for a teenager. Does Deborah really think of me as a little girl who loves pink fur just because I'm not exactly big on top?

On my hot and sweaty ride home, I decide to name my new suede journal, like Anne Frank did. Anne called hers Kitty. I choose Suki for mine because it sounds Japanese and kind of sophisticated. I want to tell someone about Suki, someone other than Deborah. I wouldn't want her to know her stupid gift has given me the idea to keep a journal. Before I go inside the house, I flip open my phone, press *Contacts*, *Mom*, and then *Send*.

"Hello, this is Sophie Burdette, musician and teacher. Please leave me a message, including your phone number, even if you think I already have it. I'll return your call as soon as my hands are free."

All I can say is, "*Mom . . .*" I close the phone and close my eyes.

Fall

Frozen

"Bye, honey. Have a great day," a mom says, hugging her daughter in the Westhaven Middle School parking lot. POW. It's the first morning of eighth grade, and I feel like someone just socked me in the stomach. Maybe it's more of a stab. Whatever it is, it hurts.

Then the woman gets back in her car, and the girl turns and walks into school with a nervous sixth-grader smile and an armful of colorful binders.

That's when I freeze. How can I continue to put one foot in front of the other when I can barely breathe? How can I smile and talk to everyone like I'm the old me, like nothing has changed?

My dread about meeting my teachers definitely doesn't help. I have a feeling at least one of them will say something annoying or do something that will catch me off guard and make me burst into tears in front of everyone. They might even try the old "complimenting my outfit to try to cheer me up" technique that my nursery school teacher used when I didn't want to let go of my mom's hand on the first day of school. I look at what I threw on this morning: a plain old white T-shirt and jean skirt. We always used to buy a few outfits before school started, but not this year.

The teachers are really the least of my worries. Everyone — worst of all, my friends — has pretty much avoided me all summer. But now they won't be able to. And everyone else . . . Well, I figure if they don't already know my "news," as soon as they find out, I'm going to be the class freak. Or the class pity project.

One girl I know from band walks by, chomping on a big wad of gum. She pushes her gum to the side long enough to say, "Hey, Corinna! Long time no see! How was your summer?"

"Um . . ."

"Not so great, huh? That stinks. Well, see ya."

BAM.

The first day of school used to be filled with the fun of seeing all of my friends after summer vacation, the thrill of carrying fresh school supplies neatly labeled with Dad's Xpress Pro label maker, and the nervous excitement about having new teachers (and hoping they would be good and not boring). But today is totally different. My head and body feel like they are moving through thick cement. I don't really want to talk to my friends or listen to new teachers. I couldn't care less about the color of my notebooks (which are not labeled this year).

I find my new locker in the yellow hallway. It's a miracle that I remembered to bring the piece of paper with my combination.

I twirl the dial clockwise a few times, the way you're supposed to, and then start in on the numbers. I think I'm being careful, but it isn't working. No clicks, no release.

"Hey, Corinna. Forget how to open a locker over the summer? Maybe you should go back to seventh grade."

A bunch of boys next to me burst into laughter. My neck and face start to sweat. When I look up, I see it's stuck-up Dylan and his immature friends, just what I need when I'm already feeling plenty pathetic.

I fumble with the locker, hoping they will get bored and leave. More kids start filling the hall. Everyone else's lockers seem to be opening just fine. Maybe I should ask for a different locker . . . in Siberia.

"Hey, Corinna," someone says a few lockers down on my left.

I pretend I haven't heard. I hope that whoever it is goes away soon.

Just when I think I'm in the clear, I see Olivia rounding the corner. I dodge around a bunch of sixth graders, but Olivia's big head comes at me anyway.

"Corinna! Love that jean skirt, girlie!"

I stare at her, probably looking like a zombie.

"So, Corinna, are you still playing on the rec soccer team or did you switch to travel?"

I can see in her face that she has a lot of questions she's getting ready to ask, and there are too many people around us.

"Uh, yeah. Rec," I manage to squeak. I want to escape Olivia before she can ask me anything else, so I say, "Ciao," like we've been doing for years, only it doesn't sound right this time.

Walking down the familiar hallways, I feel strangely alone. Alone even though there are tons of kids everywhere. Alone even though some of them are my friends. There's not enough air, and my stomach really hurts, especially on the left side right below my belly button.

I feel a tap on my shoulder, and when I turn around, it's our class "Queen Bee," Beth, wearing her perfectly matching purse, clothes, and shoes. The whole outfit. Matching. As always.

"I know we haven't talked in a long time, but I wonder if maybe you'd like to have lunch together at my family's club."

"Umm, uh. Maybe."

"They have the best Caesar salads. The dressing is delish and they never force you to eat anchovies. Aren't anchovies the grossest? Gag me. Anyway, I just know you'll love it."

I didn't think Beth even knew I existed, so her *lovely* invitation to her *lovely* club is a bit confusing. Or maybe it isn't. Maybe her invitation is proof that I'm a charity case. Her mother probably told her to invite me.

I can feel everyone's eyes on us.

"Okay, well . . . see ya," I say, wishing I could call my dad and tell him to come get me. My stomach gives another tug, and I realize what I'm most dreading today. Jocelyn.

Joci is supposed to be my best friend, but we haven't actually talked in what feels like forever. It doesn't seem possible that just six months ago we could almost read each other's minds, whether it was about boys, friends, teachers, boob development (my lack of), our favorite bubble bath, whatever. We used to text each other a gazillion times a day about everything. We practically lived at each other's houses. She sent me a card a few weeks ago but, basically, she's been MIA for months.

It's fourth period, and so far, Joci hasn't been in any of my classes. My English teacher, Miss B. B. Beatty (everyone calls her Miss Boppity Bop), comes up to me as soon as I sit at a desk in the back, next to the window.

"Corinna, I'm so sorry to hear about your mom," she whispers.

I don't hear anything she says after that. I have to block my ears and brain or I might lose it right here in front of everyone. I tell myself, "I must not cry at school or I might not be able to stop. *I must not cry at school.*" I wonder if all my teachers know, and if they do, why Miss Boppity Bop is the first to say anything to me.

The one good thing about this class so far is that Miss Boppity Bop doesn't make us stand up in front and talk about what we did over summer vacation. I've had to do that practically every year since kindergarten. What would I say? "My vacation sucked. My mom died. The end."

"Class, I'd like you to write five paragraphs about the highlight of your summer. It's due on Thursday. Make it interesting, and show me your best writing, so I know what writing skills we need to focus on this year."

The highlight of my summer? Is she kidding? At least we don't have to write it in class. Miss Boppity Bop casually says that she'll be looking for volunteers to share their highlights with the class. I don't want to turn mine in, much less read it out loud.

I rush out of English as soon as the bell rings and stop at my locker to get my lunch. Not that I'm hungry. I still haven't seen Joci, and I begin to wonder if she's absent, and if she isn't, why she hasn't bothered to find me yet.

When I walk into the noisy cafeteria, I look over at our usual spot and see Joci sitting with Olivia, Juliette, and Eliana. She sees me and waves me over. I don't know if Joci is going to talk to me about anything that's happened recently or just pretend like everything is the same as always. I have no idea what am I going to say to her, either.

"Hey, Corinna," Joci says cheerfully. "How ya doin'?"

"Hi, Joss. Hi guys."

"Hey, Corinna," Eliana chimes in. "So . . . what'd you bring for lunch?" Eliana asks with a big smile.

"Nothing much," I say, sounding pathetic.

"Did you make your own lunch today?" Eliana is still smiling as she asks this, as if she is my personal cheerleader or nursery school teacher.

How do I answer that? I look over at Joci to see if she gets how awkward this is. I'm not sure, but she looks like she's as scared as I am about how this is going to go.

Joci turns to me and says, "I can't believe we haven't had any classes together yet."

"Yeah." I nod in agreement. "Who do you have for math and social studies?"

"Mr. Spinolli and Mrs. Giamatti; what about you?"

"Me, too," I say flatly.

"Have you heard anything about them?" She's leaning in, like she wants to hear some good gossip.

"No, have you?" I sound bored.

"I heard they're the two hardest teachers in the entire school."

"Great, that's just what I need," I reply, pulling apart my sandwich as I slump even more.

"You'll be okay, Corinna. I'm sure you'll be okay," Joci says to reassure me.

"Well, I'm not so sure." I finally take a bite of my sandwich and can barely swallow it.

Out on the blacktop after lunch, there are more traps waiting. I can hear kids whispering about me.

"Can you believe it?"

"I would die if that happened to me."

As I walk by a group of girls, they go all silent. Talk about obvious. I am tempted to go to the nurse's office and ask her about my stomachaches. Maybe I could go home sick. Who would pick me up, though? Dad's at the high school, teaching.

It feels like I'm on a separate planet from everyone else. The kids at school are on Planet Normal, the planet I *used* to belong to. *Their* lives are going on as if nothing had happened. And then there's me. I'm on Planet Doom and Gloom. I don't know if I'll ever get back to Planet Normal. I was right to have been worried about school. I am obviously the unofficial and unmistakable class freakazoid. You'd think no one had ever encountered death in all of history.

Somehow, I make it through the day. Dad and I are both exhausted and eat canned chili for dinner in silence. While I'm cutting up an apple and an orange for us to share, I try to think of something to say to Dad.

"Dad, how were your classes?"

He reaches for a slice of apple.

"Fine, I guess. Not enough desks for all the students, though."

"Well, *my* first day was *totally* awkward."

Dad sits back in his chair. "I'm sorry to hear that." He sighs.

This whole day has been so *blah*, including dinner, and I'm ready for it to end.

"I'm tired. I think I'm going to go to bed early."

"Good idea. Me, too," Dad says, with zero energy. "Let's just put our dishes in the sink."

I don't go right to bed, though. Instead, I sit down at my desk to write the assignment. After about fifty sheets of paper, three boxes of Kleenex, and a supplemental roll of toilet paper when I can't find any more Kleenex for tear and snot absorption, this is what I write:

The Day That Led to the Longest and Worst Summer of My Life

My summer began last spring, on April first, right here in Bethesda, Maryland. April Fools' Day should be a day of rubber puke blobs on your desk or a whoopee cushion on your chair. But this April Fools' Day was different. My mother had surgery on that day to "make sure nothing was going on inside." My dad picked me up from school and took me to the hospital to see her. My dad never cries, but on that day, he started sobbing in the car after he told me that the doctor thought Mom had cancer that had spread to lots of parts of her body and that she probably had "three to six months to live, but it's hard to really know for sure." I went numb. Numb inside and numb outside. All I could hear or think was, "three to six months,

17

three to six months." Over and over, that's what my brain saw and heard, like those news tickers at the bottom of the TV screen that make it impossible to see anything else. We went in to see my mom, in the green hospital room with the ugly speckled linoleum floor. It sounds mean to say, but she looked like an alien, with tubes going in and out and every which way. It was really hard to look at her. I felt kind of nauseous, actually. She cried when she saw me. Two parents crying in one day. That had never happened before. Well, that's pretty much all I remember from that visit and that awful day. I didn't sleep much that night. Life as I had known it was over. My mom, Sophie Burdette, had a death sentence, but she hadn't committed a crime.

That's as far as I get. I can't answer the assignment question. There *was* no summer highlight. But I will have to turn in my essay anyway, and Miss Beatty will have to read it.

After all that writing, I take a long bath in my Blue Oasis bubble bath and listen to music quietly, in case Dad is already asleep. My usual choices in girlie music don't feel very relaxing or fun anymore, but the Blue Oasis is pretty good at getting the lump in my throat to melt. Mom used to take baths to help her relax, too, until she was too tired even for a bath.

"How many lotions and potions can a thirteen-year-old girl use?" my mom had asked after the last guest left my karaoke birthday party.

"Tons, Mom. Don't worry."

"I'm not worried, I'm shocked!"

That was the last party that took place during my old life, the one before my mom got sick and died. The one before my dad turned into a sad, sad man.

Pep Talks

I've had a lot of trouble sleeping lately, including tonight. Even though I'm exhausted, I just can't fall asleep. I keep reviewing all the things from my first day at school, and I can't shut off my brain, even after writing in my journal. Everyone at school was buzzing with energy. They had happy things to talk about.

Another reason I can't sleep is that it's raining really hard and loud. Sometimes it sounds like footsteps walking, then running for a long time, then walking again. Some people say that the heavens are crying when it rains. I guess they're really crying tonight, crying with me.

When I arrive at school for day two, I head straight to my locker and manage to get it open on the first try. Dylan and his posse start clapping. I try to ignore them while I stuff my backpack and flute inside and slam the door shut. Joci calls to me from down the hall.

"What's up?" I say, hesitantly turning to face her.

"Corinna, you didn't answer your phone last night." She sounds all huffy.

"I was tired."

"There's so much to talk about! We have to have a major catch-up session ASAP."

She's so enthusiastic and energetic, I feel like a slug in comparison.

"Yeah, I guess."

"But . . . we always compare notes on who's in what class and all the teacher gossip after our first day."

"We're going to be late," I interrupt.

"You're my best friend, Corinna," she says just outside her classroom. "Best friends share everything!"

During my first three classes, I can't stop thinking about Joci. I miss most of what is being said. But in Miss Beatty's class, I'm totally focused. She's just asked for volunteers to read the "highlights of our summer" assignments.

Only four super-perky kids read their summer vacation essays to the class.

"I went to sleepaway camp in Canada and saw five rainbows. . . ."

"My family and I spent the summer on Fire Island. . . ."

"I spent the summer helping my grandparents on their farm in North Carolina. . . ."

"The Palisades Swim Team came in first in division three. . . ."

"Great," I whisper to myself. Even if I were brave enough to read my essay, I doubt anyone would want to hear it. Summer vacations are supposed to be fun. It's a good thing soccer practice starts today because I need to run, and kick, and get rid of this awful feeling in my stomach and throat and everywhere else. I need to kick the sad out of me, at least for an hour and a half.

After practice, Coach Montgomery calls us over to the sidelines for a talk. The sky is getting darker and it looks like it's about to rain again. He better talk fast.

"You girls are looking good. We're going to have a great season, and I need you all to work hard, be your best. We need to come together and support one another, and especially to support Corinna. As you may know, her mother passed away this summer. I'm counting on each and every one of you to lend a hand, lend a shoulder, whatever you can do." There is a long awkward silence. Finally, my coach claps his hands. "Okay, girls, see you on Friday."

I think I'm glad he said something, but it feels kind of gross, too. Not gross in the usual smelly, icky way, but in the way that makes you feel nauseous because it's too intense. A few girls give me hugs, and then we gather our water bottles. As soon as I get into Dad's car, the tears begin, no longer under my control. Dad puts the car in reverse and gets me out of there. Neither of us says a word. Neither of us has to.

Later, when we sit down to dinner, my eyes are still burning, and I blurt out, "So, what's going to happen, Dad?"

"What do you mean?" He takes a sip of water and looks at me.

"Now that it's just you and me."

"Well . . ." He swallows before continuing. "We're going to do the best we can."

I use my thin paper napkin to wipe my tears, but what I really need is a roll of paper towels.

"It's not going to be easy. But we'll be okay." He touches my shoulder. "I know we'll be okay. It just might take a while."

I sit there, nodding because I want to believe him. But he hasn't answered the part of my question I've been too scared to ask. The part about what happens with me if something happens to *him*. The part I really need him to answer.

"Come here," Dad says as he reaches for me and hugs me close. My tears and nose are all running together in one big mess.

"I promise you, we're going to be okay."

The next day at school, things are definitely *not* okay. In the middle of my second period class, I get called down to the main office. The secretary at the front desk, who we call Norma the Storma, says to me, "Corinna, did your mother send in the residency form for this year? I can't find it in your file."

The other secretary chimes in, "Norma, there *is* no mother."

"Excuse me?" asks Norma.

The second one says, "I'll handle this," and walks over to where I'm standing. "Corinna, we need you to get this proof of legal residence form in by tomorrow. You're really not allowed to be in school without it, and for some reason, we don't have one for you. They're really tightening up to make sure all the students actually live in our school district. Some overcrowding problem or something." She hands me the form. "And I'm so sorry about your mother."

I'm not sure what to say.

"Thanks," is all that comes out as I turn and leave the office.

After soccer, giving Maki a walk, and taking a long, hot shower, I decide to call Joci. Even though I've been kind of avoiding her, I feel like I need my old friend back.

"Joci? It's Corinna."

"You actually called me!"

"Yeah . . . How's it going?" I twirl my hair with my free hand.

"I just got back from tennis. What's up?"

"You won't believe what happened in the office at school today."

I tell her the whole story and wait to hear what she says. But Joci stays silent on the other end of the phone. I guess she's waiting for me to continue, but I am expecting *her* to say something. She doesn't.

"Are you there?"

"Yeah, I'm here," she says.

"Well, can you believe it?" I begin to pace around my room. "I got out of there in such a hurry," I add, expecting her to finally speak.

"Yeah. That's terrible."

"To hear that lady say 'there *is* no mother.' "

"I know how you feel. Those ladies are creepy. I get the chills every time I go in there."

"Wait a second, how can you know how I feel?"

"I mean she was such a jerk. She shouldn't have said that in front of you."

I don't bother to tell Joci that my next stop was at the school nurse's office to ask about my stomachaches.

After she tells me about her new tennis coach and how cute he is, we get off the phone. I'm so ready for the weekend and for a break from all this drama.

The next morning, the doorbell rings. I can hear the lawn mower, which means Dad is mowing and I have to answer the door myself. No one is there, but I look down and see a small pink box. I recognize the famous box from Georgetown Cupcake. When I open it, I see that the cupcake has chocolate frosting and a candy heart on it that says, "BFF," as in, Best Friends Forever. I hold it in my hands, thinking about Joci. It *must* be from Joci. She knows that I love their red velvet cupcakes, and I don't think any of my other friends would have done it. I guess she's trying to get close again, but it feels so awkward, like we can't figure out how to go back to the way it was before. I place the cupcake back in the box and wonder if things between me and Joci will ever be good again. If I can trust her again.

Everything is so different now than it was before, and not just with Joci. It's as if everything in my life can now be divided between BD and AD. Before death and after death. I wish I could do something to change that. I would promise to practice my flute every day the way Mom wanted me to, if only I could roll back the clocks, the calendar pages, the years.

Mothers

Unfortunately, Norma the Storma's stupid comment is not alone in the hall of fame.

"Okay, whose mother is going to drive us home from the talent show audition on Thursday night?"

That one was at the lunch table, posed like it was some simple question. No one ever seems to get it, but if they do, then suddenly it gets quiet or someone changes the subject in a totally obvious way. I wish they would just say something to me like, "You must miss your mom a lot." I think almost everyone knows now that my mom died, but it's like this forbidden subject. On rare occasions, someone says, "I'm so sorry about your mom," or "I don't know what to say except I'm sorry." Those are both good things to say, but no one ever says anything like, "It must be hard when we're talking about our mothers." Maybe that would make me tear up, but at least it would feel like they kind of get it. They never ask me about my dad, if my dad is driving, or whatever. It's like there's this big wall between them and me.

The subject of mothers comes up in other ways, too. Our gym teacher warned us yesterday that she would call our mothers if we didn't behave. At the lunch table next to ours, some girls were complaining about their moms making lunches they don't like. In English, we're reading a book about mothers called *They Cage the Animals at Night*. It's a totally sad story in which the mother is sick and the kids go to an orphanage. Oh, and on that school form Norma the Storma wants, it asks for emergency contact information, for my father *and* my mother.

Each time the subject of mothers comes up, a red flag goes up, telling my ears to shut down. Then my brain gets a little fuzzy and I can't concentrate. It's a good thing we don't talk about mothers during math, because that's my hardest subject, and I need to keep my ears open!

Lunch can be the hardest part of the day even though it's supposed to be a time to chill, to relax. To *chillax*, as Joci likes to say. But not these days. These days I get all kinds of attention I'd rather not have.

"That's the girl whose mother died last summer," I overhear.

"Yeah, that's me," I say to myself.

And today, a sixth grader who lives on my block runs up to me and actually says, "You don't have a mama anymore!"

That one makes me freeze, but Joci speaks right up.

"Shut up, you jerk."

Joci puts her arm around me and leads me in the other direction. Having her stick up for me makes me feel like we're a team. Together. Me and Joci. Joci, Joci, Fo Foci. I think about the cupcake. I totally forgot to thank her for it. Maybe I should be giving her more of a chance.

They should make earplugs for people who are grieving, so we don't have to hear the stupid things people say, but I'd look like a dork in them. I want to tell Joci my idea, to lighten things up, but I don't. Joci is already talking to everyone about how many bands are in the talent show and how they're taking up too much rehearsal time from the other acts, including the jazz dance she and Juliette are choreographing.

I think it's cool that they are performing in the talent show, and I know I'm the one who chose not to audition with them, but I still feel left out. To be surrounded by people I know and still feel so alone is pretty weird. Too bad I can't bring Maki to school with me for company. Dogs are so much less complicated than humans, and he loves me no matter what.

By the time the last bell rings, I am more than ready to get out on the soccer field. I grab the stuff out of my locker and head to the commons, a big square hallway in the center of the building, which has the only water fountain in the whole building with cold water. Staring at the grimy floor as I walk, I can't believe the number of pencils and candy wrappers that students have dropped. When I look up, I see a woman looking right at me through the glass in the door of the guidance department. *Great.* She waves at me and opens it.

"Hi, Corinna, my name is Cynthia DuBoise. I'm the new school counselor. I'm so sorry about your mother. It must be very hard." She looks at me with big, concerned eyes. "I want you to know that I'm here anytime you want to talk. Just stop by or sign up with the guidance secretary."

I stand there, gulp, and wait for the uncomfortable moment to be over. I need to get out of here. I really don't want anyone to hear or see us talking.

"Thank you," I mumble before turning and walking straight to the door that opens to the parking lot.

Soccer practice is intense, which is just what I need. I have so much energy that I over-kick most of my shots and the coach tells me to settle down.

When I finally get through our front door, sweaty and exhausted, Maki greets me with a tail wag and a lick, and we go straight up to my room. I don't even take off my muddy cleats. Mom would have freaked about the cleats, but I don't have to worry about that now, do I? I lie down on my bed and let loose, pounding on my pillow and screaming into it at the same time. I had to work hard all day long to keep it together, to keep my head from bursting. When you don't know what's going to come at you, it makes it hard to feel safe. It's like trying to run across a street before the speeding truck that appears out of nowhere hits you and makes you go splat.

By the time we go grocery shopping on Saturday morning, our fridge is empty. Even the freezer is empty. I push the cart slowly. We haven't done a major food shopping together since Mom died. I feel a sense of danger, like I'm in a movie and a tiger is hiding in one of the aisles. Will it be in the popcorn aisle or the ice cream aisle? When we pass the Dannon low-fat coffee yogurt, I hold my breath. The next tiger is in the cereal aisle, where I see the Kashi GOLEAN cereal. Passing the Mango Tango Smoothie drinks is no easier. This sounds strange, but it's like they're neon gravestones saying MOM'S FAVORITE YOGURT and MOM'S FAVORITE CEREAL. We buy some sausages and lettuce, and a bunch of dried pasta, tomato sauce, cereal, and canned soups.

"Can we at least get some fruit?" I ask Dad, who doesn't seem to know what to put in the cart.

For dinner, we prepare the sausages and green salad we bought this morning. I chop up an apple for the salad the way Mom used to. It's so quiet and serious while we eat. I used to love it when the three of us got silly and laughed at stupid stuff. We laughed a lot, especially about my mom's random cooking. She liked combining ingredients and seeing what fabulously delicious thing would result. Most things really were delicious, but some of her inventions didn't turn out so well. Dry chicken with "mystery" sauce was one of her specialties. Sometimes the sauce curdled like cottage cheese. The texture was totally gross, and it looked like barf. I guess that's something I *don't* miss. She never got discouraged, though, and the inventions kept on coming.

"I think you're going to love this new salsa," Mom had announced.

"What's in it, Mom?"

"Jicama, sausage, and banana chutney."

See what I mean?

I would give anything right now to taste one of Mom's inventions. Even the curdled chicken. I don't tell Dad.

Our lame dinner is interrupted by the doorbell. For a second, I think maybe it's Joci, but when I open the door, it's Deborah, bringing us some of her weird bread. She must be feeling really sorry for us, because she's always dropping off homemade bread. Her bread has five trillion kinds of seeds in it, and they usually get stuck in your teeth, which then makes you look like a dental monster. She always puts a card on the bread with a message about wanting to help in any way she can, which is sweet. But sometimes she just shows up and has huge, long conversations with my dad.

"Uh . . . hi . . . again." I stand there blinking at her in her black pants and purple top.

"Hi, sweetie, I wanted to see how you guys were doing." She's looking right at me like she's studying my face for important information.

"We're great. Really great. Never been better." I didn't know I could sound so sarcastic.

"Corinna, I know this is a really, really hard time. You must miss your mother terribly."

"Uh, yeah, you could say that." The sarcasm is pouring out of me and might not stop.

She looks a little startled.

"Is your dad here?"

Dad finally comes to the door and politely invites her in for coffee, sounding almost like a windup toy that can only say a few sentences.

I turn around and storm upstairs to my room.

Too bad it wasn't Joci's mom who came by instead of Deborah. Deborah is so awkward and that makes *me* feel awkward. Joci's mom is so loving and easy to talk to. Never pushy. You don't feel like she's grilling and drilling you. When she brought us dinner back when Mom was sick, those times when Joci didn't come with her, she would sit on the floor and pet Maki. If I felt like talking, it was fine. If I didn't, that was fine, too. I never did talk much about Mom being sick. Neither did Mom.

I'm mad at Joci for a lot of reasons. But I also need her. It felt so good when she stuck up for me at lunch the other day, better than any cupcake ever could. Being so mad at the person you want on your side feels terrible.

Maki and Dad

Maki is my best bud. Thank goodness my parents let me get him five years ago, even if it was because they felt guilty about me being an only child and I had begged for a brother or sister so many thousand zillion times that they got sick of it.

"Please, please, pretty please!!!!!!!!!!!!!"

That was my broken record.

"That's enough, Corinna."

"So you'll have another baby?"

"No, honey, we're not going to have a baby, but you *can* have a puppy."

"Really?" Finally, my begging and pleading had gotten me a baby, even if it wasn't the human kind.

"But please don't ask again about a baby."

"Okay, okay."

Mom and Dad insisted on getting a non-shedding breed, so we only looked at poodles. I remember when we got the idea to name him Maki. We were making sushi rolls with sticky rice and cucumber.

"What's this black papery stuff?"

"It looks like paper, doesn't it? But it's dried seaweed."

"We're eating seaweed for dinner? Gross!"

Mom went on explaining, "The dried seaweed is called 'nori' in Japanese. When we're done making it into rolls, then they're called 'maki.' "

"How do you know all these words?"

"Remember I lived in Tokyo for a semester in high school? My host family had a daughter named Aiko, and she taught me all kinds of things. I really want you and Dad to meet them someday."

When we finally got Maki, he was a little black roll, just like the cucumber rolls, so the name Maki seemed to fit him perfectly. He is so soft, curly, and cuddly, and he's always happy to lie down right next to me. He also likes to lick my face, which I sometimes think is totally gross, especially when he's just eaten a stinky, chewy rawhide bone. I can still hear my mom's voice reminding me, "Think about where his mouth has been."

Totally ick.

On Sunday morning, I come downstairs and see Maki at the bottom step, waiting for Mom to come down in her blue flannel robe. She was the one who gave him breakfast while the coffee machine did whatever coffee machines do. That makes two of us who can't truly believe she's not coming back.

Dad's sitting on the brown leather sofa that's all faded from the sun, the one that has the red plaid blanket on it for when you need to get cozy. He's listening to The Beatles, staring into space, looking so sad.

No, he's beyond sad. He's a wreck.

Before, he was always the loud, funny one in the family. He could get my mom and me to laugh, even when we were crying or arguing about something. Now, whenever he puts on "Julia," the song about one of the Beatles losing someone he loved, I know he's thinking about Mom.

"Hey, Dad, are you okay?"

"Yeah, sure, I'm okay," he says in an unconvincing voice. He does that thing where he tilts his head from shoulder to shoulder, like his neck hurts.

"Did you eat breakfast yet?"

"No. Are you hungry?"

"I'm starving. Can we make French toast?"

"Yeah, if we have bread."

It's times like this when I feel like he barely notices me, even though we're in the same house. It's not like I am totally invisible, but more like we're separated by fog and can barely see each other.

A few minutes later, we are at the kitchen table eating Honey Nut Cheerios. There wasn't enough bread for French toast. Mom's chair is between us, painfully empty. Neither of us ever sits in her chair. We don't really talk about my mom very much. I think it was a few weeks after the funeral before Dad mentioned her name. That was weird.

Sometimes I test him. "Dad, what do you think Mom would have said about the whole situation in Iraq?"

"Dad, how did Mom get grass stains out of my shirts?"

This morning I decide to test him with another question. "Don't you think Mom would have liked the *Avatar* movie?"

He reaches out to hug me, and I knock over my cereal bowl. Neither of us reacts to the spill.

"Yeah, I'll bet she would have."

I don't mind the cold milk that's soaked into my pajama sleeve. I'm just glad we're talking about her, because it seems like since Mom's death, Dad hasn't shared much with me at all. It's like he's being more Mom-ish about it. She didn't like talking about upsetting stuff even before she had cancer; at least it seemed that way to me. She was always trying to get me to think positive when I was in a bad mood about something. I wish that I felt more comfortable talking with him about Mom. I don't mean about cancer, just regular stuff. I get the sense that it's too hard for him.

Thank goodness I can talk to Maki.

"Maki, I can't believe Mom is gone. Really gone. Forever."

Maki does his sniff and roll over routine, hoping for a tummy rub, during our heart-to-heart conversation.

"It's just so sad, isn't it, Maki? I know you miss her, too." I scratch behind his ears the way he likes me to.

"Don't you hate it when someone says my mom's death was

part of God's Plan?" I ask Maki. "Or when they say that God needed my mom in heaven or some other garbage?"

I don't believe God had a plan to make my mother die and make me motherless at age thirteen and my dad wifeless at age forty-four. Who knows how or why she got cancer, and who knows why she didn't suspect there was a problem, and who knows why the doctors didn't find it earlier, and who knows why they couldn't help her more, and who knows why the medical treatments weren't more effective. But I do know that God didn't *want* this. What kind of a God would *want* Sophie Burdette to die?

The Box

According to my dad, Mom chose the music for her funeral before she died. I guess being a musician means you really care about the music, even if you know you won't be able to hear it.

Mom never really talked about dying or funerals when I was with her, just about not feeling well and being so tired. I'd never been to a funeral before hers, so I hadn't really known what to expect.

As soon as we walked into the concert hall, I could tell it was going to be crowded. There were tons of people. From the backs of their heads, I couldn't recognize anyone. Then they started turning around and looking at me, which I didn't like. It would have been the perfect time to be invisible.

The hall smelled dusty and musty, like it hadn't been used in decades, and it was hard to believe that just eight months ago Mom had performed here with Deborah and their trio. August tenth might have been tied for the hottest day of my life, but the air inside was cool. I felt really small and wished I didn't have to go in any farther, almost like I was afraid I might get swallowed up by the rows and rows of seats. My blue skirt was tight and my blue-and-white checked short-sleeve button-down shirt was itchy. Nothing felt right.

Aunt Jennifer's cold and clammy hand was holding mine tightly, and I was squeezing hers. I wanted to turn around and go home, but Aunt Jennifer pulled me inside and somehow we made it up to the very front row of seats, where Grandma and Bapa were sitting. Everything was quiet, except for some whispers and coughs. Grandma and Bapa looked really old and sad. I could barely breathe.

"It's okay," Aunt Jennifer said quietly, though it didn't seem okay at all. "Let's sit down."

I could do that. I could sit down.

"Wow, there are so many people here who loved your mom."

I couldn't make myself look around.

"Where's Dad?" I whispered.

Aunt Jennifer put her arm around me. "I'm sure he'll come sit with us soon. Don't worry."

She was talking to me like I was a toddler again, but I didn't mind. I felt lost, like I was sinking, even though I was sitting on a hard seat. About three seconds later, Dad sat next to me and gave me a hug. Just then someone in a really loud voice said, "Where's Sophie?" It was an old man hunched over a cane. He kept asking, "Where's Sophie?" I think he was hard of hearing, and maybe he had Alzheimer's or whatever it's called when you lose your memory and you're really out of it. Some other man, who I think worked there, rushed over to him and tried to help him find a seat. The deaf guy kept asking where Sophie was, and I heard the person next to him say, "She's in the box!" as he tried to shut him up with a finger to his lips. The box with her ashes sat on the front table next to some white roses in a big vase. She loved roses.

While my neck was totally twisted to see what was going on with the loud guy, I noticed some people I recognized. Not that I knew all their names, but I saw some of Mom's viola students, plus some neighbors, including dreadful Mrs. Simmons, my pediatrician who wears Disney ties, the funky lady who cut Mom's and my hair, teachers from the high school where Dad works, Joci and her parents, Eliana and her mom, relatives I'd only seen pictures of, and tons of strangers. Because it was August, a lot of our friends were away on vacation.

Finally, the music started. A bunch of Mom's fellow musicians from the Montgomery County Chamber Symphony were on the stage. Deborah was up there, too, right in front, her long black skirt flowing on either side of her cello. The music was pretty, but sad, and it went on for a really long time. I didn't recognize any of it. Then came the speeches. One of them was given by her college friend, and my uncle read something Aunt Jennifer had written. There was also some random guy who spoke. I didn't hear how he knew my mom. I couldn't really follow what anyone was saying. Instead, I focused on how soggy my tissues were. I ended up using my sleeve to wipe my nose, which isn't exactly easy with a short-sleeve shirt.

It was so strange to think of Mom being in that small wooden box. It didn't make sense, that her body could be reduced to such a small amount of ashes, and I couldn't stop staring at it. When the service was finally over, my dad gave me a really long bear hug. His face was red and wet with tears. My throat swelled up like I was having an allergic reaction to peanuts even though I don't have that allergy, and I wanted to run out of there to breathe. All these people were coming up to my dad and me.

"We'll miss her terribly, yada, yada, yada."

"I'm so sorry, yak, yak, yak."

I felt totally trapped in a sea of tall people talking at me, over me, down to me. Finally, Aunt Jennifer took my hand and we walked outside into the thick August heat. I don't think I started breathing again until we drove away in her bright blue rental car.

After the service, a lot of people came over to our house. Joci and her parents were there and each of them gave me a big hug, but they had to leave right away to catch a plane somewhere. I wish at least her mom could have stayed. Aunt Jennifer's kids and husband came with her from California, and my cousins who live in England came, too. I hadn't seen them in a really long time because they live even farther away than the California cousins.

The kids stayed outside mostly, only coming in for food or drinks. Speaking of food, there was tons of it. Some of it was disgusting. Jell-O molds. Orange, green, and yellow. Yuck. Do they really think people like those? And like nine pans of baked ziti. Baked ziti is great, but that much ziti was kind of tough to appreciate.

The grown-ups were inside, and it was pretty hard to be around them. Some of the grown-ups hugged and squeezed me and told me to "be strong, be strong for your dad." Like I'm some kind of weight lifter. It was horrible. And *annoying*. I also was told I was "doing so well" a few times. What does that mean? That I hadn't grown horns? One totally ancient-looking stranger came up to me and patted me on the head, saying, "Don't cry." Actually, a few people did that. I'm thirteen, not two, and I'm not a dog! Who are they to say that crying is bad? I escaped back outside.

Even my grandparents — Grandma and Bapa, Mom's parents who moved from Pennsylvania to Arizona a few years ago, and my dad's parents, Gigi and Pop Pop, who live in Annapolis — didn't seem to know what to say to me. At least they gave me lots of hugs and didn't do the head-patting thing. Aunt Jennifer was the best. She told me how much my mom loved me. She didn't smother me or give me all kinds of advice. She had a baby who died a few days after he was born, so I think she kind of knew what it was like. It's totally different, but kind of the same, I guess. Before she left, she told me to call or e-mail her whenever

I felt like it, that I could ask her anything I wanted, about my mom or death stuff or girl stuff. I think she really meant it. She also said she would come visit us. It stinks that she lives in California, especially now. Aunt Jennifer reminds me of my mom. They *are* sisters, of course. *Were* sisters?

Aunt Jennifer's family had to leave two days after the funeral, because California schools start earlier than Maryland schools do, and they had to get back. Our house got really, really quiet after they left.

That night, Dad was napping on the brown sofa, so I tiptoed upstairs to Mom and Dad's bedroom. Walking through the doorway felt strange. I used to dance in there and ask them a question or show off an outfit or ask for another bedtime tuck-in. When I was sick or I wanted to watch TV in their cozy bed, I'd get under their puffy blue comforter and pretend I was floating on a cloud. I locked the door and climbed into their bed. I lay under the covers for a long time, trying to feel that floating feeling, until I started to worry that Dad would come up and wonder why I was locked in his room. My muscles got all tense and I couldn't decide what to do.

After checking that Dad and Maki were still snoring on the sofa downstairs, I went back to my parents' room. As soon as I slid open the door to Mom's closet, I could smell her perfume. I buried my nose in some of her hanging clothes. Then I touched the wrinkles in one of her shirts, left over from when she wore it the last time. I started thinking about how having her clothes there meant that a part of her was still there, too. Next, I tried on her shoes, the old-fashioned ones and the newer ones. They were too big for me, but that didn't stop me from trying them on. Clip-clop. Ever since I was a little girl, I loved the sound of her high heels.

Kanser

At lunch, everyone's all excited and chattering about tonight's Fall Follies talent show. Joci's talking with her mouth full, giving me a full panoramic view of her tuna and mayonnaise. I haven't decided yet if I want to go tonight, but everyone's pushing me to come see their acts. Joci and Juliette are doing their jazz dance, Eliana and Olivia are going to sing, and Lena is juggling and riding her unicycle.

"I don't think we should wear red tops, because it would clash with Eliana's hair, don't you think?" Olivia asks me.

Lena interrupts, "Did you hear that Mr. Spinolli is doing magic tricks? I heard he's actually a good magician."

They're talking about all the various dancers, and all I hear is "*cancers*." My mind gets stuck on the word. Cancer. CANSIR, CANSUR, KANSER, KANSIR. Lots of ways to write it, but it still is such a big, bad, powerful word.

My mom's cancer had already taken over her entire body before the doctor found it. I know that some people are luckier. Their cancer is found early or the kind of cancer they have has a better treatment than some other types. I think the doctor tried to give us hope, by telling my parents about some new chemotherapy treatment Mom could try. In April, my mom explained to us that she was willing to try anything to get better, so she did the chemo. But somewhere along the long line of appointments, we all started to wonder if it was worth it. She felt so sick and so weak. Her doctor, Dr. Rothstein, really pushed her to continue with the treatments. Even in July, after my mom had decided "no more chemo," Dr. R. kept pushing her to get blood transfusions. My dad said he thought Dr. R. was having a hard time accepting that she couldn't fix my mom. When she finally stopped chemo and all the other stuff, Dr. R. seemed kind of mad. How could she be mad? Ugh.

There were some days when I came home and Mom was so weak that she just lay there with her eyes closed. You couldn't avoid seeing her even if you wanted to, because her hospital bed was in the middle of our living room, which is practically on top of the front door. It was awful to open the front door or walk downstairs for breakfast and see her that way.

My mom told me, "Corinna, I know I should be talking to you about everything that's going on with me. Everyone tells me I should. But it's just too hard."

I told her, "It's okay, Mom."

My dad was the one who shared a lot with me during the time when Mom was sick, maybe too much, like about different chemo treatments and stuff like that. I liked having talks with him, feeling included, but sometimes it was just too much for me, hearing so many scary things. I didn't tell my friends. I didn't want anyone to know. If they knew, then it would be even harder for me to block it out.

"I really wish you were in the show with us," Lena is saying when I tune back in to the conversation. "Remember last year?"

Last year, the six of us did a skit in the talent show, called "A Brighter Future," about energy conservation. Our social studies teacher made us do it because she liked our class project so much, but the audience didn't know if it was supposed to be funny, and we felt really stupid.

Joci makes a loud announcement: "Ever since my mom saw Juliette and me practicing our dance, she has been driving me crazy with all her warnings to keep it 'appropriate.'"

My back stiffens and I quickly tune out again to avoid what to me feels like fingernails scratching on the chalkboard.

I know moms can be annoying, but she's lucky to *have* a mom. I used to complain about my mom, just like everyone else does about their own mom. It would be totally fake to pretend we didn't ever get mad at each other. Of course we did. I remember when I was in first grade and I kept changing my mind about what I wanted to be for Halloween. She made me a Tweety Bird costume after I told her I really, really, absolutely wanted to be Tweety Bird. She spent days cutting and sewing it. But the costume was so *yellow* and didn't have feathers and didn't look at all like the real Tweety Bird, and there was just no way I could be *that* Tweety Bird. I had a total spaz attack and then she had a total spaz attack and . . . it was not my best Halloween.

Now when I look at the Tweety Bird in my ginormous stuffed-animal collection, I can't believe I ever liked him. He has a grand total of three eyelashes per eye and one sorry tuft of hair on top. His eyes are open big and wide, but with a look of terror, like he's about to fall into a huge bottomless pit with no way out. It's not a happy face at all. It's a seen-too-much look, like he's freaked out about something. I wonder if my eyes looked like that when Mom was dying in our living room. I think I should get rid of Tweety Bird as soon as I get home from school today so I won't have to see that look, so I won't have a three-haired bright yellow reminder of how I felt when I looked at my mom.

"Corinna, let's go," Joci's saying as she touches my shoulder.

Suddenly, everyone is getting up from the lunch table and I'm thrown back into my school world.

"Corinna, we need to have a little talk," Dad says when I walk into the kitchen. He's using his serious voice, like when he told me about Mom's diagnosis. His words send my heart down into my stomach. But instead of devastating news, Dad starts lecturing me about my forgotten social studies homework, which he found out about thanks to an annoying call from Mr. Spinolli. As soon as he's done, he goes back to fixing the faucet, and I walk over to the computer. Rather than telling Joci about Mr. Spinolli, like I would have done before, I start on my homework. I type three paragraphs about the causes of World War I and print them out before going online to check my e-mail, which I haven't done in ages.

A minute later, I get an IM from a girl in my grade named Clare, who moved to our school in the middle of last year. She plays soccer, too, but she's on a travel team in a different league.

soccergrlc: *hey Corinna, what's up?*

maki226: *not much. U?*

soccergrlc: *just wondering if u knew my dad died 3 years ago?*

maki226: *no. wow. I'm so sorry.*

soccergrlc: *thanks.*

maki226: *so you were 10 when he died?*

soccergrlc: *the big one zero.*

I can't believe it. I'm not the only one in the entire eighth grade — no, make that the entire middle school — who knows what it is like to have their parent gone, dead, lost, whatever. I'm sad her father died but also happy that I'm not actually completely alone. I type like crazy.

maki226: *how'd he die?*

soccergrlc: *heart disease*

maki226: *was he sick a long time?*

soccergrlc: *yeah*

maki226: *that must have been so hard*

soccergrlc: *ur right*

maki226: *do u ever get over it?*

soccergrlc: *no, I don't think so, but it gets a little easier. tiny bit by tiny bit*

maki226: *ouch*

soccergrlc: *yup*

maki226: *so was it hard to concentrate?*

soccergrlc: *totally. I don't remember very much from 5th grade*

maki226: *yeah, tears and exponents don't mix. haha*

soccergrlc: *let's keep this on the DL*

maki226: *yeah, totally*

soccergrlc: *good*

maki226: *no way am I talking about this with anyone else at school*

soccergrlc: *yeah they don't understand*

Suddenly, it makes sense that Clare was one of the few kids who sent me a note after Mom died. Then I think about Joci. I'm not sure Joci will ever "get it."

The ref blows the final whistle of our Saturday afternoon soccer game, and I'm relieved. It's hot, I'm tired, and I'm glad the official season is more than half over. Maybe it's good I didn't switch to the travel team. They're much more serious and intense. In today's game, I messed up big time. I had the perfect shot on goal and I missed it. I hate that. My team hated it, too. We lost, 0–1.

"Girls, you've got to stay focused out there," my coach says after the game. "You've got to concentrate."

I know he's talking to me.

Tonight as I'm trying to fall asleep, I see that play over and over.

After a lot of tossing and turning and reliving my pathetic shot on goal, I finally drift off. At some point, I start dreaming. Three lion cubs are walking in the tall grass. They seem lost and their mother is nowhere in sight. They don't know yet that she's dead. My first thoughts when I wake up are: Will they be able to survive without her to feed them and teach them how to hunt? Will they find another adult to care for them? Will their father appear? I tell myself that the cute little cubs are going to all survive, *somehow*.

During my daytime reality, it turns out I have my own Animal Planet to deal with at school. Dumbhead Jake, who I somehow had a crush on last year, looks up when I pass him in the cafeteria and says to Dylan in his totally annoying, sarcastic voice, "I sure hope her dad knows how to cook."

Dylan laughs really hard and says, "He should. He probably works at McDonald's!"

I want to kill them! In a split second, I have to choose whether to a) say something back, b) give them "The Look," c) ignore them altogether, or d) vaporize them. Since I can't destroy them, I decide to ignore them. It's easier, and I don't have the energy to fight back. Besides, it's hard to think of just the right come-back to say to those jerks. I never seem to have something ready to say in situations like this. Next time, maybe I'll try bossy Beth's "Whatever" expression that she uses whenever she gets insulted. I can learn something from our eighth-grade Queen Bee without having to eat her club's super Caesar salads or follow her ridiculous fashion rules.

School seems so irrelevant, especially math. I just don't care about math equations and solving for x and y. Other subjects are *too* relevant, like in biology, where our review of Punnett squares reminds me of how I got my green eyes and heart-shaped face from my mom. When Mr. Spinolli talks about World War I and the piles of dead bodies and the rats that were big as rabbits from feasting on them, it's hard not to think about my mom's body. But Mom's body is now ashes, and those ashes are in an urn in my house, in our living room, safe from rats.

By the time I get home, have a snack, do homework, and eat dinner, it's eight o'clock. We are supposed to learn new· pieces for band because we're performing at a retirement home next week, but practicing flute is the last thing I feel like doing. Clare and I made plans to instant message on the computer tonight. During the day, we have to save up our questions, because when we're at school, we have to keep on our protective armor. There's a look we give each other, a knowing look, the way you might if you were part of a secret club.

Tonight, Clare tells me that her dad wrote her a letter before he died. Her mom gave it to her when she turned twelve. I totally wish my mom had done that. After I get off the computer, I check with Dad.

"Did Mom write any kind of letter for me?"

"She wrote you cards on your birthdays. Is that what you mean?"

"No, I mean for the future. Like for my sixteenth birthday or my wedding or something."

"Not that I know of."

Dad seems clueless.

There are so many things I want to ask my mom and even more things that I want to tell her. One of the things I wish is that I'd said more of a good-bye. I never really found the right moment. Even after I finally figured out she was dying, it was so hard to know what to say. So hard to *think*. So hard to feel. Much easier to be on "autopilot," as Dad would say, getting through each day, taking care of things, helping out my dad or the nurses, trying to ignore the ache in my belly.

I still have stomach pains. I don't think that was one of Mom's symptoms, but I can't help but worry that the different aches and pains I get might be some kind of cancer, or something else really serious. Some of my stomach pains might be connected to the Joci situation.

Joci was the first one to find out that Mom was sick, just after school ended in June. I had stopped inviting friends over. I guess my parents told Joci's parents, and they told Joci. Right after she found out, I saw her in CVS. We were picking up more medicine, and she launched right in.

"Corinna, are you scared?"

"Um, yeah, I guess so."

"Well, my mom said to tell you that we want to help."

"Okay, thanks. Can you do me a huge favor, though? Please don't tell anyone."

"Why not?"

"Because I just can't deal with it now. Everyone will talk about it. Everyone will know. Plus, it's freaky seeing my mom connected to an IV."

She scrunched up her face, then said, "Gross." I stared at her in shock and then closed my eyes while she continued. "I'm sorry, but I hate medical stuff."

"Joci, I'm serious. Please, please don't tell anyone."

"Okay, okay."

I took that as a promise.

Joci's family invited me to come with them to the beach for a week, and my parents thought it was a good idea, so I went. That meant that I missed most of Aunt Jennifer's visit when she came to help Mom. After Aunt Jennifer left, Joci's mom started bringing over dinner two nights a week, which was really sweet of her. Mom could only handle liquids by then, so it was just Dad and me eating what she brought. Joci came with her one time in the middle of July, but that was the one and only time. She stood in the doorway, with only her eyes moving. I'm sure it freaked her out. In a way, I don't blame her, but still, it hurt that she didn't come back again. She called me, but not very often, and it felt so awkward. Neither of us knew what to say.

There were lots of times when all I wanted to do was go for long walks with Maki or watch TV, but I tried to find things to do to be helpful. I could feed Mom ice chips or give her a foot rub like Aunt Jennifer did, or open a can of chocolate Ensure for her to sip when she could still sip. I tasted the Ensure one time, thinking it would taste like a chocolate milk shake, the way the picture on the label promised. Man, was I wrong! It tasted like watery, chalky, fake chocolate toothpaste, but without the mint. Yuck. My mouth gets all puckered when I think about that awful taste.

Sometimes I read cards to her from people trying to sound cheerful. "Get well soon" certainly was popular. The white basket now sits on our coffee table, and it's overflowing with cards to her and cards sent to us after she died, a reminder of all the people who cared about her. We still get cards once in a while, when someone else hears about her.

Sometimes I just sat there next to Mom. She was so weak that we didn't really talk a lot. Kind of like she was half there, half already gone. There were lots of times I couldn't sit with her, though, when I just needed to get away from all those smells and boxes of rubber gloves. I usually got out of there when Deborah was with her, not to get away from Deborah, but because I needed a break.

There was all this pressure to do the right thing to help her, and then she was gone. Going, going, gone. I can't believe she's gone.

Most people feel sorry for me that my mom died, but they don't really get it. They don't understand that my life has changed forever. *Forever.* They also don't have a clue what it's like to be terrified that your other parent might die. That could be the worst part. I don't have a backup plan.

The great thing about Clare is that she understands the serious stuff. Another great thing about Clare is that we can joke about things that no one else gets, like baked ziti. We have even developed an online ziti routine. I don't think they would welcome it in any talent show.

> maki226: *did ur family eat a lot of ziti after your father died?*
> soccergrlc: *I don't ever want to c baked ziti again. we ate it every night for a month.*
> maki226: *my neighbors think baked ziti is what everyone needs when they're sad.*
> soccergrlc: *do they want us to eat ziti so we get all ziti?*
> maki226: *haha*
> soccergrlc: *do u still have some in your freezer? maybe we can have a ziti party & put some on our faces for a serious case of teenage zits?!*
> maki226: *LOL!*

It took me about five minutes to stop laughing about the ziti. Laughing with Clare is the best. But I don't like hearing her mention her mother's boyfriend.

I'm staring out the car window, looking at the trees. There don't seem to be as many bright red trees as I remember from other

Octobers. I ask Dad to pull over at the farm stand so we can get a pumpkin, and I pick out a big round one. When we get home, there are three phone messages waiting for us on our answering machine from some random person trying to schedule an earwax cleaning. I never even knew that there were professional earwax cleaners. What a gross job. The messages get madder and madder. It sounds so crazy and bizarre with him yelling at us, like we did something wrong. Besides the wrong number calls from the screaming earwax maniac, we also have a message from Deborah. She asks if I want to go out to lunch with her, like it's something we've done a thousand times.

"Are you going to call her back?" Dad asks.

"Maybe someday."

I can't explain why, but I just don't feel like it.

Deborah used to be at our house all the time. She and Mom would take over the house for their rehearsals, and during her divorce, Deborah would sometimes stay for dinner. During the time Mom was in bed so much, Deborah would come over and play sad cello music for her.

I know Deborah is just trying to be nice to me and get me talking, but I don't want her poking and squeezing me about my mom.

The last message on our answering machine is from Mrs. Simmons, the neighbor who keeps calling to invite us to dinner. Before I even finish listening to it, the phone rings. As soon as

I hear the deep voice on the other end, I know it's her and I wish I hadn't answered. She has always been pushy. My parents used to tell me to "be kind, be patient; remember she's old and lonely," but I can't stand her. Her voice sounds like she smokes five packs of cigarettes a day, not that I've ever seen her smoke.

"Corinna, dear, this is Phyllis Simmons. You and your father *must* come have dinner at my house this week. How's Tuesday?"

My eyes roll back into my head when I tell her, "I'll get my dad, hold on."

Dad makes up some excuse, which saves me from telling Mrs. Simmons that I am never going to set foot in her house.

About ten o'clock, I'm lying in bed reading the last few pages of my English homework. I can hear Dad on the phone.

"I'm just not up for it yet," he says.

What is someone asking him to do, I wonder? Go out on a date? Now I have something else to worry about. I can't fall asleep. The streetlights are humming louder than usual. After I get up and go to the bathroom, I see that Dad's light is still on, so I decide to knock on his door.

"Dad, you awake?" I whisper through the door.

"Yeah. What's wrong?"

I open the door. Dad is lying in bed with a book on his chest.

"Who was that on the phone?"

"Mike."

"What did he want?"

"He was asking me to play tennis or basketball with him next Saturday," Dad says, trying to sound upbeat.

"Well, are you going to?"

"Nah. Not this time."

"You should, Dad," I say to encourage him, but he doesn't seem to hear me.

"Good night, Corinna."

"Night," I say as I close the door.

On Saturday, I'm the one with plans. The eighth grade is having two car washes this year to raise money for our graduation dance. While we're getting soaked by sponges, hoses, and soap, Joci invites me to see a movie in downtown Bethesda with her tonight.

"Come on, it'll be fun! We can get that yummy custard ice cream or go to Georgetown Cupcake after the movie. My mom said she can give us a ride."

"Who else is going?"

"Just us. Okay?"

"I think so. I'll check with my dad. Not a sleepover, right?"

"That would be great!"

"But . . . that's not what I meant. I mean, movie and cupcakes, but then your mom can drop me off, right?"

"Yeah, fine."

I don't tell Joci, but I worry about Dad feeling too lonely.

A few hours later, Dad picks me up from the car wash.

"Good news, Corinna," he says with excitement in his voice.

"What, what is it?"

"Aunt Jennifer called and asked if she can come visit us over Veteran's Day weekend."

"How soon is that?"

"In a few weeks. She's leaving the kids at home with their dad."

"Yahoo! That's great."

"I thought you'd be happy."

It's great to have something to look forward to. Something positive to focus on.

My focus has pretty much gone missing so far this year, and it's been hard to concentrate in all of my classes. Algebra is the worst. Algebra equals Mrs. Giamatti, and right now, Mrs. Giamatti, who is also known as Hawk Lady because of her sunken eyes and glued-down hair, is walking around the room, looking like she's ready to pounce. She stops two inches from my desk. "Corinna, you missed two out of four assignments last week."

"What?" I stammer.

"You only turned in two problem sets."

Mrs. Giamatti's gray eyes feel like daggers piercing through my pride.

"But I know I did all four of them."

I start flipping through my papers, desperately hoping to find them. No luck. Then I start digging around in my backpack and pull out some crumpled papers. No luck there, either. By the time I get to my English binder, she has already walked back to her desk and everyone is whispering. Amazingly, I find the problem sets in the poetry section of my English binder. Without looking at her or anyone else, I walk up and put them in her assignment basket and slink back to my desk.

"Nice save," says Alex, the cute boy who sits behind me.

After my complete and total humiliation in math class, I can't face the cafeteria scene today, so I escape to the school library. The library has its own dramas and noise problems, including the librarians' never-ending battle to shush everyone. I overhear Beth and her gang passing on the gossip they've been reading in the latest *People* magazine. I could move somewhere else, but I'm stuck. It's like I have glue between my butt and the chair. Butt glue. What a lovely thought.

"Wait up, Corinna," Lena calls as she comes up to me in the hallway before our next class. She's very petite and looks younger than most people in our grade.

"What's up, Lena?"

"I just want to say, I'm *never* going to juggle in front of anyone again. Everyone was laughing at the talent show, and that made me mess up even more."

"I know the feeling. It's an awful feeling. But we have to try *really*, *really* hard not to let our mistakes get us down."

Soccer practice helps me relax and forget about Mrs. Giamatti. Dad picks me up, and two minutes later, he goes right through a stop sign. We almost run into a police car. Police lights start flashing and Dad pulls over. The cop looks angry.

"What is not clear about that stop sign you just ran?"

"Nothing, officer. I didn't see it."

"Yeah, I've heard that before. Got your head in the clouds?"

"I'm sorry, sir."

"You idiots are going to get yourselves killed."

Dad's spacey-ness makes me feel sick and scared. We really could have been hit or hit the cop, we could have died, or we could have killed someone else. I'm worried that he isn't paying attention to important stuff, and I need him to get his act together.

Twists and Turns

It totally irritates me when I walk through the hallways and I see hundreds of kids acting like their same old immature selves, like nothing has changed. Well, maybe nothing has changed for them. Yeah, yeah, yeah, maybe once upon a time their beloved gerbil or goldfish died. You can always buy a new goldfish. Or maybe one of their grandparents died. I'm sorry, but that just isn't the same, not unless the grandparent was raising them. I hate that they can just go on like normal and I can't. My world is upside down and inside out and scrambled like mush and it's really horrible, and I feel like I have this great, big, giant emptiness inside of me. Not all day, every day, but a lot of the time. And even knowing that Clare is here doesn't always help, because I still don't have my mom and I never will. Why did this happen to me, why *my* mom? Life is so unfair.

I'm in a terrible mood because we ran out of bread again this morning and Dad got all annoyed when I wasn't ready.

"Dad, there's nothing to make for lunch."

"There must be *something* you like."

"We wouldn't *be* out of bread if Mom was here."

Mom used to make our lunches before Dad and I went off to school. We always had good bread — without a ton of seeds in it — and other sandwich-making supplies in the house. She made sure we had other good stuff in our lunches, too, like apples that weren't mushy. I hate mushy apples. Now our mornings are hectic and discombobulated (love that word, hate that feeling). Mom was the queen of lists, so we never ran out of milk, either, like we did two days ago.

Dad promised we'd buy six loaves of bread after school today, but I'm still feeling totally annoyed by everything in my life. I see Franklin walking down the hall, smiling, minding his own business. I don't even know Franklin; I just remember his name because it's so unusual.

"What are you so happy about?" I ask.

"Nothing. What's wrong with *you*?"

"You want to know what's wrong? I'll tell you what's wrong. It sucks to have your parent die."

"Yeah, it probably does."

"Probably? You don't know how lucky you are to have two parents alive."

I don't even know if Franklin has two parents, or if he has two dads or two moms or what.

"You shouldn't go around making assumptions that everyone else's life is just perfect. Everyone has problems." Then he practically screams, "Life's not great for me, either."

That shuts me up.

Thankfully, no one else is in the hall with us, but it's almost as if the guidance office has antennae and heard about it. I get a note the next day, passed on by Miss Boppity Bop, asking me to go to Ms. DuBoise's office. I've been avoiding the hallway near her office, but I guess she decided she'd waited long enough (or she *does* have hidden antennae). At least she didn't call for me over the loudspeaker!

When I get into her office, she says, "It must be hard sometimes when the kids don't know what you're going through."

Talk about uncomfortable. What's she going to do, make me talk? I feel trapped. She doesn't push me, though. She tells me that there are a few kids who have had a parent die in the last few years and she's thinking of starting a group for us to meet together. I'm surprised to hear that besides Clare, there are other kids like me. That keeps me listening. But I also feel scared. What would we have to talk about and what if I don't feel comfortable? What if it's totally cheesy and fake? She says she has to send home permission slips and she'll let me know when the group is starting. Then she tells me she really thinks it would be a good idea for me. Seventy-five percent of me wants to say, "No, thanks," on the spot, but I keep my mouth shut.

On Tuesday, all outdoor sports practices are canceled because of heavy rain, and my dad has a meeting, so I go home with Joci after school. I give her mom a big hug when she meets us at the door.

67

"Corinna, Corinna. So good to have you here, sweetie."

I've been there so many times since our very first playdate when we were both in Mrs. Medvin's second-grade class. Whenever Joci was being too bossy or wouldn't let me have a turn, her mom always seemed to notice. If I fell off their swing set, her mom was there to comfort me. She always made the best snacks, like warm chocolate chip cookies or banana muffins, and she taught us how to make them, too. Sometimes, I even felt more comfortable asking her about awkward things than I did my own mom, like the time I asked her how babies are made. She was good at answering stuff like that, and she never made me feel bad for asking. She never said, "Why don't you ask your own mom," which I was glad about because my mom got so uncomfortable with hard questions.

"Joci is so lucky to have you as her best friend," her mom practically sings.

"Me, too," I reply, but I'm not sure if it's true anymore.

We go upstairs to Joci's room to hang out. Her room is twice as big as mine and has matching beds. We always pretended to be twins whenever I used to spend the night. We *were* twins in a lot of ways. We liked the same movies, books, singers, colors, and candy bars. We would stay up late making up songs about silly stuff. Another thing we liked to do was spa night, when we did each other's nails, hair, and makeup. That seems like a long time ago.

Joci starts complaining to me about her tennis coach and

some of the girls on her team, and I'm trying to listen, but then I get distracted when I notice her new jewelry organizer. It's one of those picture-frame things that has holes for earrings and hooks for necklaces. I walk up to it for a closer look and I can't believe my eyes.

"Joci, when did you get that bracelet?"

"Which bracelet?"

"The silver one with sayings on the beads."

"Uh . . . I don't remember."

"I had one just like that but I lost it last year. My mom gave it to me for my birthday. I've looked *everywhere* for it."

"Oh, well, I'm not sure where it's from. Maybe it's my sister's."

"Hmmm."

"Do you want it? You can have it. I never wear it."

"Uh, well, yeah, I guess so."

I'm not sure what to believe about her story. I can't imagine Joci stealing anything from me. But it's hard to imagine it's not the bracelet I've been missing. Joci quickly gets us off the subject.

"Let's go eat. You want our favorite?"

"Sure."

"Oh, yeah, love that PB and B."

That's what we always used to say to each other, "Love that PB and B." I put the bracelet on and we go downstairs for our peanut butter and bananas. It doesn't taste so good, though. I call Dad a few minutes later and ask him to pick me up. Joci is a great friend in some ways, but after what happened with my bracelet, on top of blabbing about my mom to who knows how many people last summer, I really don't know if we can stay friends.

"You're leaving already?" Joci asks.

"Yeah. I have a ton of homework," I lie.

I wave bye to Joci's mom, who is on the phone in the kitchen, and slam their fancy stained-glass door behind me. Dad's not here yet, so I press *Mom* on my speed dial. She had known how upset I was when I lost that bracelet.

"Hello, this is Sophie Burdette, musician and teacher. Please leave me a message, including your phone number, even if you think I already have it. I'll return your call as soon as my hands are free."

"Mom, you won't believe where I found the silver bracelet you gave me. It was in Joci's room. This might sound crazy, but I think my own best friend stole it from me. Maybe I left it there one time and she just didn't get her act together to return it. I guess it's possible that she didn't know it was mine, but how could she not at least make an *effort* to find out who it belonged to? Ugh."

When I get home, I go to my room and cry. And cry and cry.

I spend the next few days in shock about the bracelet before I finally e-mail Aunt Jennifer to tell her the whole story.

On Wednesday night, I have to get out of my Blue Oasis bath two times to answer the phone. The first call is from Beth, inviting me to her makeup and spa party. I say no to Beth right away because she gives me the creeps.

"What a fake," I tell Maki. Thank goodness she hasn't brought up lunch at her swanky club again. I would rather eat anchovies than have lunch with her.

The second call is from Olivia, inviting me to her movie star sleepover. I'm supposed to come up with a stage name so she can make us personalized party favors, but I'm torn about whether or not to go. I like parties, and I want to do something besides hang out at home with Dad. Even though Olivia can be a lot of fun, she sometimes gets on my nerves. And honestly, I've avoided her since our major conversation in July in the shopping center parking lot. Dad and I had gone to CVS again for more medical stuff for Mom, and Olivia was there buying candy. I called out to her, and when she saw me, she had a strange look on her face.

"Are you okay, Olivia?"

"Uh, yeah. What about you?"

"Okay, I guess."

"Really?" She looked surprised.

"What do you mean?"

"Well," she said, looking down at her bright green high-tops, "I kinda sorta found out about your mom."

Since my stomach was already doing its "thing," it was hard to feel worse, but I did.

"Who told you?"

"I just heard it somewhere."

"But from who? I need to know."

"You really want to know?"

I folded my arms across my chest, trying to hold myself together, as I nodded yes.

"Joci told me. But she only told us so we could understand what you were going through."

Olivia looked down at her shoes again. Without saying another word, I turned and walked away as my eyes filled with tears. Olivia didn't try to stop me.

All of this flashes through my head before I give Olivia my answer about her party.

"Well, I'd like to come, but I can only stay until ten. My dad won't let me sleep over because we have some stuff we need to do in the morning."

I lie to Olivia because I feel kind of guilty about abandoning my dad, and I don't want to do a sleepover yet. I didn't know you could miss someone even though you're still living with them and eating breakfast and dinner together almost every day. But I miss the old dad, the one I knew before Mom got sick. The one who laughed and made *me* laugh. I feel like I should be the parent and make him go out with his friends or play tennis or something. He goes to work and comes home. He watches TV, sort of, and he grades his students' papers. If I need help with homework, he's always good about that, even when his neck and back hurt and he's attached to his heating pad. Sometimes he calls old friends or some people in our family, and he still plays that Beatles CD a lot, the one with the "Julia" song. He also helps at my soccer practices when he doesn't have teacher meetings.

Dad is totally into soccer. At least he was before Mom's whole thing. This fall, Dad hasn't missed a single game, home or away, but he's kind of like a scarecrow. He stands there in his khakis and Orioles baseball hat, silent, tall, thin, kind of blowing around in the wind. This might sound paranoid, but I get the feeling that the other parents don't talk to him the way they used to. Before he became a w-i-d-o-w-e-r. That's a new vocabulary word I had to learn.

Starbursts and Ziti

Now that I'm a teenager, I'm not so sure about going out for Halloween. I'd rather stay home and hand out candy, but Joci really, really wants me to go around with her in her old neighborhood like we always have. She's practically begging me.

"It's our tradition, Corinna. You have to."

Lucky for us, her mom had saved the dice and box of popcorn costumes from Joci's older sister, so we don't have to throw something together at the last minute. The costumes are actually really cute.

We're surrounded by tiny superheroes and princesses. Seeing them holding their moms' hands is sweet *and* hard. One enthusiastic mom says to her Superman son, "Look at the box of popcorn and the die."

I hadn't realized I was a *die*. Creepy.

The day after Halloween is a day of recovery. I'm having a disgusting reminder of why you're not supposed to go crazy stuffing your face with candy. I think I ate twenty or thirty

Starbursts, a few Milky Ways, and some peanut M&M'S. Who knew Starbursts and chemotherapy have something in common? I discover the similarity as I hug the toilet bowl. I stay home sick from school the next day, so I'm home for the dreaded mail delivery.

It used to be that I would rush to see what I got in the mail — good catalogs or magazines or maybe even a letter or invitation. But after Mom died, getting the mail fills me with dread. There's always something addressed to my mom. Mrs. Sophie Burdette. Seeing mail addressed to her feels like getting sharp needles stuck into the emptiness inside of me. Don't they know she's dead and can't read their stupid catalogs or contribute to their organizations?

Then there are the phone calls, which are just as bad. That night, just as I'm beginning to feel better, the phone rings.

"Hello, this is Eleanor from the Sierra Club calling. Is Sophie Burdette there?"

"Um, no, she's not."

"Can you tell me when I can reach her?"

"Um, well, you can't."

"Well, I can call at a more convenient time."

"No, you really can't. Um, I mean, um, she's dead."

"Oh, I'm so sorry."

She gets off the phone as fast as she can, and I am stuck with more pain. At least I can write about it in my journal.

If you'd told me back in September that Clare would become a regular member of our lunch table by November, I would never have believed it. No one changes where they sit unless there's some big fight or something. That happened in seventh grade, when Beth tried to control what everyone at her table was wearing: First it was capris and glittery eyeliner every day, then it was French braids. For a while, they went along and looked like Beth clones. Finally, Sydney told her to "shove her stupid rules up her butt." Now that was a memorable moment.

Our table doesn't really have a leader, although Olivia is always issuing fashion alerts and analyses of everyone else's clothes, shoes, and accessories. She's a milder version of Beth. Clare's mix-and-match style of clothing has shaken things up, in a good way. She likes to combine things that no one else would think of combining, like plaids and stripes, or peach-colored capris and cowboy boots. Then there's me. My fashion don'ts aren't on purpose. The fact that a lot of things are getting too small for me doesn't help.

Instead of joining in on the daily clothing commentary, Clare and I tend to discuss other important things, like the cute new art teacher or ziti.

"Got any baked ziti in your lunch?"

"Maybe tomorrow."

We laugh and laugh. In Clare's case, make that snort and snort. No one else gets it, of course. Their lives are ziti-free.

Ashes

"I've been meaning to talk to you about something," Dad says while we're driving home from soccer practice. I'm thinking he might be about to bring up the C on my progress report, or maybe the trip to Japan that we were saving up for before Mom got sick. Then I realize he's about to tell me he's sick, too, and my stomach goes on high alert.

"What, Dad?" I ask, trying to prepare myself for what he's going to say.

"About growing up. I can't believe you're almost fourteen." He's looking straight ahead, and so am I.

"Yeah, well . . ." *Where is this going*, I wonder.

Dad starts pulling at his left ear.

"I know Mom talked to you about some of the body changes girls go through. She was certainly more of an expert on those kinds of things than I am, but if you have questions about that stuff, maybe you can ask Aunt Jennifer, or Deborah, or . . ."

"Yeah, Dad, I know. Thanks."

"Well, I just want to be sure you know I'm here, even if I can't do it the way Mom would."

"Yeah, okay," I say, turning to look at the trees along the side of the road.

"Talking about these things with your parents isn't exactly easy. I remember *my* dad trying and failing miserably. Man, oh, man." He smiles, which helps a little, and we pull into the driveway.

"Yeah, I can just imagine Pop Pop." I turn to the backseat and gather my soccer bag. "Okay, Dad, thanks."

He keeps talking as we get out of the car.

"Oh, and one last thing, honey. When you need supplies at the drug store or the grocery store or wherever you buy those things, just go ahead and toss them in the cart, okay? I don't want you feeling embarrassed."

"Okay. Got it. Can I go now?"

"Okay. Ciao, honey."

The talk. We had the *talk*, or at least part of the talk. I know he tried, and I guess he did all right. Dad rarely calls me honey. I guess the birds and bees were on his mind. He's doing his best to be a dad *and* a mom.

As soon as I'm sure that Dad is safely watching the Orioles-Yankees baseball game in his room (*their room*) upstairs, I head downstairs to the living room, turning on every light we have, one by one. Mom's ashes are on the mantel above the fireplace in a jar. Not a glass jar like the kind they use for pickles and jam, but a Chinese ginger jar. Mom had a collection of them, and Dad thought that using one for her ashes would be nicer than the wood box from the funeral home. It's kind of like a vase with a lid on it, decorated with blue and white flower designs.

I hate to say it, but at first, Mom's ashes creeped me out. I tried to imagine what they looked like in the box, and what her body went through to turn into ashes, but then I reminded myself that dead bodies don't feel anything. That's what dead *is*. Dad still hasn't told me when or where we're going to spread her ashes. Isn't there some sort of a deadline for these things?

I don't think I'll be pointing out the ashes to any of my friends, because it might freak them out. But it's comforting to have a place in the house where I can go to think about Mom and feel closer to her, or talk to her and ask her questions. Tonight, I ask her lots of things about growing up — *in my head.* It would be way too embarrassing if Dad came downstairs and heard me. *When did you get your period? When you said you were a late bloomer, is that what you meant? When am I going to get mine? Almost all of my friends have theirs already. Is there something wrong with me? Does being sad make your period come later? What else do I need to know about growing up that I can't find out from my friends or Dad?*

I don't get any answers.

If only ashes could talk.

I also want to ask Mom about flute and if she would care that much if I quit. I never practice, and band is boring except for seeing that cute boy, Alex. But if I'm honest, I do know what Mom's answer would be to the flute question.

Seeing Orange

I first noticed Alex Doherty in sixth grade. He has freckles and brownish hair, and he's one of those boys who wear shorts almost every day, even when it's freezing. He has an orange shirt that he wears all the time, and it looks really good on him. Maybe he has a few of the same shirt? On top of that he has the most beautiful smile. Maybe you're not supposed to use the word *beautiful* for a boy, but his smile is gorgeous. When he smiles, he lights up the whole classroom. I haven't ever really talked to him, except the very rare times when we are assigned to work together in a small group.

I'm trying to solve an impossible math problem when I hear, "Alexander Doherty, would you like to share your fascinating conversation with the class?"

"No, Mrs. Giamatti. Sorry."

Everyone turns around and stares at him. I know what that feels like. Mrs. Giamatti makes him move his seat, and I am so mad because now he's two rows away. He still sits behind me in social studies, but I am too nervous in social studies, with Mr. Spinolli waiting to yell at anyone who gets a question wrong, to let myself relax in there, much less look around and stare at Alex. He's also in band with me, but he's always busy with his drums in the back of the room. What is it with boys and drums? I still don't know if he knows I exist, and if he does, does he just think of me as "the girl whose mother died" or "the pathetic flute player with big ears"?

I did learn something about *him*, though. The entire grade had to write haiku poems for English. Everyone's poems were then hung up in the hallways. So much for privacy. I'm glad I didn't write mine about anything personal. Clare and I searched until we found Alex's.

> *caught in the middle*
> *like a print behind the glass*
> *sharp cuts if broken*

"That sounds serious," I say to Clare.

"Yeah. Not much about nature and seasons in that one."

As soon as I get to my next class, the fire alarm goes off. After lots of moaning and groaning, everyone marches outside into the rain. I find Joci and Clare with a bunch of our girlfriends, all huddled together. Everyone is complaining about how miserable they are.

"Can't they do fire drills on nice days?"

"This is horrible."

Our hair and clothes are getting soaked. At least it's not that cold today. We're finally allowed back in the building in time to grab our stuff and go home.

When I get to my house, there's a message from Joci asking me to call her as soon as I can because she has an extremely urgent question about the English homework. I'm soaking wet and starving, so I change into my most comfortable flannel pants and sweatshirt and eat a bowl of cereal first.

"Hi, Joss, I just got home. That fire drill was horrible, huh. I got your message. What's up?"

"When is the English essay due?"

"Next Monday," I say, sitting down with Maki on my lap.

"Oh. Phew. It is unbelievably hard. I just don't get what she's asking for. Do you? Does your dad help you with your writing since he's a high school teacher?"

"Sometimes, but not much."

"You're so lucky. My dad says he was terrible at English, and that's why he became a banker. My mom wants to help, but she gets too involved and we always end up fighting."

She sounds majorly frustrated, and I don't know what to say other than, "Really?"

I can't imagine her mom fighting with anyone.

"So, what have you and Clare been up to lately?"

"What do you mean, *up* to?"

"Well, I feel like we don't hang out together as much as we used to, and I see you with Clare all the time."

I pull Maki closer to me.

"Well, yeah, I mean, I like Clare, and she really understands what it's like since her dad died."

"So you just want to hang around with kids whose parents died?" Joci says in a mocking tone.

"No, that's not what I mean."

"Well, what *do* you mean?"

"I only said that because you asked me about Clare."

Now I'm feeling like I have to apologize for spending time with Clare.

"Well, I feel sorry for you," she continues.

I can't tell if her voice sounds sarcastic or concerned.

"Um, well, I don't think I want you to feel sorry for me."

"Well, if my mom died, I would just *kill* myself," she says with her best drama-queen imitation.

I feel like I got punched in the stomach. What a thing to say to me! I mean, how insensitive could she be? When I catch my breath, I manage to say, "Joci, is that supposed to make me feel better?"

My anger kicks into high gear and I want to scream at her. Before I can figure out what to do next, she answers, "I'm just saying it must be *awful*. I don't know how you go on. I don't think I could."

"Well, I don't really have a choice, do I?" I say with sarcasm oozing through every word. Joci is silent, so I quickly add, "I have to go. I have homework."

Now I'm really not so sure our friendship will survive. And that would be sad. We've been friends for so many years, and I really love her mom.

Space

I feel so alone and scared sometimes, scared that the pain will stay with me forever, that I won't ever go back to having a normal life. I try to remember the times before Mom got sick, when Dad wasn't so sad and quiet. He had a funny laugh. Mom used to tease him about sounding like an otter (whatever an otter sounds like). Lately, the only laughter I've been hearing at home comes out of the TV.

Dad used to play all of these jokes on us, like putting a king-size Tootsie Roll on my pillow. *"Corinna! Come look at what Maki did in your room! Did you forget to walk him?"*

He also used to be full of stories, like the one when he stayed in the woods for twenty-four hours with only three matches and a bandanna. It was at his camp in Vermont, and he had to do a "solo" hike to get a certain wilderness survival rating that he really wanted. He was only thirteen. I can't imagine doing that at this age. He built a shelter out of branches and everything. I would be so scared. He used to tell us camp stories all the time, until Mom and I were sick of them. He had school stories, too. He must have told me a million times about the disaster that happened when he wrote a love note to his second-grade crush, and his teacher snatched it and read it aloud to the class.

I wish Dad would start telling stories again, even the ones about camp. I'd like to hear more stories about my mom, but I feel unsure about bringing her up too much. Stories about Mom still make me feel sad, even if they are happy stories. Maybe that's why I don't feel like spending time with Deborah, even though she keeps calling and making these sweet offers to have a girls' lunch together.

One thing I really like is finding different stashes of Mom's things around the house. It's kind of like finding pieces of her, parts of a puzzle or a treasure. I've put a few things in a memory box, which I call my Mom Box. It's a wooden tea box that she brought home from Japan and used for storing hats and gloves. So far, it contains her perfume bottle, her watch, her brown leather gloves, and her special cashmere scarf.

Today, I'm searching for more "Mom things" when I find a shoe box stuffed with photos in the basement. Mom did make a few albums, and she filled in my baby book, but the albums only go through my first four years. The other day, I found a bunch of pictures of my mom when she was a little girl and a teenager. She was beautiful, with her long wavy hair and soft green eyes. But some of the outfits she wore are unbelievable! I can't believe yellow corduroys and culottes with vegetable-print fabric were ever in fashion. I like looking at pictures of her and imagining what she was thinking about then. What were her worries? What was her favorite music group? Who was her best friend? Did she ever fight with her parents? Who did she have a crush on? Was her body healthy or did she already have a seed of some cancer back then? I don't want to forget what she looks like. I mean, what she *looked* like. I'm also worried I'll forget the sound of her voice. It's already fading a little, even though I have her cell phone message. We do have some movies Dad made, but that's not the same as hearing it in your head.

I decide to call Aunt Jennifer.

"Hi, Aunt Jennifer, it's Corinna."

"Hi there. How are you doing, sweetie?"

"Okay, I guess."

"Really?"

"Kinda."

"Tell me the worst thing and the best thing that happened to you this week."

"Well, the best thing was having good laughs with my new friend Clare. And the worst . . . was when I raised my hand to ask a question in math and everyone laughed at me."

I didn't mention that Alex witnessed my humiliation.

"Oh, that's terrible. How did your teacher handle it?"

"She said, 'There's no such thing as a stupid question,' but I still felt stupid."

"Oh, honey, those moments are so hard. But I'll bet other

kids had the same question and were relieved that you were brave enough to ask."

"Yeah, well, it still felt awful. I *hate* when people stare at you or laugh at you." I think of Lena and her juggling fiasco.

"I know, I know."

"So you're still coming next weekend, right?" I ask, needing reassurance that the long wait is almost over.

"Definitely. I can't wait to see you and your dad."

"Me, too."

Now *there's* an understatement!

Panic

Dad never stays on the phone for very long, so when he does, my ears perk up. It's like when Maki is quiet and you don't know what he's up to, you get suspicious that he's stolen some food or a dirty sock out of the laundry. The moment I hear Dad on the phone, I can tell he's talking about our situation, so I make my way closer to the source.

"What would she want me to do? I don't know. I don't know. I wish I knew." There's a long silence — I guess the person is talking a lot.

"What would I want *her* to do? I don't know that, either." Another long silence. "I guess I would want her to take really good care of Corinna, to make sure she was okay. And to continue with her music. Music was so important to her."

Then come a lot of "uh-huhs," before he starts talking about some other friend they both must know, someone I've never heard of, but apparently this guy is changing jobs or something. I quickly tiptoe out of the hallway, just in case he opens the door. When I see him later, he tells me that Mike had invited him to go hunting and to get facials.

"What? That's totally weird. You don't even hunt."

"How about the facial part?"

"Even weirder. I've never heard of guys getting facials."

"Well, his wife works at a spa or salon or something and she's been getting on his case about needing one."

"Are you going to do it, Dad?"

"Nah, those aren't really my thing."

I guess the conversation about Mom's music reminded him that I play the flute, because in the morning, he asks me if I've been practicing. The silver music stand is still in the living room, next to Mom's two violas. I haven't touched it.

"Not so much," I admit without looking at him.

The next day is the second-to-last day of the first marking period, and our teachers are driving us crazy with tests. Clare and I are walking to lunch, quizzing each other on the math formulas. Clare knows how nervous I am about tomorrow's huge math test and wishes me luck.

"Thanks. I need all the luck I can get."

Just then, my old English teacher walks by, the one who was so critical of everything I wrote last year. She's got lipstick all over her teeth, which I'm trying not to stare at. When I turn away, I see Alex looking right at me, right into my eyes. He's only two feet away from me, and he's wearing his orange shirt.

I smile but I can't think of anything to say. That frozen-but-hot-and-sweaty feeling takes over my body. It's an unforgettable moment, for sure. I finally start breathing again when we get to our table, where I ask Clare, "Did you see what I saw?"

"He just totally checked you out!"

"Is he hot or what?"

"Oh, yeah. Orange boy is *totally* hot."

I signal to Clare to zip it so that the whole table doesn't get involved in discussing my love life. She's good at reading my signals and keeping secrets, unlike some people. Just then, Joci looks over at us with a sad expression and then turns to whisper something to Juliette.

I definitely need Clare to find out more about Alex for me. Amazingly, she IMs me that her younger brother is friends with Alex's younger brother, and she says she'll "work her sources."

Even though I go to bed early, I wake up late and barely get my stuff together. I forget to bring my science poster project that's due today. There goes ten points. And when I lean over in social studies to pick up the pencil that rolled off my desk, I notice that my socks are two different colors of blue. In the bright lights of the classroom, they're an advertisement for what a loser I am. I don't hear Mr. Spinolli, my scary social studies teacher, call on me, because I'm lost in space . . . again.

Everyone starts giggling before I realize he's glaring at me with those turn-you-to-stone eyes and waiting for me to answer him. I hate him! I want to disappear. Of course, I have no idea what he just asked me. He repeats the question in the voice he uses when he's annoyed, and I can just imagine him calling my dad again to say I was goofing off in class. Lucky for me, I know the answer, but my face is burning up.

Finally, it's lunchtime. Joci, Clare, and I meet up in the cafeteria, plop ourselves at the table with Lena, Eliana, Juliette, and Olivia, and begin to eat our sandwiches and salads. Even though I'm sitting with my friends, I feel trapped. I'm torn between wanting to scream at everyone and everything, and wanting to run out of there and jump on my bike to freedom. Nothing is going right. I feel like Alexander in the book *Alexander and the Terrible, Horrible, No Good, Very Bad Day.*

I packed my lunch last night, including a chocolate cupcake Dad bought me at the high school bake sale. I even made a special tent out of tinfoil to protect the frosting. When I open it up, I see that not only the frosting, but the whole cupcake is totally smooshed. No one else's lunch is smooshed. I want to crawl into a hole, one with soft flannel padding and no sound.

In the afternoon, I'm spreading out my notebook in biology, minding my own business. Beth turns around in her seat and says in a loud whisper that everyone in the entire room can hear, "Hey, Corinna, you have something in your teeth."

She almost sounds happy when she says it. Maybe I should be thankful that she is saving me from something even more embarrassing, but I'm definitely not. I spend the rest of class moving my tongue around, trying to clear the monster — *Is it lettuce or one of those seeds from Deborah's bread?* — out of my teeth. I had been hoping that Alex would come over and talk to me, but it's a good thing that he doesn't.

By the time I get to soccer practice, I'm more than ready to run. It's a tough workout, and I'm starving and thinking about dinner before practice is even half over. When it finally ends, my teammates are getting picked up, one by one or in carpools, but my dad is late.

Usually, Dad sits in the car reading or stands on the sidelines while we're finishing up, but sometimes he just pulls up as practice is ending at five o'clock. Even when Mom was alive, he was usually the one to get me because she was always giving viola lessons in the afternoons. He's never late, unlike Olivia's parents, who are late all the time. Well, today, he is *really* late. I'm the last one here, except for the coach, who can't leave until everyone is picked up. I'm trying not to panic. It's not working. I'm freaked, which is beyond panic. What if something happened to him? What if he was in a car accident? What if he had a heart attack at work or while he was driving? What if a drunk driver hit him? Who would come tell me? Who would I live with? My mind is going crazy. I have the most horrible, horrible feeling in my entire body. My coach is trying to distract me by talking about our last game, but I can't really follow what he's saying. I call Dad on my cell, but he doesn't answer. I try again, he still doesn't pick up, and I don't see any sign of our Toyota.

Finally, Dad pulls up. It's 5:25. I am so mad and so relieved at the same time, I can't decide what to say first.

"Daaaaaaaad!"

"Sorry, Corinna, traffic was terrible."

"Dad, I thought something happened to you!"

"No, no, just traffic."

He's eating a bag of barbecue potato chips, crunching away.

"How could you do that to me?"

"I didn't do it on purpose; I just got stuck."

He puts another chip in his mouth.

"Dad, do you have any idea what it felt like to have you be twenty-five minutes late?" I say, with my voice going up higher than normal because my throat is so tight. My tears are rolling all over the place, and Dad is acting all chipper.

"I'm sorry I made you worry."

"I can't go through that again."

"I'll do my best to be here on time. I usually am."

"I know, I know, but this was *awful*. You totally freaked me out. I thought you were dead."

"I should have called you."

"Well, I called you, and you didn't answer."

"I didn't hear my phone; it was in my briefcase."

He finally puts down the chip bag and looks me in the eye.

"I hear you. I'm really sorry. I don't ever want to make you feel that way. I'll do my very best not to."

"Please, Dad," I plead.

"I get it. Shall we go home and take Maki for a walk?"

"No, I don't feel like a walk."

"Well, how about a nice dinner? What do you feel like having?"

"Spaghetti. I'm starving, and we haven't had spaghetti in ages."

"Your wish is my command."

Dad's cell rings, and he fishes it out of his briefcase. It's Aunt Jennifer confirming plans for her trip. I can't *wait* for her to get here. Maybe she can give Dad some lessons.

Jewels

Clare's investigative talents are awesome. She found out that Alex Doherty and his brother live with their mom. His parents are divorced, but he sees his dad, who lives somewhere far away, on some vacations. It's a relief to hear that his life's not perfect, because it's hard for me to be around people who seem to have a perfect life. I find myself doodling hearts and practicing my future signature, Corinna Burdette Doherty, on the inside cover of my notebook during the last minutes of class when Mr. Spinolli drones on.

With my mind on my future with Alex, I go up to my parents' room after dinner. Dad is busy grading a stack of papers at his desk, so it seems safe to do a little investigation of my own.

As soon as I walk in, my eyes go to Mom's oval-shaped jewelry box, which sits on her dresser. When I was little, I loved looking through the wooden box's two layers of jewels and hearing stories of who gave her what and when. It sounded so romantic. Mom once told me that the delicate chain necklace was from someone named Hugh, but I don't remember if he was from high school or college. I wonder if eighth graders ever give jewelry to one another. Now, when I run my hands through the chains and earrings, I still feel like I'm touching treasure.

Mom didn't wear jewelry very often, but when she dressed up, she looked beautiful. She said she worried that she would scratch her viola if she wore earrings or necklaces. I bring the oval box over to the bed, sit down on the puffy comforter, and begin going through everything. I think about wearing some of it, but what if I lose it? I do have a bit of a track record of losing things . . . like when I lost my brand-new winter coat in fourth grade. That might have been the maddest I'd ever seen my mom.

"Corinna, I can't believe you lost your coat! If your head wasn't attached, you'd lose that, too!"

I thought she was going to explode.

Mixed in with the fancy jewelry are the one-of-a-kind Corinna specials. I smile when I look at the big plastic bead necklaces I made for her when I was younger, remembering how happy I was when I presented them to her. She would smile and say, "I love it, sweetie, thank you." I loved how she called me sweetie and Cori. Even though she didn't wear my necklaces more than once or twice, she always appreciated them and made me feel like an artist.

In the middle of my jewelry daydreams, Dad calls me downstairs to say that Aunt Jennifer's whole family has the stomach flu and she has to cancel her trip to see us this weekend. *Arghhhh.*

I'm so mad at her, even though she can't help it. At least it's not because of her work.

Last week was the start of the second marking period. My new elective is called survival sewing, and I'm surviving it with the help of the wonderful and stylish Ms. Carey, whose hair is very spiky and looks like it belongs in a fashion magazine.

It's so funny to see kids my age using sewing machines, especially the boys. First, we learn how to make a straight seam connecting two scraps of cloth. You have to be careful not to let your fingers get in the way, and when you press the foot pedal, you can't press too hard or the machine will gobble up your fabric *and* your fingers. I love making mine go really fast, until I can barely control the fabric and the machine starts to vibrate. It's kind of like bike riding in that way, where you want to see how fast you can go before disaster strikes.

Ms. Carey told us she sews her own clothes, all of which have zigzaggy uneven hems that she says are on purpose. She's super-creative and she encourages us to find our "inner artist." Mom was like that, too, always getting out craft projects for me to do with my friends or by myself in the kitchen while she was making dinner. Ms. Carey also loves to talk about her little kids, which makes me think she is a fun mom. She told us that her son's preschool class was talking about what they are thankful for, and he said he was "thankful for tortellini!" So cute.

I, on the other hand, am having trouble thinking of something I am thankful for.

I'm not sure if Ms. Carey knows my mom died or if I should tell her. No one ever told me if our principal told all my teachers or just Miss Beatty. I don't want Ms. Carey to feel sorry for me, or change the way she treats me, but it seems kind of strange not to say *something* to her, as if I don't trust her or don't really want her to know me. I feel really comfortable with her, and my mom's death is a big part of me. That's the thing — I feel private about my mom, but if I don't tell people, I have the risk every day of them asking or saying something that hurts.

"Did you show your mom?"

"What's your mom's job?"

"Don't you hate it when your mom won't let you wear what you want to school?"

"Why don't you ask your mom?"

"Get your mom to write you a note."

Blah, blah, blah. Even the people who do know sometimes forget and ask me something about my mom, as if she's still alive.

You know what I really want? For someone to ask me, "What can I do to help you feel better?" Not that I would necessarily know how to answer them, but it sure would feel good to at least be asked. This part is confusing, because I also don't really want people to think of me as "the girl whose mother died" or to bring it up when I don't want to think about it. It's hard to explain.

When people ask: "How are you?" I sometimes don't know what to say. Do I give an honest answer, or do I say, "Fine," to shut them up? "Life sucks sometimes" doesn't go over well with adults, and the sarcastic option, "Well, my mom died, but other than that," leaves people with their mouths hanging open.

I'm in the girls' bathroom between classes, having just checked again to see if I got my first period. I'm paranoid that it's going to come at school. Joci walks in while I'm washing my hands. After looking under each stall to be sure no one else is in here, she says, "Corinna, we have to talk."

"Okay."

I start squirming inside and turn off the water.

"It's really bothering me that you didn't want me, your best friend since second grade, to know that your mom was dying."

"Uh . . ."

I want to go back into the stall and avoid this conversation.

"And now you're all mad at me for telling other people when all I wanted to do was to help you."

She looks really upset and angry.

"Joss, I . . . I didn't want to tell *anyone*. I didn't want her to be sick. I couldn't believe she was dying."

I'm talking to her reflection in the mirror instead of looking straight at her.

"I wanted life to be normal . . . at least *outside* of my house," I continue.

"But I'm your best friend!"

"It wasn't about you. . . . I was scared."

Joci leans in and hugs me.

"Oh, Corinna, it must have been awful."

I don't say anything, but my tears start flowing. The door opens and a big group of girls comes in. They're talking loudly. We quickly separate and Joci starts washing her hands. I pull a bunch of paper towels out of the dispenser, turning my back to everyone. As soon as they leave, I wash my face and notice that Joci does the same.

The day before Thanksgiving is a half day. It's hard to get myself out of bed after another bad night's sleep. I choose sweatpants and a sweatshirt, and I stuff my hair into a messy ponytail, which is not my best look. Walking in the east wing toward my locker, I become aware of someone walking toward me. I don't feel like looking up, but when I do, I see it's that jerk, Jake. I keep on walking. Then his gruff voice barks, "Corinna, you're a walking disaster today."

What a thing to say, and his tone is disgustingly sarcastic. Yeah, I *am* kind of a mess. But who thinks it's okay to say things like that?

"Jump off a bridge, Jake."

So what if my hair looks like one of those wacky twig-headed mannequins in the store window? And what's it to Jake anyway? Why is he picking on me?

Telling Jake to jump off a bridge feels good, but later on, I start thinking about Joci saying she would kill herself if her mom died. It's been eating away at me. Even though things are getting a tiny bit better with Joci, I decide I have to tell her how much that comment hurt me. I can't decide if I should try my relaxation technique before or after the conversation, which I know will be dreadful. Words are zinging around in my head.

Maki starts scratching on the door, which is his way of signaling for a walk, so I take him out. I start to run, and Maki has to struggle to keep up. It's not very pleasant for Maki, but I *need* to run. When we get back, Maki lies panting on the cool tile floor in the kitchen, and I head up to start a bath. After rehearsing possible conversations while submerged in my Blue Oasis, I wrap myself in my terry bathrobe and fluffy slippers and call Joci on my cell. I almost hang up because I'm nervous, and her mom might be in the same room as she is.

"Remember when you said you would kill yourself if your mom died?"

"Oh . . . hi, Corinna, I thought that was you. So . . . um . . . yeah. I remember that."

"Well, it's really been bothering me."

"I thought we were over all this."

"I'm trying to get over it, but I keep getting stuck because that was such a horrible thing to say."

"I'm sorry. I didn't say it to be mean. I wanted you to know I understand how hard it must be."

"Understand? Are you kidding me? You think you understand what it's like for me?"

"Well, I'm trying to, but . . ."

"Well, I think you're going to have to try harder. That's the thing. People think they know what it's like, but unless you've been through this, you have no idea."

"I'm sorry. It's just that . . . I . . . I don't know . . ." she stammers.

My mind is racing, trying to think of what to say. I keep thinking of things that I probably should *not* say if I want our friendship to survive. I take a deep breath and blurt out, "So even though I hate it when you say things like that, or broadcast to the entire world about my mom having cancer even after I asked you not to, I just hope we can be real friends again, like before."

Joci is quiet for what feels like forever, and then, in a high-pitched voice, says, "I didn't know we weren't friends. Best friends, I mean. You've always been my best friend, ever since second grade. We're practically twins, remember?"

"Well, it didn't feel like we were best friends when you stopped coming over."

"Yeah . . . but . . . well . . . it was really hard. I felt so uncomfortable. I didn't know what to do. I didn't know what you wanted me to do."

"Uh. Well . . . I didn't really know what I wanted you to do, either, but I wanted you to show you cared."

"Of course I cared."

I stay silent.

"It's so sad."

"You could say that." The meanness in my voice is shocking even to me.

"How can I make it up to you? I mean, I can't help it if my parents didn't die like yours and Clare's."

"Of course not. Joci, all I want is for things to be normal. Normal with us, normal in my life."

"Well, me, too."

She's pleading with me. My best friend, and I don't want to lose her.

"Well . . . I guess . . . everyone makes mistakes."

"Yeah," she says, sounding relieved, and I am, too. "Do you think we should try to hang out together the weekend after Thanksgiving? My mom said she could take us to the mall."

"Yeah, okay. I guess we could do a spa night or something. Not a sleepover, though. Well . . . I have to take Maki for a walk now," I tell her, even though I just came back from taking him for a run.

Poor Maki is still tired and panting, but walking seems like the best thing to do after a conversation like Joci and I just had. I throw on my sweatpants and sweatshirt and grab my cell phone on my way out the door and call Mom. Hearing her voice is heavenly.

Thanksgiving

I wake up and remember that I had planned to make cranberry sauce to bring to Gigi and Pop Pop's house. Dad and I didn't feel like doing anything for Thanksgiving, but Gigi and Pop Pop insisted. I'm nervous about celebrating a holiday with other people, and without Mom. I can't imagine eating turkey and pumpkin pie without her.

I make the cranberry sauce according to Mom's recipe, and when it cools, I put it in a Tupperware. After showering, I decide to get dressed in some of Mom's things, to kind of have her with us. I put on her silver chain necklace with a tear drop pendant and a cozy purple sweater that she loved. It's huge on me, so I roll up the sleeves.

Thanksgiving used to be my favorite holiday. Mom and I would do lots of baking and decorate the table with flowers and homemade place cards. Usually we had some cousins and aunts and uncles and grandparents come to our house or we would go to their houses. A few weeks ago, Dad asked me if I thought we should invite Deborah and her boys, and I said, "Definitely not. Gigi and Pop Pop would not be happy about that."

Besides, Gigi is not the world's best cook. She serves canned cranberry sauce. She even leaves those ridge marks on it, from the inside of the can, like a tube of red goo. Gross. That's why Mom and I always made fresh cranberry sauce. I have to keep up the tradition.

When we arrive in Annapolis, Gigi asks me to help set the table. I put my sauce, along with a folded index card labeled SOPHIE'S CRANBERRY SAUCE, right next to the plate of thick red goo. After everyone is served, Gigi makes an announcement.

"Corinna made the cranberry sauce in the blue bowl. You might want to mix it with the other kind, unless you like it tart."

"Thanks, Gigi," I mutter to myself.

Somehow, I manage to get cranberry sauce all over my sweater sleeves, but I don't care. Dad spends most of his time on the sofa watching football with his brother. Everything about this Thanksgiving feels so wrong, so fake, so empty without Mom. I don't know if I should try to act cheerful and "thankful," or if it's okay to sulk and feel jealous of my cousins, who still have a mom. Uncle Patrick and Aunt Vicky, my father's brother and his wife, are both trying to be thoughtful and make an effort to talk and sit with me away from my loud and hyper cousins. All the grown-ups ask me the same question: "How's school?"

I think people are avoiding talking about Mom, which is really weird, because we're with our own family. It's like everyone is trying to protect one another by not bringing her up, but it's so obvious that she's on everyone's minds. Well, maybe not my little cousins' minds. They're busy being kids. The only thing I'm in the mood to do with them is zone out in front of some stupid TV shows.

Since she couldn't be with us and I need to laugh, I decide to e-mail Aunt Jennifer when we get back home and ask her to tell me a funny story about my mom when they were kids. She writes back and tells me about the time Mom had a crush on a boy in ninth grade. She baked brownies for him and dropped them off on his porch and did the old "Ding, Dong, Ditch" because she would have been too embarrassed if his parents had answered the door. It turned out that the boy was allergic to tree nuts. What had she put in the brownies? Walnuts. Lucky for her, he didn't eat any of them. My grandmother had insisted that because the recipe called for walnuts, she had to use them. No wonder Mom liked inventing her own recipes! I print out the e-mail and put it in my Mom Box.

Maybe we can be thankful with Aunt Jennifer's family next year. I'll bet she'll appreciate my cranberry sauce. I sure hope future Thanksgivings will be easier.

Winter

Wishful Thinking

We have a plaster mold of my hand that I made in preschool. I must have been three or four years old. I like to squeeze as much of my hand into the mold as I can, imagining that my hand fits in perfectly, and I get transported back in time to that age and size, and my mom is still alive.

There's another trick I do with candies. I've always loved candy, and so did my mom. Sometimes I use M&M'S, but I've also used Koppers, Jujubes, jelly beans, Gummi Bears, and salt water taffies. Anything with a lot of colors. Chocolate Easter eggs wrapped in colored foil would be good, too. First, I sort the candy into color groups. Then, I make designs with them. I tell myself that if I get the right combination and eat them in a special order, then I might somehow unlock a secret passageway and be magically transported to heaven (or wherever her spirit is), and my mom will be sitting there smiling at me like she's been waiting for me. Yeah, yeah, I know that sounds crazy. But it feels good to wish . . . and the candy tastes good.

I'm daydreaming about my candy trick when our band teacher

interrupts with his usual preconcert speech: "We have a big concert this Thursday and I expect everyone to know their parts! Okay. One, two, three, four, one, two, three, four."

After we play the first two lines, he stops us and says, "That was terrible, guys. What's going on in the flute section?"

Eliana answers for us. "Mr. Morgan, my keypad is sticking."

· She doesn't tell him that I'm the one who missed all the C-sharps.

"Let's try it again. Flute section only. Ready? One, two, three, four."

Band practice drones on for what seems like another five hours while I'm wishing I could be invisible. Then Mr. Morgan says, "Corinna, is something the matter?"

"I'm sorry, Mr. Morgan."

"Corinna, why don't you sit this one out."

My hands are sweaty and my tears ignore my orders to stay dry while the flutes play the same passage over again. Talk about public humiliation! I think I'm going to croak. I fear that Alex is witnessing my tears and this musical disgrace even though I can't see his face.

"Corinna, can you stay after class for a minute?" Mr. Morgan asks.

When the bell finally rings, everyone packs up and leaves. All except for Alex, who is busy adjusting his drums. When he walks to the door, he turns around with what looks like a little smile, and says, "See ya."

It would be thrilling, except for the fact that Mr. Morgan is standing right here, obviously waiting to pounce on me with some vitally important teacher conversation and my eyes are surely looking hideously puffy. Mr. Buzz-Kill Morgan takes a long sip out of his Redskins mug, swallows loudly, and wrinkles up his face, like he's gulping down some foul-tasting cleaning chemical.

"Corinna, how are you doing?"

"Not so great."

"Because your playing is not what it used to be, not what I know you're capable of. You seem distracted."

"Yeah, kind of," I mutter.

In his gentlest voice he asks, "Is it your mother?"

"Um . . . yeah."

I'm still looking at my flute case, fiddling with the latch.

"Well, if there's anything I can do . . ."

I know he means well, but this is really awkward and I don't know what to say.

"No, not really. Thanks."

"Well, if there's any —"

I'm halfway to the door when I turn around and say, "I don't know if I even want to play the flute anymore."

"What makes you say that?" he says as his eyebrows go straight up. He looks like he's scared of me.

"I just don't enjoy it."

He takes another sip out of his mug, swallows a few times,

and says, "I think everyone goes through periods of being less enthusiastic about their music."

"Yeah, but I never say to myself, 'Oh, I think I'll go play my flute.' "

We're both quiet for what feels like a superlong time before he says, "Your mom would be sad if you quit."

"Well, maybe, but my mom's not here," I say, looking right at him.

"Right, but wouldn't she want you to continue?"

His effort to send me on a guilt trip rubs me the wrong way.

"Yeah, Mr. Morgan, she probably would. But what about what *I* want?"

"Okay. Well, then, why don't you think about it, maybe talk about it with your dad, and then let me know. I'd hate to see you drop band. You're a good musician, Corinna."

Thanks for the punch, Mr. Morgan. And thanks for ruining my perfect chance to talk to Alex.

I'm glad Clare is coming to my house tonight for a movie and dinner. I need a major distraction.

I can't believe it's December and this is the first time Clare is at my house. It just hasn't felt right to invite someone over when my dad is so down. I've wanted to have her over ever since she sent me that first IM. The one about us both being part of the same Parent-Who-Died Club that no one wants to be a part of.

"I have so much to tell you!" I blurt out as soon as I open the door.

After a snack of tortilla chips and salsa, we take Maki for a walk. When we pass Mrs. Simmons's house, I tell Clare about how she visited umpteen times during Mom's cancer.

"That lady drove me crazy. She would just show up, take up space, and jabber away at my mom, my dad, and me."

Clare's answer surprises me: "I'll bet she thought she was being helpful."

"Yeah, real helpful. One time, I caught her taking pictures of Mom, so I said to her, 'What are you doing?' Mrs. Simmons acted all innocent. 'Just taking some photos of your mom. I want you to have them. Doesn't she look better today?' I wanted to scream at Mrs. Simmons, but not in front of Mom, who was half awake. I said to Mrs. Simmons, 'Could you please come into the kitchen for a minute?' As soon as we stepped into the kitchen, I said, 'Mrs. Simmons! What are you doing? Stop taking pictures of my mom! We have good pictures of her, thank you very much, and we don't need you taking pictures of her dying.' Mrs. Simmons was clueless. 'Oh, Corinna, dear, I'm sure she doesn't mind.' "

I tell Clare how my dad wasn't there when I needed him to deal with Mrs. Simmons. Then I describe how my cheeks were exploding with the words I had wanted to scream back at her, *"Well, I mind. In fact, I mind a lot. If you don't delete those pictures,*

I'm going to smash your camera and you will never come into this house again."

I'm glad I'm finally telling Clare about this horrible experience. She's the one person who might understand.

"I *still* cross the street or walk the other way whenever I see her. I can't deal with her."

From the way Clare looks me in the eye, makes a face, and even shudders her shoulders, I can tell she gets it.

Dad is asleep in his chair when we get home, so we go to the basement to watch our movie. Clare's mom picks her up after Clare and I make a pot of spaghetti for our dinner.

The rest of the weekend is pretty boring until Dad's announcement. He tells me that we're going to dinner tomorrow night at Deborah's house. It will be the first night we've had plans to go out for dinner since before my mom died. Dad seems nervous as he's telling me. I can tell by the way his eyes and mouth look. I'm nervous, too. What will we talk about? Will Deborah ask me for an update on the furry pink journal she gave me? Will her sons ask me uncomfortable questions about my mom? Will she hog my dad's attention? Will she go on and on about music and pressure me about my flute?

Deborah is cooking when we arrive, but we don't eat until at least an hour later, by which time I am starving. The food is pretty good: chicken without any of her strange bread seeds, baked potatoes, and, unfortunately, brussels sprouts. I can't stand brussels sprouts. Even the smell of them makes me sick, and these smell burned and cabbagey. I leave them on my plate, but so do her two little sons.

Deborah makes a toast in the middle of dinner.

"Here's to Sophie."

"To Sophie," Dad echoes.

"We miss you," Deborah goes on, sounding sad and looking right at me.

I manage to hold up my water glass while I look down at the brussels sprouts on my plate.

I think everyone is unsure of whether or how much to talk about Mom, kind of like at Thanksgiving. Of course she's totally on our minds. I practically have a red light that flashes "Mom" on my forehead.

Deborah tries to get me to laugh by saying, "Remember when your mom's music stand fell down and she just kept on playing? Has that ever happened to anyone in your band, Corinna?"

I swallow and put on a smile, though I'm not sure who the smile is for. The boys are busy playing with their action figures on the table. Dad is definitely being more talkative than I am, more talkative than he's been in a long time. He must be feeling really brave, because he asks Deborah, "How's the chamber music going for the Bellagio Players?"

"Oh, pretty well. We've had lots of gigs, including one at the governor's big fund-raiser. Sophie always wanted to play there and check out the acoustics in that beautiful historic building."

"Remind me who you got to play viola?"

"Well, no one can replace Sophie, but Alan Peterson joined us. He's this super-serious guy who never laughs, even when we make mistakes in rehearsal. He just sits there, really, with no expression on his face. Sophie and I used to laugh so hard we practically peed in our pants."

That part makes *me* laugh. There were lots of times Mom would tell me stories about when she'd almost wet her pants laughing. She really did love to laugh.

Dad doesn't do anything crazy or embarrassing, but Deborah sure does. Right at the end, when we're saying good night, she announces that she'd really like to go to the Parents' Night at my school since Dad has to be at work as a teacher at his own school that night.

"No, it's okay," I tell her, because the last thing in the world I want is for people to think Deborah is my mom.

"But I'd like to."

"No, thanks."

"Oh," she says. "I didn't realize I was stepping on toes." She actually seems surprised that I don't want her to come.

Talk about awkward. On the drive home, Dad says to me, "She was only trying to be nice."

He doesn't look at me when he's talking; he just stares straight ahead. I want to say, *"Well, she's not my parent,"* but I don't let the words go past the part of the throat where your tonsils hang down like a gate.

If Only

I can't help it, but I wonder whether my mom could still be alive if only she had gone to the doctor sooner, before the cancer spread. What made her wait? Did she know or even suspect she had something wrong for a while before she went to the doctor? Did she wait because she was too busy with me or her job? Was there something my mother did that caused the cancer? Something she *didn't* do? My head sometimes spins with so many questions, questions that I will never have the answers to.

I've thought about writing her doctor, Dr. Rothstein, but I haven't because I didn't think she'd listen to a kid. Today, I decide that the only way to get some of these things out of my head is to actually write the letter, not because I'll get answers, but because I want her to know some things. I take out one of Dad's red correcting pens and a piece of computer paper.

Dear Dr. Rothstein,

I don't know if you remember me, but I remember you, and I remember some things I want to share with you. I hated it when you

119

visited my mother's hospital room and you always seemed so rushed. You spoke so technical and scientific, like my mom was some kind of science experiment and we were part of the machinery. What was THAT about? Maybe when you deal with cancer all the time, you forget about the person. If I get cancer, I'm going to find a doctor who knows how to talk to me and my family like people, not machines that don't have feelings. I hope you will do a better job of listening to your patients and their families about their choices from now on. You made us feel bad about choosing to stop the treatment. It felt awful.

Sincerely,

Corinna Burdette

I show it to Dad, who says, "I understand how you feel, but you can't send that."

"Why not? You always tell me how it's important to be honest."

"Yes, but . . ."

"Dad, don't you think Dr. R. needs to know her strengths and weaknesses, just like your students?"

"Well, yeah, but . . ."

"So, I'm sending it. I think Mom would be proud of me."

That shuts him up. He goes back to sucking on his butter-scotch Life Saver, which I can smell from ten feet away. I don't think Dad will give me the address, so I hunt for it on one of those millions of pages of medical bills, in the piles on his desk, that he's so stressed out about.

I spend the next three days trying to decide if I should mail the letter. Maki doesn't give any useful advice, so I consider calling Aunt Jennifer to ask her what she would do if she were in my shoes. I decide the choice is up to me. When I finally walk down to the mailbox on the corner, I open the door and hold it flat for a long time. Will Dr. R. even read it? If she does, will she say, "Oh, that little kid doesn't know what she's talking about"? I finally let the mailbox swallow the envelope.

Trapped

Just before lunch, we get our eighth-grade school photos back, and I am horrified by mine. They are *awful*. I mean truly terrible. They don't even look like me, unless I look a lot worse than I thought. Maybe my whole sense of reality is off because nothing much feels normal. When we meet up in the hall, Joci and Clare look at them quickly, smile, and then start to talk about going to the mall after school. I must look hurt, because they apologize, but the apology doesn't make it better. Not only am I being excluded from the mall, but I have hideous pictures. I think about throwing them away or burning them. My ears are sticking way out and my smile is more like a grimacing Halloween mask. I thought the green V-neck shirt would look good with my green eyes, but it makes me look like I've just thrown up. If there was an ad for what *not* to wear for school photos, it would use that disgusting picture. At least my hair is neutral-to-good, thanks to Olivia's French-braiding skills. Joci's photos are gorgeous, with her long brown hair perfectly in place and her beautiful blue sweater and big boobs. Even her braces with matching blue rubber bands look okay. Clare's are kind of dorky-looking, but she doesn't seem to mind. Her smile is nice, and that's the most important part. I can't even think about the fact that my hideous picture is going to be in the yearbook for Alex and the rest of the world to see. Mom would have told me not to worry, that's what the do-over days are for, but I don't feel like dealing with it.

I stuff my pictures into my backpack and look for Eliana. I'm supposed to go to her house today. I did manage to get out of bowling. She's always asking me to go bowling. Her dad manages a bowling alley, so I haven't wanted to break the news that I actually hate bowling and think it's the most boring thing in the world.

When we get to her house, we scarf down some strawberries, cinnamon-raisin English muffins, and apple cider, and then go up to her room. It's all color coordinated and looks like it could be in those decorating magazines they have at the checkout counter. She shows me her scrapbooks, which are all neatly lined up on her bookshelf, and there's this really cute page of all her school pictures since nursery school. I'm relieved to see that her fifth-grade bad hair day rivals my eighth-grade disaster. She had drawn bushy curls in black pen all around her red hair to cover it up. We both have a good laugh about that. I take one of my photos out of the big white envelope and use Eliana's Sharpie to give it some black bushy curls to match hers.

We look through her scrapbook with all its cute paper shapes and borders, and I see some recent photos of Eliana, Joci, Clare, Olivia, Juliette, Lena, and their moms, all dressed up.

"What are these from?"

"Oh . . . those are from a tea party thing."

"A tea party? Where was I?"

"Well, um, I think Juliette didn't want you to feel left out so we were supposed to keep it hush-hush. I told her we should wait or maybe change the theme, but she didn't want to."

"The theme?"

"Yeah. It was a mother-daughter theme."

"Oh. Oh, wow. So everyone went with their moms."

"I'm so sorry, Corinna."

"I can't believe Joci and Clare didn't tell me."

"They were probably just trying to protect you, like I was. I'm really sorry."

"Alrighty then. This calls for chocolate. Do you have any?"

"Hershey's Kisses."

"Perfect."

I can't decide if I should confront Joci and Clare about not telling me about Juliette's mother-daughter tea thing. I ask Aunt Jennifer what she would do. I figure she'll have better advice than Dad would on this kind of thing. She e-mails back a few hours later.

That's a hard one. They probably were trying to protect you, but it was a big risk, since you might find

out. I'm glad it wasn't one of them who hosted the party. Do you think you would feel better if they knew you know and that it hurt you when you found out about their secrecy? With a hard choice like that, it sometimes helps to think about what you would have done if you were in their shoes.

It doesn't exactly give me a clear answer, but when I ask myself that question, I understand the problem in a new way. I put off a final decision because either way feels bad.

In my e-mail, I also asked Aunt Jennifer if she knew if any of Mom's friends in middle or high school had a parent die.

Yes, one girl's mom died in an airplane accident. The whole school freaked out. But it wasn't a close friend, so I don't think Sophie was very involved.

I wish, wish, wish Aunt Jennifer lived closer to us. It would be so great. I've thought about asking her to consider moving. Or asking Dad to move there. Maybe I should go to college in California. Then we'd at least be in the same state.

A week before winter vacation, Miss Boppity Bop asks me to have lunch with her in her classroom.

"I've been thinking a lot about you losing your mom, and how hard it must be for you."

She starts to get these icky spitballs in the corners of her mouth. Maybe she does that when she's nervous. She does seem nervous, and I know I am, too. I don't think my mouth has spitballs, and I certainly hope I'm not close to the age when you start developing them, but I wipe the corners of my mouth just in case. She tells me that her mom died a few years ago, and that even though she's a grown-up, it was still hard for her to lose her mother.

"Tell me more about your mom," she says. "What was she like?"

"Well, she was a violist. . . . She loved music and Japan . . . and creative cooking."

"What do you miss the most?"

"The projects. We used to do lots of projects together. All kinds of crafts. Oh, and cooking. We both loved baking and cooking."

After a while, I ask her, "What was it like for you after *your* mom died?"

"Well, it gets easier over time, but there are still things that make me have a big wave of missing my mother. Sometimes, it's something like Mother's Day. Other times, it's seeing a certain flower in the garden or eating homemade chicken soup."

That makes me swallow hard, but it feels really good to talk. A few tears drip down my face. Even though I'm crying at school after I vowed not to, it doesn't feel so bad. She gets a little teary, too. The best part is that she doesn't tell me to stop crying. I finally get up the nerve to ask her what the two Bs stand for in her name.

"Beatrice Betty."

I can't believe her parents named her Beatrice Betty Beatty.

"Did you ever worry that people would think your mom did something that made her deserve to die?"

Miss Beatty looks startled.

"Is that something you've been worried about?" she asks me.

"Well . . . kinda . . ."

"Some people may think that, but it's not true, and it's hurtful."

I still wake up in the middle of the night with stomachaches a few times a week, which makes me worried that there might be something wrong inside. I remember that phrase Dad used when he explained why Mom was having surgery: "To make sure nothing's wrong inside." Yuck. I have a page in my journal where I keep track of my stomachaches.

Last night was one of those nights when my stomach hurt a lot, but today I feel better after lunch. I drop a note on Joci's desk when I walk by on my way to the pencil sharpener, asking if she wants to do something after school. She mouths "Yes!" When the bell finally rings, we make a plan to walk to Bruce's Variety, which is a store with everything you could ever possibly need for any art project or holiday decoration and tons of school supplies. It's so crowded with junk you can barely fit in the aisles, especially if you're wearing a backpack like we are. We love to go in there and look around.

We're standing in the section with sequins and glue-on jewels when I realize that we have to leave immediately. I tap Joci and say, "Let's go."

"We just got here." She sounds annoyed.

"I have to get out of here."

"Corinna, what's up, we just got here!"

"I *have* to go."

"Can you just wait a minute? I have to get some stuff for my social studies poster."

"I'll wait outside," I say, walking away, pulling down on my shoulder straps.

"What is *up*?"

I turn around and say in my most serious voice, "Just trust me."

"Okay, okay, I'll be out in a sec."

When she comes out, Joci is all irritated.

"Geez, you're so impatient."

"Sorry," was all I could manage to say.

It was like I couldn't breathe in there. All those times I'd been to that store with my mom came flooding back. I knew I had to leave right away, but Joci didn't get it and I don't want to have to explain everything. I probably seem crazy to her. *She* doesn't have to worry about freaking out in stores.

I'm really cold by the time I get home, so I make myself a cup of wild berry zinger tea using Mom's favorite mug. It's white with hand-painted dainty blue flowers and green vines, and I gave it to her for her birthday a few years ago. I kiss the rim of the cup and feel the warmth from the tea. Then I do a really dumb thing. I put the tea on the shelf in the basement and I stand on a chair to reach up to the top of the cabinet to lift down my bead collection. Yes, it's a swivel chair. Yes, it's an incredibly stupid move. I drop two plastic jars of seed beads, which scatter everywhere, and the next thing I know, I knock over the precious cup. I'm so worried about the cup, I dive for it. Kind of like a soccer goalie move. Lucky for me, I save it, except for a tiny chip on the rim, but I land really hard on the tile floor on my elbow. And it's not the soft kind of tile. It hurts big-time. I ice it for a while, hoping that will help numb the pain. If that cup broke, it would be like a part of *her* smashing. Really. I want to have it as long as I live.

Mom drank tea, too. Green tea. Her host family in Japan used to send her tins of fancy green tea at New Year's. Whenever she made it, the whole house smelled like green tea, which to me smells kind of like wet decaying grass. I could never imagine wanting to drink that smell. We don't smell that smell anymore.

Two days before vacation, my hawk-eyed math teacher gives me a note from the counselor, saying that the grief group will be starting at lunchtime on January fourth, the day after we get back. It's been so long since Ms. DuBoise told me she might do a group, I'd forgotten about it. I wonder why she waited so long. The note makes me dread that it will be totally cheesy or uncomfortable, but I'm also a little bit curious about who else will be in it.

The idea of having a time and place where I am supposed to talk about Mom at school seems strange. I've been trying so hard *not* to think about her at the grocery store and random places like Bruce's Variety store, but it's hard to control. It's kind of like when you're walking behind someone who's smoking a cigarette and the smell and smoke keep catching up to you and surrounding you no matter how hard you try to avoid it.

Just as I'm thinking about coughing and choking on smoke and grief, I see Joci down the hall and rush to catch up with her on the way to lunch. Walking right in front of us is our principal, Mr. Maroni, in his pinstriped suit. He's always trying to get into conversations with students, the same kids who call him Maroni the Moron behind his back. We slow down so that we don't have to talk to him, and Joci starts elbowing me.

"What?"

She laughs and points to his shoes. A long piece of toilet paper is stuck to the bottom of his left shoe. He stops and talks to some teachers. We're dying with silent laughter. We pretend to be looking in our lunch bags while we wait to see if the teachers notice. Will they tell him? Will they burst out laughing? It's almost impossible not to shriek. I practically pee in my pants . . . just like Mom. The suspense is too much, and we end up turning around and using a different hall to get to the lunchroom. There's nothing like a good laugh with Joci.

When I get home, I pick up the mail, which is mainly

catalogs. Without looking at the mailing labels, I start paging through, looking for pants. Mine are all getting too small. I fold down the corners of pages with some options so that I can present my case to Dad.

"Dad, I need some shirts and pants and shoes. Can we order them for my Christmas present? It's okay if they don't get here in time."

"How will you know what size to get? Didn't you and Mom always go to stores to try stuff on?"

"Yeah, but you and I haven't exactly been doing that."

"You're right. But I thought Joci's mother offered to take you to the mall."

"Yeah, Dad, she did. But you're my parent. Parents take their kids shopping. Why don't you like shopping?"

"I've always hated shopping."

"But I need stuff."

"Okay, okay, show me the catalog." Dad sits back in his chair, waiting for the torture to start.

"Maybe when Aunt Jennifer comes to visit she can take me. She likes shopping and so did Mom."

"I don't know when Jennifer is coming," Dad says, sounding vague.

"She said it would be soon. She promised me she would after she had to cancel."

If she doesn't come here, then I am going to have to go out there. I really need to see her.

Vacation

I haven't been to Joci's house since the bracelet "incident," so I'm a little nervous when I accept Joci's invitation for a sleepover on the first night of winter vacation. She's invited me lots of times, but I've managed to avoid it. Joci's parents are so sweet and welcoming, and I hug both of them. Her mom asks me what we're doing for vacation.

"Nothing much."

Her face has that concerned look, so I say, "But that's okay. We don't want to travel this year."

Joci's dad makes us a nice bowl of buttery popcorn, just like when we used to hang out all the time and watch *Gilmore Girls*, *Glee*, and reruns of *High School Musical*. Then her parents head up to their room to watch the news, and we go into the family room with the big TV. There isn't anything good on live TV, so we look at the movie channel and decide on this old movie, *Meet the Parents*. There's a scene when the dorky guy is at his fiancée's parents' house. They're at the dinner table having a totally awkward conversation. It's hilarious and we're both

132

laughing. But then, the guy opens a bottle of champagne and the cork flies and hits the dead grandmother's urn on the mantel. It falls, and her ashes spill everywhere. Joci continues laughing, but not me. I put my hand over my eyes and hold my breath. It's one of those OMG moments that I will definitely have to write about in my journal. Even though it's supposed to be funny, it's horrifying to think about. I can't *imagine* my mom's ashes being knocked over. They feel sacred. As soon as the movie ends, I announce that I need to go home.

"But I thought you were going to spend the night," Joci says.

"I was, but now I'm worried my dad will be too lonely."

"Corinna, you've got to start doing more things. Everyone's been talking about how you're always saying no to things."

"Who's everyone?"

"You know, the girls at school."

"Well, I *am* beginning to do more."

I pull out my cell phone and start to call my dad.

"So stay the night," Joci practically commands.

"I don't know."

"Please? We'll have so much fun. You can sleep in your twin bed, and we can have chocolate chip pancakes in the morning."

"Well, I just have to check on my dad."

I'm not sure how I feel about her shaming me into sleeping over.

"Hi, Dad."

"Corinna, is everything okay?"

"Yeah, Dad."

"Are you sure?"

"Yeah, I'm sure," I answer with a wobble in my voice.

"Are you worried about something?"

"No. Not really."

"Okay, call me in the morning."

"Good night, Dad."

"Night, Corinna."

In the morning, her mom asks me if I want to go to the mall with them.

"I know it will be a zoo with everyone doing their holiday shopping, but Jocelyn needs some things before we leave on our trip to Florida."

I instantly feel jealous that her mom is paying attention to what Joci needs (and that they're going to Florida). But I also know this is my chance to get what *I* desperately need so I try to stuff it back down. And when I call Dad to make sure it's okay, he sounds relieved.

After breakfast, we head out to Montgomery Mall. The mall is smothered in Christmas decorations, and crowds are swarming everywhere to the tunes of holiday music that repeat over and over. As soon as we get inside, Joci's mom says, "Let's go to Victoria's Secret. Joci needs some bras, so let's do that before you start looking at other stuff."

We walk past the guard at the front door of the store, who is surrounded by pink underwear, bras, and nightgowns. He's busting out of his navy security suit and he looks sound asleep. His Santa hat makes him look even more ridiculous. Joci's mom turns to me.

"Corinna, what size are you?"

How does she know that's what I need? Is it that obvious? At least she uses a quiet voice.

"Um, I don't know."

"Well, you're probably a 30A. Let's try one and see."

I hope she knows what she's talking about, because I don't want the saleslady to get involved.

I never imagined that my first bra would be bought by someone else's mom.

I'm inside one of the tiny dressing rooms filled with other people's rejects, some of which are gigantic and look like they still have breasts in them, when Joci's mom whispers, "Corinna? How are they? Can I come in?"

"Just a sec."

I open the door about an inch.

"That looks great. Is it comfortable?"

"Yeah, it's fine. I guess I'll get it."

"Well, let's get a few so you can rotate them in the laundry."

I've been feeling more and more self-conscious about being flat when all my friends are filling out and moving from exercise bras to real bras. My body seems to be stuck. I've thought about what I could do to get it going but haven't been able to come up with any ideas. I even did a Google search on that, hoping that no one at Google headquarters would be able to see what I was searching. I did find "How to Put on a Bra 101," which I must confess I watched.

When I finally come home with three bras, I feel like a grown-up. I just wish my mom had been the one to get them with me. It's one of those things you're supposed to do with your own mom. I suppose there are other girls in the world who don't have moms to do that with them, either because their moms are dead or not around, or they have two dads and no mom, or they don't feel comfortable with their moms. But in my grade, among my friends, I'm pretty sure I'm the only one who hasn't had the experience. I go to bed wearing one of them under my pajamas. I have some catching up to do, and I'm thrilled to be joining the bra sisterhood.

I have a dream about my mom. She's not sick or dead, she's just normal. It feels so good to see her with hair and looking like herself. Her wavy brown hair is so soft and beautiful. I can even smell her Neutrogena shampoo. I wake up in a happy mood and hope I will have more dreams about her like that, looking healthy and normal. Up until Bra Night, all of my dreams have been with her being sick and looking like she did at the very end. Thin and almost bald and really pale. Two weeks before she died, I told Dad, "She already looks dead."

He nodded and said, "I know, I know."

It's been hard to get that scary image out of my mind.

Holiday Blues

We don't get a tree, and the house feels empty. After our painful Thanksgiving, Dad and I decide not to go to someone else's house for Christmas. I don't know if it's the right decision. We rent a bunch of movies and buy a ton of Jiffy Pop. Dad decides we should eat Mom's favorite holiday meal, which was leg of lamb, but instead of making real leg of lamb, we buy frozen dinners. The lamb is hard to swallow, even though I usually love lamb. It's not that the meat is so tough. It's the swallowing part that is so hard. I make some wild berry zinger tea to try to soothe my throat. Later, as I load Mom's cup into the dishwasher, the whole handle snaps off in two pieces.

"Oh, no!"

I'll have to use it as a pencil holder or something.

The next few days, I don't do much of anything other than walk the dog, listen to music, and open holiday cards from happy families. Practicing the flute has no appeal, it's too cold to ride a bike, indoor soccer practice is canceled until mid-January,

Joci's having fun in Florida, and Clare is visiting her friends in Connecticut, where she used to live.

Eliana calls with her usual offer.

"Do you want to go bowling tomorrow?"

"No, thanks, we're really busy."

Not. But bowling sounds worse than doing nothing.

At least Beth hasn't called, trying to get me to eat Caesar salad at her club.

Deborah and her kids are in New Orleans, so even *she* isn't stopping by. Dad has been around every minute of every day.

The phone rings. After a few minutes, Dad tells me to get on the phone. I try to get him to tell me who it is, but he just hands me the phone.

"Hi, Corinna. It's Grandma and Bapa."

"Oh, hi. Thanks for your Christmas card."

"We sent you a package. Didn't it get there yet?"

"I don't think so. I'll ask Dad."

"How's the weather there?"

"Cold."

"You should have come to Arizona. Here it's sunny and hot every day."

After they moved from Allentown to Phoenix, we didn't visit them very often. Mom didn't seem that close to them. I think we all felt closer to Aunt Jennifer. Mom and Aunt Jennifer were always talking on the phone. With Grandma and Bapa, phone calls are always about the weather. Hot, cold, rainy, dry. Oh, and windy. Can't forget about windy. What's up with that?

I can't think of anything to say to them. They end the awkwardness for me by wishing me and Dad a happy New Year.

The sound of the front door shutting wakes me up. I wonder where Dad's going. When I get downstairs, I see a note on the kitchen table telling me he went to the post office to pick up the package of presents from Grandma and Bapa, so I run back upstairs to my parents' bedroom. I want to finish looking in the nooks and crannies of Mom's closet. Maybe I'll pick out some clothes.

Hanging on a hook at the very back of her closet is a huge canvas flowered duffel bag I've never seen before. At the very bottom is a red cloth notebook with blue and yellow stripes. And it looks like a journal! Two seconds after I find it, I hear Dad pull into the driveway, so I quickly put it back and go into the hall bathroom, where I try to catch my breath. Mom had a journal? What did she write about? Dad calls through the door to say he's home and asks if I want to go swimming at the Y before it gets crowded.

"I was just going to take a shower, but I guess I can take one after the pool."

Dad looks ridiculous in his huge goggles, so I'm glad I don't recognize anyone at the pool. No one recognizes me, either, which is a bonus. During my boring laps of freestyle and breast-stroke, I remember Dad's story about me being an early swimmer and how I swallowed a lot of water because I was smiling so much with my mouth open.

I take a real shower when we get back, to get rid of that chlorine smell. After choosing one of my many lotions to counteract my lizardy dry skin, I can't stop thinking about the notebook. I'm dying to know what's inside, but I also feel guilty about even finding it. To get my mind off all that, I force myself to go back to sorting boxes of photos. It's one of those projects that could take forever.

I come across a picture of Mom standing next to some guy I don't recognize. It's definitely not my dad. It's so weird to think about her having other boyfriends besides him, but maybe it's not a boyfriend. Maybe he's some random dude. She looks kind of happy for it to be a random dude, though. The question is, should I ask my dad? Maybe he was some secret boyfriend. Maybe he was her math tutor. I know she had a math tutor in college just to help her pass. Maybe he was a musician in the college orchestra. Maybe he's a prince who went to college with her and she almost married. Then she would have been a princess, and I would have been, too, like in that movie, *The Prince and Me*. Maybe he was enchanted by her viola playing and fell madly in love with her, despite the king and queen's instructions not to date an American girl. I guess the point is that there are some things I'll never know about my mom because she's not here to tell me.

While I'm busy making a pile of photos to ask Dad about, I'm sitting in one position for so long that my leg falls asleep. I hobble and hop around and do a lot of moaning as I try to wake it up. Dad is reading in his chair and doesn't seem to notice.

"Hey, Dad, can you tell me about some of these pictures?"

"Sure, show me what you've got."

First we go through the ones of me and Mom at Glen Echo Park when I was little. Dad tells me how much I loved the slides and swings, but I apparently never wanted to stay on the fancy carousel ride.

Then we get to the ones from my fourth birthday party, and he starts laughing. "You kept trying to hand out the goody bags before the end of the party. Mom and I didn't know if it meant that you were ready for the guests to go home or if you were just so excited about giving them to your friends."

I guess I wasn't so easy to figure out sometimes. That's still true, especially since Mom's cancer. I'm such a crazy mixed-up bowl of feelings.

The doorbell rings. It's Mrs. Simmons. She has nerve, that lady. Even though she shows up with a plate of cute little snow-man cookies, I still think she's evil and nosy. She pushes past me and looks around the living room. Then she starts asking about Mom's clothes.

"Have you decided what you're going to do with them?"

"No," Dad replies quietly.

"Well, have you gone through them yet?"

"Not yet," Dad says, sounding awfully chill.

Waving her veiny hands in the air, she informs us that it's definitely time that we get rid of them. At this point, I'm at the kitchen table trying to look like I'm reading the newspaper. She goes on and on, and Dad is trying to get rid of her.

"Isn't it depressing to see them every time you open the closet?" she asks.

Dad replies, "We haven't had time."

But she doesn't get the hint. "I know you will be relieved to have it done," she continues, oblivious. "Why don't you let me help you?"

I can't stand it any longer. I've learned that the wishy-washy approach doesn't work with people like her. I grip the seat of my chair for strength before booming, "Can't you see that we don't want to?"

Dad's eyebrows jump up to the top of his forehead and he quickly puts his hand on my shoulder.

"Corinna, that's not a very nice way to talk to Mrs. Simmons."

"Well, she doesn't get it. Since when is she an expert on when it's the right time to give away a dead person's clothes?"

"Well, Corinna," she begins, "my mother died a long time ago, and I remember how helpful it was when people offered to sort through and donate things to charity."

"Well, maybe you were ready." I cross my arms over my chest. "But we're —"

Dad interrupts my rant. "Mrs. Simmons, thank you, but Corinna and I are just fine. We'll do it when we're ready."

Who does she think she is, telling us what to do, when to do it, and how to do it? She's not even close to us! I'll bet she was hoping she could have Mom's good coat or something.

As soon as she leaves, I crank up my music on the iPod speakers Dad gave me for Christmas. The loud music helps drown out my anger.

That reminds me. The other day, I heard my dad telling someone over the phone that I've been spending a lot of time in my room and that I was playing a lot of sad music. Like he hasn't? I wish I knew what the other person said, because then my dad said, "Yeah, we're kind of going through the motions of life, doing our best."

Motions. It's more like slow motion, with Dad around all the time. I mean *all* the time. He has only been going out for short dog walks, which has made further investigations into the secret life of Sophie Burdette almost impossible. Even if I had the chance, though, I do wonder if I really want to read what's in that book. What if it's filled with details that daughters don't want to even think about?

My music therapy helped a little bit, but I'm still angry about Mrs. Simmons, so I decide to go for a long walk. Between Dad and me, Maki sure is getting a lot of exercise.

I'm all bundled up in my coat, hat, and gloves, and my nose is running all over the place as I walk around the block, looking at the neighborhood houses all lit up for the holidays. They're no longer just houses or scenery. Each one of them is a story.

I start thinking about who lives in the gray house, the yellow house, the tan house. I watch them going about their business, turning on their holiday lights, setting out the trash. Life as usual. In our house, life is *not* "as usual." We didn't put up our decorations. Our house is permanently changed. Our house is filled with sadness, not holiday cheer. Our house is missing someone. Our house is the one with the mom who died, the one with the girl who lives alone with her dad. I don't know if it makes people feel sorry for me or makes them feel lucky that they are *not* me. Or both. Maybe some people don't even notice. A recycling-bin detective would, though. No more cans of Ensure. No more empty bottles of Mom's favorite shampoo or Mango Tangos.

New Year

We didn't exactly ring in the New Year last night. Dad got really mad at me about my messy room. It was kind of shocking, because he never gets mad at me, especially about things like that. He's just not a yeller. But last night, he walked into my room and started yelling about the dirty clothes on the floor and my unmade bed. I reminded him that it's *my* room and I can keep it the way I want. Then he started telling me I have to practice my flute. He's only done that once before. That was always Mom's job. The last part of our fight was when he announced that his parents, Gigi and Pop Pop, had decided to come visit us for New Year's since they haven't seen us since Thanksgiving and we didn't make the trip to see them for Christmas. I'm not looking forward to it, to say the least.

I spend the morning writing in my journal and making my New Year's resolution, which is to start a conversation with Alex about *something* no later than January thirty-first.

Dad calls up the stairs to remind me that Gigi and Pop Pop

are arriving in a few short hours. I still haven't cleaned my room, and I'm not going to. I get up and slam the door.

Two hours later, I'm still in my pajamas when I hear the doorbell ring. Maki starts barking like crazy. "Oh, wonderful," I say out loud to my stuffed animals surrounding me on my bed. I know that's not a very nice thing to say about your grandparents, but today, it's the truth. Hearing their footsteps on the stairs, I hold my breath.

"Corinna, we're here," Gigi sings in her Southern Maryland accent.

I don't move.

In barges Gigi. She takes one look at me and tells me to cheer up because it's a new year. Her hair is wild looking, and she has on a huge green down coat. She looks like a green Godzilla.

"Cheer up?"

"Well, you can't just sit there all day. Happy New Year! Get dressed, come down, and help me unload the car. We brought you some goodies."

I still don't move and feel like I might start crying.

"Honey, we're only here for two days. I don't want you to spend them in your room. Let's have some fun!"

"But I don't really feel like having fun right now," I tell her.

"Well, it's not going to help you feel better if you stay sulking all the time."

"I'm not sulking. I'm having some peace and quiet. There's a big difference."

"Well, when you're done with your peace and quiet, honey, I'd love to see you downstairs. Your Pop Pop is waiting for you. And it's a new year!"

Yeah, it's a new year on the calendar. But not in my heart. I just want her to leave me alone. She's almost as bad as Mrs. Simmons! Gigi never ever stops talking. It used to get on my mom's nerves, too. Mom would go off and practice her viola even more often when my dad's parents were around.

After two long days of hearing about Great-Aunt Gladys and second-cousin-twice-removed Walter's boring lives, Gigi and Pop Pop leave to go back to Annapolis. I think Dad is also glad when they finally drive off in their old-fogie-mobile. I'm hoping it will be a long time before I have to listen to their yammering again. Sometimes, actually being alone feels better than the alone feeling you get around other people who don't have a clue and are being totally annoying.

We begin our recovery from their visit with a trip to the grocery store. Before we leave the house, Dad announces, "Okay, enough canned chili and cereal. Let's make a list of things to cook."

A list? Dad's making a shopping list?

"I need help thinking of things," he says, as he sits down with a paper and pen.

I'm shocked. "That sounds great. I was wondering when you would finally get sick of that stuff."

"My taste buds must have gone into hibernation."

"No, really?" I'm glad to see the smile on his face.

"Yeah, yeah, I know."

I notice that our grocery store doesn't feel quite as much like a Red Alert: Danger Zone. Yes, I'm still reminded of Mom when I pass by her coffee yogurt, but it's kind of a *nice* reminder of something she loved. I ask Dad if we should get some of Mom's yogurt and to my surprise, he says yes.

Neither of us eats it, though.

It's a relief to get back to school after "vacation" and to see friends, even if I still feel so different from them most of the time. I'm super-glad to see Joci and Clare, not to mention Alex, but I still need to sort out some stuff with Joci. It's hard to let down my guard with her. What's a best friend for if she can't keep a secret?

I'm also glad to return to survival sewing and Ms. Carey. I have an idea for my final project that I thought of on one of my cold walks with Maki. Who would have thought this soccer girl would like sewing and even have daydreams about it? I guess I got some strong creativity genes from Mom.

Some kids choose to make stuffed animals, aprons, locker organizers, or plain old pillows as their final sewing project. Not me. I have a different plan that involves Mom's clothes. I'm just glad that evil Mrs. Simmons didn't succeed in forcing us to give them away.

I decide not to ask my dad if I can cut up some of Mom's

clothes because I'm worried he'd say no or maybe try to take over and choose *for* me. I want it to be *my* project. It does seem kind of wasteful to cut up perfectly good clothes that we could donate to the poor, but I plan to transform them. The first thing I cut is a flowery silk scarf. It's a good thing my scissor skills have improved since kindergarten. My teacher back then gave me a U for unsatisfactory scissor skills. Actually cutting the fabric *is* incredibly hard, but not because I'm holding the scissors wrong. Slicing through her clothes . . . it's almost like cutting a person's skin.

Choosing which clothes to use is tough. Things she loved? Things she wore on special occasions? Her blue flannel bathrobe or the flowered nightgown she wore when she was sick? Favorite clothes that she gave to me? Some Japanese napkins or place mats? Things that are soft like her skin? Things that are green like her eyes?

Ms. Carey has started playing music during class, once she knew that no one was about to sew their fingers together and everyone was moving along on their projects. Wouldn't you know, she likes the Dixie Chicks. When I hear one of their songs, my entire stomach, chest, and back tighten up. The Dixie Chicks were my mom's favorite group and she used to sing along really loudly in the car. Annoyingly loud, sometimes. I used to whine, "Mooooooooooooom."

"Without you, I'm not okay, and without you, I've lost my way . . ."

Talk about having your throat close. Those words zing right through me. Music can actually feel dangerous when you're in a public place like school and you don't want to cry. Eliana brings me back to reality when she practically yells, "Dude, dude, dude, could you please pass me the scissors?"

Group

It's lunchtime on January fourth, and I slowly walk down to Ms. DuBoise's office. There are five of us here for the first grief group meeting, all seventh and eighth graders: me, Max, Chris, Robert, and Yasmine. It's incredibly uncomfortable for the first fifteen minutes. Ms. D. explains that we're all here because we have something in common: Someone very close to us died. She tells us we'll have eight meetings to share our stories and learn about grief, and then she asks us to go around in a circle and say who died and how. Some of us say it like we're reading a recipe. "My name is one cup of sugar and my two cups of flour died." Chris gets really choked up when he says his dad died from diabetes three months ago, and that makes *me* choke up. I had no idea these kids existed.

"My mom died in August . . . from cancer," I manage to push past the huge blockage in my air supply.

Some of the stories are really shocking. Yasmine's father was in the U.S. Marines and got blown up in Afghanistan about eight months ago. Max's dad committed suicide. Robert's stepfather died in a car accident when someone ran a red light. Yikes. I want to know more about all of them, but especially the suicide.

Ms. D. seems okay, even if she does smell like she's wearing a gallon of perfume. She doesn't try to lecture us or make us do anything too weird, which is also a relief. Clare isn't in the group, maybe because her dad died three years ago. I stupidly didn't ask her if Ms. D. had told her about it. I guess I was trying to block the whole idea out of my mind. Ms. D. explains that we have to respect one another's privacy, which means that we can't talk about what people said outside of the group. My first thought is that it will be really hard not to talk about it with Clare.

No one eats lunch during the meeting even though it's our lunchtime. Some of us doodle with markers on the table, which is covered with brown paper. When Ms. D. asks us if we want to name our group, no one has any good ideas. The usual group names like The Tigers or The Hornets just don't apply. The Death Group doesn't sound so hot, either. Since no one has a good idea, we decide to go nameless.

As soon as I see Clare at her locker, I ask her, "Why weren't you at the group today?"

"What group?"

"You didn't know about it?"

"What are you talking about?"

"The group for kids who had a parent die."

"What is it?"

"It's like a discussion group. We share our stories and it's private, so I can't tell you more, but you should come."

"Well, what am I supposed to do? Maybe the counselor didn't want me there."

"That's ridiculous. She probably just forgot. She seems kind of disorganized. Let's go see her at lunch tomorrow and see if you can join. Unless you think you don't need it."

"Just because my dad died three years ago doesn't mean I'm over it."

"So let's go see her. But I'm warning you, it's hard to breathe in her office because she reeks of perfume."

The next day, we head down to Ms. DuBoise's office at lunch period. Without even saying hello, I blurt out, "Just because her dad died three years ago doesn't mean she's over it."

Ms. D. stops writing whatever she's writing and looks a little surprised. Then she turns to Clare and says, "Well, Clare, would you like to participate in the group?"

Clare nods yes and says, "Yeah, I think it would be good. I don't think grief just ends on a certain date."

"I agree. You're right about that. I guess I didn't think of you because your father didn't die when you were a student here. I'm really sorry I didn't include you. It was my mistake. Our next meeting is on January eleventh, and I hope you'll be joining us then. We still have seven more meetings before I have to switch over to a kids-of-divorce group."

Oh, how I like it when grown-ups admit their mistakes.

Stories

I can't stand it any longer. Dad is out getting a haircut, and I go straight for the red, blue, and yellow notebook in the back of Mom's closet. I flip through it, hoping to see it fully filled with juicy nuggets of info about my mom or me or something, but I'm disappointed to see that unlike *my* journal, hers is mostly blank pages. The air goes fizzing out of my big shiny balloon of hope. I decide to let myself read only one page at a time since there are so few and I want to make it last.

I haven't written in a journal since I was a little girl, maybe age eight or nine? I would write in it when ever I got super-mad at my parents or Jennifer, and that was often! When a friend sent me this journal, I decided to try again as a twenty-six-year-old, to see if maybe it would help me find the words to express myself better. Contrary to stereotypes about men and women, Daniel, my wonderful husband, is actually more expressive than I am. He's a man of words and historical analysis. I seem to use music to express myself. I wonder if all musicians are like that.

I can answer that one, Mom. *No, not all musicians are like that.* Then again, I'm not a real musician; I just happen to play the flute. I think writing about my feelings is much, much easier than making beautiful music.

On Thursday, we have our second grief group meeting. Clare is here this time, but Robert, the boy whose stepfather died in a car accident, isn't. We all wonder what happened to Robert, because someone saw him in school today. Ms. DuBoise says she doesn't know. We go around and tell our stories again. It's kind of like starting all over, since Clare is new. She tells everyone that her dad died from heart disease three years ago.

Ms. D. asks Clare, "I wonder if you could share with everyone how the second and third years have been for you, compared to the first year after your dad died?"

Clare squirms around in her seat and stays silent for what seems like a very long time.

"Well . . . I guess in some ways it's easier, but in other ways it's not. It feels more real, like you realize he's really not coming back."

Everyone is quiet, waiting for her to say more.

"And another thing is, I can't remember his voice anymore."

After more silence, Ms. D. asks Clare if she wants to share more about that.

Then Clare stuns us all when she tells us, "I think forgetting is worse than remembering."

In my head, I start listing all the ways I can try to remember Mom, especially her voice. I really hope I don't forget Mom's voice.

The room gets a little less heavy after Max offers to share his Doritos and the sound of crunching and the smell of Doritos dust fills the room. Ms. D. points out that even though everyone's story is different, there's a lot that's kind of the same. I think people are more comfortable this time because they ask questions like:

"Did you ever wonder if they are really dead or if somebody made a mistake about that?"

"Don't you hate it when people try to give you advice?"

Ms. D., who is having another perfume-overload day, asks if anyone else has been given unwanted advice. Every one of us has heard lots of "You should do this" or "You shouldn't do that," so there's lots of nodding and even laughing. "Be strong" is another one we've all heard a million times.

I feel really sorry for Max, whose father killed himself. That must be the worst because, in a way, his dad chose to die. Maybe his dad didn't think he had a choice, but if I were Max, I think I would see it as a choice. Max's eyes seem to have this haunted look (a little bit like that look in Tweety Bird's eyes). I can't tell if they're saying, "Stay away from me," or "I don't want to be here." Maybe they're saying, "I might snap if you get near me." Maybe he saw something truly awful? I try not to look at him too much, but I can't get his eyes out of my mind. I really want to know more, but I'm afraid to ask him. I wonder if he saw the dead body and if it was all bloody or what. He said that his mother still hasn't told him that his dad killed himself. She thinks he thinks it was a heart attack, like she told his siblings. I wonder if she'll ever tell him, or if he'll ever tell her he knows, or if he'll ever tell us what exactly happened. Maybe it's just too hard.

I realize I haven't asked Miss Boppity Bop how her mom died, and she hasn't told me. I guess some people share that information and some don't.

Rags

Everyone is making progress on their projects in survival sewing, and Ms. Carey continues to entertain us with cute kid stories, which always puts me in a better mood. Today, while Ms. Carey is busy in the back of the room trying to fix someone's machine, I get the first comment about my project.

"Why are you using that ugly fabric?"

I don't even bother to look up to see who said it.

Then Billy Bradley, the class dork, chimes in, "Well, what are you *doing* with those rags?"

I look up at his pale face, staring straight at him, and I say, "What does it look like?"

"Like ugly scraps. Can't you afford any new material?"

I remain silent.

"Why aren't you making a locker organizer or an apron like everyone else?"

I'm ready to kill him. In my mind, I rehearsed what I would say if someone made fun of my project. I want them to know how important it is to me, but if I tell them, maybe it would feel like they know too much of my personal life. I could say, "I doubt anyone would ever make a quilt out of *your* clothes because no one would want to remember you after you died," but that would be cruel and probably start a war. I don't have the energy for that, so I say, "Get a life," and get back to work.

I hang back after class ends, waiting until everyone is gone. Everyone but Ms. Carey. It's time to tell her why I'm making Sophie's Quilt.

"Did you know that my mom died this summer?"

"No, I didn't. Oh, Corinna, I'm so, so sorry. What a great idea to make a memory quilt."

Then she gives me the most wonderful hug. In that moment, I don't care if anyone sees me with my quivering face hugging my sewing teacher, spiky hair, crazy hem, and all.

On Thursday, our group meets for the third time. Robert still hasn't come back. No one knows why he dropped out, and Ms. DuBoise doesn't have a very clear explanation, either. Either she doesn't know or she can't reveal it to us. Maybe it's one of those confidential situations.

The best thing about the group is that people *want* to hear your story. They listen in a different way than most kids. Even though our stories aren't all exactly the same, everyone seems to get it and even asks questions. Chris, who is usually pretty quiet, tells us that his mother still cries all the time and he doesn't know what he is supposed to do or say to her.

"I just go in my room and leave her alone."

Yasmine says she has had trouble sleeping ever since the day the military man came to their door to tell them about her dad dying when he was serving our country.

"What are some strategies you have used when you can't fall asleep?" Ms. D. asks us.

"Listen to music."

"Read a boring book."

"Pray."

"I don't have any. I just lie there."

"Take a bath."

Then she tries to teach us some breathing and relaxing exercises, but we end up in giggles. Clare snorts, which makes us laugh even more.

We also play Jeopardy! Death Jeopardy. Sounds fun, right? Actually, the questions are pretty good and lead to some pretty funny stories about some of the things that happened at funerals and hospitals. We all agree it was weird having people we didn't know at the funerals. One of the Jeopardy! questions is about using the word "died" versus "passed away." Most everyone's families say "passed" or "passed away." That leads to a discussion about whether "passing" is about passing gas or about death and we all laugh again. Plenty of our answers aren't funny, though.

Another question is, "Share a fear or worry you've had since the death." Every single one of us is scared our other parent might die. I also say that I'm scared that either my dad or I might get cancer some day.

Max reads the next question. "How do you feel when someone says 'I know what you're going through' or 'I know how you feel'?"

"I hate that."

"Ditto."

"It drives me crazy."

"How can they possibly know?"

"Yup."

Ms. D. speaks up. "Having people *listen* instead of telling feels much better, doesn't it?"

I jump in and explain to them about the random earwax removal calls we got last year. "The people who aren't good listeners should get their ears professionally cleaned!"

The kids laugh, even if they don't really get what I'm talking about. I wonder if that kind of thing happens to Alex, with people telling him they know how he feels about his parents' divorce.

For the next meeting, Ms. D. tells us to bring in photos or other things that remind us of the person who died. I know right away which picture I want to bring. The one of me and Mom and the Japanese decorations at my last birthday party, and the teddy bear I gave to her when she was sick, who sits on my bed along with the rest of my stuffed animal collection.

As soon as I walk into social studies, Joci comes rushing over and asks, "Where were you and Clare at lunch today?"

"We had a meeting."

"A meeting? What kind of meeting?"

"Tell you later."

I don't really want to, though.

Four days later, I wake up to a huge snowstorm. Dad's still in bed. He must have gotten the early morning teacher call saying school is closed. Joci texts me to see if I want to go sledding. After a bunch of texts to coordinate times and places, Clare, Joci, and I go sledding on the golf course. I'm hoping we'll run into Alex and his friends, but luck is not on my side. When we're done sledding, we trudge back to my house for hot chocolate. I'm relieved that we bought milk recently and have enough cocoa powder.

After they leave, I lie down on the sofa. I'm exhausted, the kind of tired you feel after being in the snow for hours. Dad asks if I want to go with him and Maki for one last walk before bed, but it's too cold and I've had enough snow for one day.

"No, thanks."

The night walk is usually short, so I know I have to be quick. Without even stopping to lock the door, I go directly to Mom's closet and pick out two sweaters since Dad still hasn't taken me shopping. Then I decide to bring her striped notebook into my room, just in case he comes back even quicker than usual.

Daniel is always pushing me to tell him how I feel whenever he senses I'm mad or upset. It's not easy! Maybe I'd know how if I'd grown up in a family that did that. One thing that's clear is that we both worry about our finances, about whether he's going to get a raise, and how we're going to get by on a musician's and a teacher's salaries. He makes a lot of jokes about us both choosing low-paying professions and why couldn't one of us have been a computer geek.

The front door squeaks open and I stuff the notebook down to the bottom of my bed, inside my sheets. It will have to wait.

My radio alarm comes on at six thirty A.M., blaring a commercial for a furniture store that's having a blow-out sale. I rush downstairs to make my perfect winter breakfast of instant oatmeal with maple syrup before I remember the notebook at the bottom of my bed. It's going to have to wait some more, though, because Dad and I are running late for school.

When I get there, I see Robert and Alex in the main lobby. I smile at Alex, but he doesn't see me. Robert is walking toward me, but when he sees me, he looks away and starts fiddling with his pencil case. I'm about to look away, too, but then I decide it's too weird not to ask him about why he disappeared from our group. I hesitate before asking him, in my best attempt at a joking voice, "Robert, what's up with you not coming back to group?"

He turns and says, "Oh. Hey, Corinna. You know . . . I didn't feel right in there. My situation is different."

"How's it different?"

"Well, the truth is . . . I hated my stepdad. I'm not going to pretend I miss him."

"Oh, wow. Okay . . ." I focus on my sneakers, anything but his face. "Well . . . um . . . I guess I'll see you later."

I understand why Robert feels different from the rest of us in our group. He probably thinks we wouldn't want to hear that he actually *doesn't* miss his stepfather. I bet his mom doesn't want to hear about that, either.

I come home from school with a fever and chills. Dad thinks it's the flu. I go to bed and tell Maki to stay off the bed because I'm so hot and sweaty, and he's like a little furry heater.

Dad does an okay job of taking care of me, but I miss Mom.

After a full week of the flu, the homework piles up. I go to see Miss Beatty to get the assignments I missed.

I ask her, "Does it get any easier?"

"What do you mean?"

Maybe she thinks I'm talking about school or sentence diagrams.

"Do you get used to not having your mom alive?"

"Yes and no. But you know what's important to remember? Our mothers will always be a part of us and your mom's love will always be inside of you. No one can take that away."

Missing

I'm sitting at Dad's huge desk, which is actually a wooden door on top of two filing cabinets. He has a couple little smooth boxes made out of different kinds of wood, and I'm fiddling around with them, spacing out, thinking about Mom instead of doing my homework.

Mom was so much fun before she got sick. (Although, there were certainly times when she was annoying, like when she kept bugging me to practice my flute or clean my room or even to clean out the slimy disgusting spit buildup in my flute.) Sometimes I can only see her in my mind when she was quiet and thin and weak and kind of scary-looking. But other times, I can see how she used to be. Pictures are good in that way. I have one in my room of us holding hands at the beach. I'm in a purple turtleneck and diaper, and she looks really young and pretty. Pictures help me remember her when she felt good, when she could do things with me. I have so many good memories, too, of summer vacations at the beach, parties we had, crafts projects we did together, birthday cakes we baked and decorated, plants we grew in the garden together, bike rides to the park, cuddling up next to her when I felt sick or sad, playing soccer in the backyard. Soccer was better than any games using your hands, because as a musician, she was always worried about hurting her hands.

I can't believe that she is really gone. Gone forever. That is just too much to believe. It's comforting to think about what Miss Beatty said, that she's not really gone, she's a part of you forever. I get what she means. My mom *is* a part of me and I have my memories. And I do talk to her, sometimes in my head, sometimes out loud, but *still*, she's not coming back to our house, to be my dad's wife, to be my mom here and now. She won't be there for all my graduations when everyone else's mom will, or for my wedding.

I decide to IM Clare.

maki226: *hey Clare. I've been thinking about weddings. not necessarily about Alex, but just about wedding days, yours and mine. do you ever think about who's gonna walk u down the aisle at your wedding since your dad can't? maybe my dad should walk u and your mom can do mom stuff with me.*
soccergrlc: *wooh, that's heavy, but yeah, sometimes I do.*

Dad comes over and stands next to me with his nose buried in his calendar. I click on the weather icon so he can't see my chat on the screen.

"I need to go to the Spy Museum and check it out for a possible field trip for my eleventh-grade classes' biography unit. You haven't been there yet, right?"

"Right. I was sick on the day my class went last year."

"You up for going this weekend?"

I agree to go, so on Saturday afternoon, we drive downtown past the monuments. We're circling around F Street, looking for a parking spot along with hundreds of other cars. We're both getting annoyed.

"I don't get how this connects to biographies in your history class," I moan.

"My class is reading various biographies connected to World War Two, and there are a lot of people in the exhibit — Julia Child, Alfred Dreyfus, Josephine Baker. I thought it would add an interesting angle to their research, but I want to be sure there's enough there to make it worthwhile."

After slowly making our way through the crowds of groups in their color-coordinated shirts, I'm standing on my tiptoes, trying to read the signs. We're both admiring the totally cool James Bond gadget car, when I say to Dad, "Wow, so many secret lives. Do you think their families knew they were spies or helping secretly?"

"Good question. I suppose if it would have put the families in more danger, then they wouldn't have told them."

"But don't you think it's bad for families to keep secrets from each other?"

"Yeah, in general, I agree, but it depends on the situation."

"So, if you were a spy, you wouldn't tell me or Mom?"

"I'm not a spy, Corinna."

He may not be, but I feel like a bit of a spy for sneaking into my mom's notebook.

I remember to put the notebook back in the bag the next time Dad starts watching a basketball game, but not before I finish the page about their money problems.

How will we ever afford to buy a house? We don't even have kids yet and I'm already worried about how we'll be able to send them to college. At least we are rich in love.

Old Spice

Clare and I never finish the wedding conversation, but I guess there's plenty of time before we have to figure out all that stuff. There are other things we have to deal with before our weddings to Alex and her crush, Tyler. Now that Clare and Joci are hanging out with each other, I have to be a little careful about how much complaining I do about Joci to Clare. Sometimes, I can't help it, though, like tonight, when I call her after dinner.

"Clare! Joci keeps complaining about her mom not letting her talk on the phone past nine. She's going on and on about it, every time I see her."

"Ugh."

"I hate it when she does that."

"Me, too. She doesn't know how lucky she is. Guess what happened to me tonight?" Clare asks. "I was at a soccer goalie clinic and the trainer asked me if my dad was a soccer player. Even after three years, I get that dread when I meet new people and I start wondering if they know, or am I going to have to go through the whole story and all that. I still get that pounding feeling in my heart whenever the 'Dad' topic comes up."

"Oh, Clare, that must have been so hard."

The next morning, I make scrambled eggs and one of the eggs has two yolks in it. I call Clare immediately, to ask her if she thinks it's a sign that something really special or magical is going to happen, like getting a message from my mom. She doesn't laugh at me when I come up with stuff like that, and that feels really good.

Not all of our conversations are about Joci, Alex, or death, though. On Wednesday, Clare and I are at CVS, killing time while Dad is at his weekly faculty meeting. We spend five minutes debating between the Smartfood Popcorn and the Doritos. When we finally make our choice to get the popcorn, we get in line to pay behind this big group of boys in seventh grade. They're all in their North Face jackets, each one chewing huge wads of gum, talking about the great qualities of the supersize red sport deodorant that each of them is buying. The cloud of spicy deodorant smell is so strong it makes us gag. They think they're so big and cool, and we try hard not to burst out laughing. Yuck.

As soon as we get outside and around the corner, I let loose. "Did you see the size of those deodorant sticks? What's up with that? It's enough to last for five years!"

"Well, some boys really need it. Have you noticed how the school hallways have that BO smell? I think it's about time they took some responsibility for their stink!"

I ask Clare if she remembers when she first started using deodorant.

"Yeah, I begged my mom to get me some in third grade. She told me I didn't need it yet, so I went and bought one myself out of my own money. There were like fifty choices, so I started opening and sniffing each one. My nose couldn't smell anything by then, so I chose a really gross one and didn't use it more than a few times. I couldn't stand the smell of myself."

I laugh at Clare's story and then tell her mine. "My mom told me the same thing, but when I asked again in fifth grade, she did get me one. She got me the same brand and scent she used."

"I wonder if anyone's parents actually suggest their kids start or if parents are like the last to realize the kid needs it?" Clare asks.

"Maybe they like their own kids' smells!"

By the time I get home from CVS, Maki is desperate to go out for a walk. While I'm out, complaining to him about the stupid assignment Mr. Spinolli gave us over the weekend, two bicycles whiz by. I didn't see who they were, but they looked like they were about my age. A boy and a girl. From a distance, I see the orange shirt on the boy's back. My back stiffens. Could it be

Alex? His house is on the other side of town. I looked that up in the school directory weeks ago. Why doesn't he have a coat on? Who is he with? Why didn't he say hi? He didn't even turn around. Am I that invisible? Does he have a girlfriend who goes to a different school? I'm devastated. But I can't be sure it was him. As Joci is always telling me, I shouldn't jump to conclusions. I'm still devastated, though. It's going to be another night with too much to think about.

At school the next day, I see Alex in the band room.

"Alex, were you out riding your bike yesterday?"

"What?" he says, looking up at me with his gorgeous eyes.

"I thought I saw you riding a bike on my street yesterday."

Just then, Mr. Morgan taps his baton and everyone has to get to their seats and hold up their instruments to show "readiness." He wants kids to take band seriously, so he threatens to reduce our report-card grades by one point for every time someone's not quiet and ready to play. I'm going to have to find another way to bring up the bike thing with Alex.

Two long days pass before I see Alex again. Either he was absent or he was avoiding me. When I finally see him at his locker, his back is toward me and he's talking to Juliette. I start freaking out. Does he already have a girlfriend? Am I just a blob to him? There's no way I'm going to go up to him and risk total humiliation.

Since we're not allowed to have cell phones on at school, I go to the bathroom and text Clare.

does Juliette like Alex?

Her reply comes at the end of the next period:

will investigate

The boys aren't the only ones who smell up our school. Mr. Spinolli, my social studies teacher, has terrible blue cheese breath and a mean personality. He probably eats moldy cheese for breakfast every day. Everyone talks about how we dread having to go up to his desk because of his deadly smell, much less having him yell at us for getting something wrong. His poison goes beyond his smelliness.

"Miss Burdette, please bring your paper up here."

"Umm, okay."

Everyone is staring at me as I stand up and start walking toward his desk. I want to disappear into the walls.

"Miss Burdette, march yourself directly to the main office and wait for me there. I'll be there as soon as this test is over."

"But, Mr. Spinolli . . ."

"No buts."

I can't believe this. Is he accusing me of cheating? In front of everyone? How horrifying. And confusing. I didn't do anything wrong. I wasn't cheating. I didn't look at anyone else's paper. I didn't have any notes on my arms or in my desk or on my water bottle. I wasn't using my cell phone. What's his problem? By the time I get to the office, I'm raging. Rage and confusion are not a pretty combination. My ears are burning, too. I sit on the bench for fifteen minutes before he comes stalking down the hall with a super-serious look on his face. His comb-over hair is partially flopped in the wrong direction, so he looks stranger than ever. I've had plenty of time to panic about the embarrassment this is going to cause my dad, the teacher. And to think about Alex the Magnificent witnessing my horror scene, even if he does like Juliette.

"What is this?" he demands like a fire-breathing, cheese-breathed dragon. He's holding our textbook with a paper sticking out of it.

"A history textbook."

"And it was under your desk, Miss Burdette."

"But I keep mine at home. It's in the kitchen on the bench."

"Then why was this under your desk with some very important dates and vocabulary conveniently sticking out of the book? This is not the kind of thing you want following you and your records that go with you to the high school."

"I don't know; it's not mine. I didn't know it was there, Mr. Spinolli. I didn't do anything, I swear."

Mr. S. opens the book and his megabushy eyebrows go way up above his wire-rimmed glasses.

"Hmm. Seems it was issued to someone else. I'll have to investigate some more. You may go to your seventh period class now."

No apology or anything. He should be fired for humiliating students. That is the worst — well, almost the worst — thing a teacher can do. Somehow, I get myself to my biology class. As soon as I sit down, Joci passes me a note that reads, "What happened?"

"Tell you later," I mouth.

I brief her in the hall while we're changing classes.

"I would have freaked if he did that to me."

Her mouth opens superwide when she says the word *freaked*, which makes it seem even worse, but it also looks so funny that I start laughing.

"Yeah, I did freak."

"But you survived."

"Barely."

Joci's face lights up. "We should start a petition against him for that. That would teach him a lesson, wouldn't it?"

I grab my flute out of my locker and rush to band. I wish I had eyes in the back of my head so that I could really check out the drum section and confirm if Alex is or is not looking at me like I'm a criminal or a piece of cardboard. Instead, I try to act normal.

Dad doesn't want me dropping band in the middle of the year because it would mess up my schedule, but I have my own reasons to continue. And I don't mean because Mom would have wanted me to. I make myself a promise during band that I will practice three times a week. I need to avoid any more humiliation in front of Alex.

As soon as I get home, I move the music stand up to my bedroom and perform my band pieces for Maki. It's hard not to think that even if I am doing all of this for a cute boy, Mom would still be happy that I'm actually practicing my flute.

I Am

We have to do this poem thing for our next grief group meeting. It's called an "I AM" poem. Here's mine:

I AM . . . a daughter that loves her mother
I WONDER . . . if she could have lived if the doctor found
the cancer sooner
I HEAR . . . her voice
I SEE . . . her face
I WANT . . . to ask her so many things
I AM . . . a daughter that loves her mother

I PRETEND . . . to be with her
I FEEL . . . sad without her
I TOUCH . . . her pictures
I CRY . . . at night
I AM . . . a daughter that loves her mother

I UNDERSTAND . . . she's still part of me
I SAY . . . "But it's not fair" .
I DREAM . . . of when we were together
I TRY . . . to get through each day
I HOPE . . . it gets easier
I AM . . . a daughter that loves her mother.

I can't imagine reading it out loud to the group, so I think I'll plan on asking Ms. DuBoise to read it for me or use the "I pass" rule.

After I write my "I AM" poem, Joci calls and starts asking all kinds of questions about the group. I explain to her for the tenth time that we're not supposed to talk about what goes on in the group.

"Come on, Corinna. No one's going to find out if you tell me what happened to Max's father."

"Yeah, but if I tell you, then he might tell someone else one of the things *I* shared in group."

"But he'll never know."

"Sorry, Joci. I just can't."

As soon as I get off the phone, I dial Clare.

"You won't believe what just happened."

"What? Tell me."

"You know how we're supposed to respect the privacy of our group and what people say? Well, Joci called and she was trying to get me to tell her some gossip about Max's dad."

"Poor Max."

"I know, right?"

"So what'd you tell her?"

"I told her I couldn't tell her anything, but she sounded pissed."

"She probably wanted to know all the gory details."

"Well, so do I, but if he doesn't feel comfortable telling us in our group, then he certainly isn't going to want everyone else to know!"

"I totally agree."

"So what should I do about Joci?"

"I have no idea," Clare moans. "I guess we can't expect her to understand."

"Yeah, I guess she didn't mean any harm, but it still bugs me."

"Guess what?" Clare asks, her voice sounding very chipper.

"What?"

"I have some news for you."

"Yeah . . . ?"

"Juliette does not like Alex."

"That's good, right?"

"It's better than that."

"What?"

"Alex was asking her about *you*!"

"No way."

"Way."

Happy Birthday

My birthday is coming at the end of February, and I'm not sure how we're going to celebrate it. A birthday without Mom is beyond my imagination. My dad thinks we should invite some family, like my Arizona grandparents, or Aunt Jennifer and her kids, but I'm not so sure. Having houseguests means you can't be alone when you want to be. I don't really feel like having a party with my school friends, either. My mom and I used to have such great parties with themes that we worked on for weeks. Mom loved doing that stuff. She even kept a little note-book with lists and party themes, games, and favors. My favorite was the rainbow theme. Dad isn't good at those things and, besides, it just wouldn't feel right. He'd be better at planning a camping trip. I'm starting to think that maybe we should go on some kind of a trip, so we won't be sitting around the house. Maybe going to Aunt Jennifer's would be good. That would also make it easier if one of my friends asks me what I'm doing for my birthday.

A few days later, Dad brings up my birthday again. I get brave and tell him what I really want: "How about we take a trip to California?"

He seems to like the idea and says he'll check on flights and all that. I'm still hoping for the UGG boots that I've been wanting forever, the chocolate brown ones. I'm tired of people saying, "Nice boots," when I wear my clunky winter ones. Another thing I want really badly is pierced ears. My mom said I couldn't get my ears pierced until my sweet sixteen because *she* got some terrible infection that spread all over when she got hers pierced. She was worried that I would, too.

That doesn't seem like much of a worry now. The thing I *am* worried about is if Aunt Jennifer or I will get cancer, since she's the sister and I'm the daughter and we have a lot of the same genes. I've heard that some cancers can run in families, so I decide I better Google that or ask my dad to ask my doctor, to see if I need to be doing something to prevent getting it.

At dinner, Dad tells me he talked to Aunt Jennifer and the airlines and we're good to go to California for a long birthday weekend. I can't believe my ears.

"Dad, that's great. Thanks! What's for dinner?"

"Um, how about breakfast food?"

I'm tired of breakfast for dinner. We've been doing that at least twice a week for months, even after he made his famous shopping list right after New Year's.

"Okay . . . unless you want me to make some soup and grilled cheese."

"Actually, that sounds much better."

I serve up the tomato soup and grilled cheese, and we sit down in our usual chairs. The empty one is awfully empty.

"Dad, am I going to get cancer, too?"

"No, honey, of course not."

"How do you know?"

"Mom's situation was really unusual."

"How?"

"It just was."

I go back to blowing on my soup.

The Chair

Our next group session is almost a disaster. I forgot to pack the picture of Mom and me and only remembered the plan when Maki stole the teddy bear off my bed and started throwing it around, playing catch with himself. I did forget my "I AM" poem, but maybe that was sort of on purpose. Max forgot to bring everything, and I feel bad for him. He acts like he doesn't care, though. Seeing everyone else's pictures of the person who died is pretty powerful. It makes them even more real.

After sharing the stuff we brought from home, we answer a list of questions about the person who died and write them on sticky notes. Each of us has an extra chair next to us, and we plaster it with sticky Post-its. Then we take turns introducing our chair.

"This is Ralph. His nickname was Ziggy. He was thirty-six. He loved steak and fries and pumpkin pie. His favorite music was jazz. I miss his cooking the most. He taught me how to play drums. If I could, I would tell him that I miss him and he was a great dad. I feel bad that I didn't get to say good-bye to him."

Hearing Chris introduce his dad like that makes it hard to breathe. I'm sitting next to him, which means that my turn is next. As soon as he finishes, I make a quick exit to the bathroom, and then bravely return to Ms. DuBoise's office, hoping that I'll be able to breathe again. Yasmine is in the middle of saying she still feels terrible about an argument she had with her dad on the phone the day before he died. I'm now the only one who hasn't had a turn.

"This is Sophie. She was forty-one when she died. She played the viola and she liked to sing in the car. Her favorite dinner was leg of lamb and roasted carrots. The thing I miss most about my mom is . . ."

I pause. A few kids nod.

"It's hard to put into words."

"It's okay. Take your time," says Ms. D.

"Well, she loved to laugh and she helped me plan really fun birthday parties. I could list a million things."

Some of the things the other kids miss are pretty intense, like: "the hugs he gave me," "his smile," "that safe feeling," and "laughing together over stupid stuff." Max says he feels bad that his dad didn't get help for his depression and that he couldn't prevent his suicide. Clare wishes she could tell her father how much she still loves him. Yasmine wishes no one ever invented bombs.

I pull up the hood on my sweatshirt, trying to warm up. It's not until I get home, make some tea, and cozy up with Maki on the sofa that I finally feel warm. While I was busy making the tea, Maki must have pulled Mom's teddy bear out of my backpack and started chewing on the eyes, because now the eyes are all scratched and damaged.

After rescuing the teddy bear and scolding Maki, I decide that I want to keep it forever. There are some things that seem weird to keep, like Mom's toiletries. When Dad asks me about rearranging or giving away something that belonged to Mom, I usually tell him I'm not ready. Of course we want to keep most of her things, but we can't keep every little thing *forever*. The first things we threw away were her old toothbrush and underwear. What about her glasses? Whenever we throw some small thing away, it kind of feels like we're removing a part of *her* from our house. I guess I'm glad my dad asks me for help, but it's really hard, too. How do you know when you *are* ready? At least he's not asking Mrs. Simmons for advice!

Meanwhile, I need to get some new clothes *into* the house for me, especially if Alex is actually going to be noticing me. Maybe I should get an orange sweatshirt. Except for the few things I ordered from the catalog, the bras I got at the mall, and my loose soccer clothes, everything is getting too tight or too short. When I remind Dad that I need to go shopping, he says, "Soon," or "Maybe later." But we never do anything about it. And I don't want to ask Deborah. Things are complicated with her. I guess

I'm going to have to rely on Joci's mom, which means I better get over my problem with Joci and focus on her good qualities.

I finally find an excuse to go see Miss Boppity Bop before school. I can't stop thinking of her as Boppity Bop, but of course I call her Miss Beatty when I'm with her. I bring her a pumpkin muffin that I baked last night using Mom's recipe. I bring two, so we can eat them together. She thanks me, and then she says she's going to save it for lunch, so I leave mine in my backpack even though I'm hungry. My voice quivers as I ask her, "Miss Beatty, how did your mom die?"

She sits down and adjusts her pretty scarf. "I guess I never mentioned that, did I? Well, she had multiple sclerosis. Have you ever heard of that?"

"Is that MS?"

"Yes. That's right. She was sick for a long time."

"That must have been so hard."

"Yes, it was. You know that better than anyone, right?"

"Yup."

I bite my lip. A few seconds later, the bell rings.

"Thanks, Miss Beatty."

"Thank you, Corinna. Have a good day, sweetie."

The band concert is Thursday night. We have to wear white shirts and dark bottoms. I put on the only pair of black stretchy pants that still fit me, and they make me look like I'm going to an exercise class. Meanwhile, Alex is wearing his cool black shirt

186

and gorgeous smile. I guess drummers can get away without the white shirt. I miss a few notes and I'm late on one entrance, but I hope they don't stand out too much. No one turns around and stares at me or anything. The clarinets squeak a lot, which makes the flutes sound better in comparison. After the concert, I spy Mrs. Simmons in the hallway. What is she doing here? I try to avoid eye contact and look busy fixing my flute case, but she comes charging up to me like a bull. I worry that she's stalking me, but she announces that she was here to watch her grandson, Steven, who plays the trombone.

"Isn't it great that Steven was asked to audition for the All State Band?" she says, bragging.

I had no idea that Steven is her grandson. I instantly start feeling sorry for him. Then she asks me about all the signs covering the hallway walls.

"Oh, they're just reminders about the Valentine's Day fundraiser for the student council."

She's probably trying to set me up with poor Steven.

I'm still deciding who to send Valentine's Day candy-grams to — Clare, Joci, Eliana, and Miss Beatty are definites, but I'm still unsure about Ms. Carey and Alex. I don't want them to think I'm weird. Steven is not even under consideration.

I find Dad waiting in the lobby, acting like he's in a rush to go, so I don't get to say bye to Alex. On the drive home, Dad says, "I know your mom would have wanted to see you play."

I don't say anything back.

Questions

Our group meets again on Valentine's Day. The girls in the group, including Ms. DuBoise and me, are all wearing some kind of pink. None of the boys are. We each write questions and then put them in a basket, without saying who wrote what. Then we take turns holding an unplugged microphone and fake-interviewing someone else, using one of the questions from the basket. I get asked, "Did you ever feel angry at the person who died?"

I answer, "Yes, I sometimes feel mad at her *for dying*, even though I know it wasn't her fault. I also got kind of mad sometimes when she was sick and we couldn't do anything because we were always taking care of her."

Chris, the boy whose dad died from diabetes, says, "How could you be mad at the person who died?"

That makes me feel terrible. Actually, I already felt terrible about having had that thought, but the truly honest answer is *yes*. I'm glad when Ms. D. says something about how lots of people feel mad at the person who died. Max says he's incredibly mad at his father for killing himself and mad at his mom for lying to him. Then he says something that really bothers me. He says, "I'm glad my father didn't die of a disease."

The room goes quiet. The silence lasts for a long time. Finally, Ms. D. says, "I think everyone is trying to understand and accept how their parent died. It's a really hard thing to do."

When it's my turn to read a question from the basket, I ask Yasmine, "Have you ever had a strange feeling when you ate something?"

Yasmine, whose father was the one who died in the military, answers, "Yes, whenever I eat string beans, it reminds me of my father. He loved string beans." No one else laughs, but I'm struggling to stuff down my giggle. Then I think about the coffee yogurt still sitting in our fridge. It's expired, but neither of us wants to throw it away.

The question I wrote to put in the basket is: "Do you ever dream about the person who died?" Clare reads that one aloud to Max, and I get a pit in my stomach, expecting to hear him talk about some gruesome details. He still hasn't told us exactly how his dad died or even how he figured out the truth. I think we're all afraid to ask him directly. I guess he's really private about it. I wonder if he knows that kids have been asking questions about how his dad died. I have noticed that he uses the "I

189

pass" rule more than the rest of us. Max tells us his dream about finding out that his dad is still alive, that it had been a case of mistaken identity, and that his dad came back to live with them.

Ms. D. reminds us that we have only two more meetings because she has to start the divorce group. Maybe Alex will be in that one. From the sound of his haiku poem, he could use it.

When I make it back to the class after group, the student council reps are handing out the candy-grams. I get one from Joci, Clare, Olivia, Chris from our group — which is kind of a surprise — Eliana, and "a secret admirer." I'm hoping the secret admirer is Alex, but I have no idea. The handwriting doesn't give any clues because it's in block letters. I chickened out of sending one to him, but I hope he is braver than I am.

The phone rings. Could it be Alex?

"You never call me anymore," Joci says in an accusing tone.

"Yes, I do," I say defensively.

"Well, not very often. What's wrong?"

"Nothing."

"What are you doing for your birthday?"

"We're going to California to visit my aunt," I say flatly.

"That sounds fun, but what about a party with your friends?"

"Nah, we're doing the trip instead."

"Bummer."

"Well . . . thanks for the candy-gram. See you next week."

"You know, I didn't do anything to you, Corinna. I'm just trying to be nice. I didn't steal your stupid bracelet, and the only reason I told anyone about your mom last summer is because I thought people should know so they could be helpful."

"But I asked you *not* to!"

"If I screwed up, I'm sorry. I already said I'm sorry, and I'll say it again. I don't know what else to say. I hope you can get over it."

"I'm trying to. It's just not that easy because you really hurt me."

As soon as I hang up, I call Maki to my room and go to bed. Packing for our long weekend in California will have to wait until morning.

Before we leave for the airport, we drop off Maki at this lady's house who boards dogs. Saying good-bye to him is sad, but I know he would hate the plane ride, and it's too expensive to buy him a seat.

Dad and I watch *Shrek the Third* and nap on the plane. I'm disappointed that Alex doesn't happen to be on the same flight to California. Talk about a serious case of wishful thinking!

Aunt Jennifer and my cousins all come to the San Francisco airport to meet us. She looks so cute in her brown suede boots and stylish jeans. I think she looks more stylish than my mom ever did, and taller. My cousins are both wearing shorts. How can it be warm enough for shorts in February? I only packed long pants and long sleeves. Maybe I can borrow a pair of shorts so we can kick around a soccer ball since I'm missing practice.

My cousins tell us about all the outdoor activity options we can choose from while we are driving back to their house.

"We can hike on the trail, but you have to be careful not to let the mountain lions get you. You have to act big and scary."

It's great to be laughing with them, and my body starts to relax a little.

The next day, which is my actual birthday, we spend a long time looking through photo albums, with Aunt Jennifer telling me funny stories about when Mom had chicken pox and their parents tried so hard to keep them separated so Aunt Jennifer wouldn't catch it. Mom and Aunt Jennifer kept sneaking into each other's rooms because they were so bored. Aunt Jennifer didn't get it until two years later. Then there was the time when Mom broke her leg skiing in seventh grade and had to cancel her first big viola recital. Her teacher almost fired her as a student, as if she had done it on purpose. One of my favorite stories is one I'd heard before from Mom. It's the one about the gourmet sandwiches. Aunt Jennifer and Mom used to make: peanut butter, pickle, mayonnaise, and jelly. They loved grossing everyone out, especially their mother, as they ate the dripping, oozing sandwiches. As she's telling me these stories, I try to decide if I should tell her about Mom's journal, but I decide to wait.

When Aunt Jennifer and I go out to walk their dog, Pepper,

I bring up the subject of ear piercing, but Aunt Jennifer doesn't think she should go against Mom's wishes. I had been hoping that she could help me convince Dad to let me get them. Then she starts asking how Dad is doing and what things I'm worried about.

"Sometimes I worry about Dad. And I'm still hurt about how Joci treated me."

She keeps asking, "What else?" like she's looking for a different answer.

I don't really want to bring up the subject of Deborah and how she seems to be trying a little too hard to help us. That whole issue wigs me out, so instead, I tell her that my other big worry is that Dad will get cancer, too. She tries to reassure me but it doesn't work. In fact, while she's making dinner, I do a Google search on her computer on "cancer family risk." It doesn't exactly bring relief.

"Knowing whether your relatives have had illnesses like cancer can help predict your risk of developing the same diseases. Five to ten percent of all cancers are thought to be hereditary."

Great, huh. Dad's not actually related to Mom, he was just married to her, so that's good. But what about me? It's not easy tuning that info out of my head. In fact, I'm kind of freaking out. What a mistake to look it up on my birthday. Stupid me.

My cousin Audrey comes up to me at the computer in the middle of my freak-out and announces that her mom wants me in the kitchen. She's laughing, so I kind of suspect something is up. I log off the computer and follow Audrey into the unmistakable lovely smell of something baking. Then I see the chocolate cake with raspberries on top. The corners of my mouth perk up into a smile, and I turn to Aunt Jennifer to give her a big hug.

"I hope you still like chocolate cake."

"You're the best, Aunt Jennifer."

For some reason, I can't sleep tonight, and I don't think it's because of the combination of barbecue chicken and chocolate birthday cake in my stomach. I go down the hall to the bathroom but stop when I hear Dad and Aunt Jennifer talking quietly in the living room. I stand where they can't see me, but I can still hear Dad's voice.

"I wish Sophie talked more about her cancer. It was just this huge elephant in the room."

After some sniffling, I hear Aunt Jennifer say, "She barely talked about it with me, either. She was always trying to stay upbeat about it, not complaining, always asking about me and my kids, changing the subject."

"Yeah, she prided herself on not being a whiner."

"Do you think she talked with her friend Deborah about it?"

"No, I don't think so. Even though she knew she was going to die, she just didn't want to talk about it."

They're both silent, except for some nose blowing.

After a long, long silence, my dad says, "I wish I'd pushed her harder."

"How could you have known?" she asks. I think she means about pushing Mom to talk or something.

"I guess she thought she was protecting us."

Aunt Jennifer agrees with him, and I hear more crying sounds. Then Dad starts talking again.

"She must have been so scared about dying. She told me she wanted to keep on living. She didn't want to think about dying."

"It must have been so, so hard for you and Corinna. I feel terrible I didn't visit more, help out more. I can't forgive myself for only visiting that one time while she was so sick."

Dad says, "You had a lot going on, too. She understood that. We all did."

"Yes, but she's my *sister*. How could I have been too busy for my sister? If only I'd lived closer, I would have been there."

Then his voice starts shaking. He can barely get out the words.

"It . . . was . . . just . . . awful, watching her get weaker and weaker and thinner and thinner. And quieter and quieter. It was like she faded away. . . . God, I miss her."

"Yeah, me, too," I whisper to myself.

The last thing I hear Dad say is, "I'll never love anyone else the way I loved her."

I tiptoe back to my room without going to the bathroom and hug my pillow supertight. Too bad the quilt I'm sewing wasn't done in time for this trip. I could use it right now.

I finally fall asleep, and the next thing I know, Aunt Jennifer is waking me up to get ready to go to the airport for our eight twenty A.M. flight. Because the airplane food was so awful on the flight here, we stop at Subway to get turkey sandwiches. We polish them off in the first ten minutes after take-off. After flipping through the cartoons in Dad's *New Yorker* magazine, I ask him if he'll go through more of the picture shoe boxes with me when we get home. That seems like an easier thing to ask about than anything related to the conversation I overheard last night. I'm not so sure I want to ask Dad about why Mom never did really talk to me about dying. Maybe I already know all there is to know. What's done is done.

We have a really annoying person next to us, who keeps calling the flight attendant for more screwdrivers. At first I wonder why he's asking for a tool. Doesn't he know that no sharp objects are allowed on flights? Then I realize he's talking about an alcohol drink with orange juice. Yuck. The flight is full, so we can't change to another row. Finally, the flight attendant tells the guy that she won't be able to serve him any more. He's pretty drunk and smells of alcohol, and of not having showered in a while. Double yuck. Even though Dad is the one sitting next to him, I can still smell his stink and it makes me even crankier about having to go home already. He definitely needs one of those megadeodorants the middle-school boys worship.

After picking up Maki, who barks and gives me lots of kisses, I spend hours writing to Suki about the whole California trip: the fun times and sunny weather *and* the gut-wrenching conversation between my dad and Aunt Jennifer that I can't get out of my head.

Spring

Back to School

I miss California: the weather, my relatives, the laughter. Our house seems so quiet compared to Aunt Jennifer's. School is never quiet, though, and my heart leaps whenever I spot Alex in class or the hallway. Today, I see him on my way to lunch in Ms. DuBoise's office. His orange shirt makes it easier to spot him even from halfway down the hall.

Ms. D. asks our group to come up with a list of advice for kids or grown-ups who know someone whose parent died. It's harder to do than I would have thought. We all have an easier time coming up with things people should *not* say. "Don't cry" is out. "I know just how you feel" is *really* out. So are, "Everything is going to be just fine," and "Everything happens for a reason."

We agree that there is no one right thing to say or do, but that somehow you have to let the person know you care, and that the worst thing to do is to ignore them or pretend that this huge thing didn't happen. We also agree that saying "I'm here for you" or "I'm sorry about your mom or dad" is good. Or

201

"I'm so sorry," or "I don't know what to say except I'm sorry," or even, "I don't know what to say." A few people mention sending cards as a way to show you care, and I nod my head in agreement. Clare and I start joking about the importance of ziti and Jell-O mold deliveries, but the other kids apparently love ziti and Jell-O. I guess there's no agreement on food dos and don'ts.

Speaking of dos and don'ts, I'm disappointed that Dr. Rothstein never answered my letter, but I guess I'm not surprised. I just hope she read it. I wonder what it's like for her to have her patients die. I wonder if she gets used to it or if each death is hard for her. In some ways, I think I'd like to have a career helping sick people. I was planning on being a newspaper journalist like my Aunt Jennifer and Uncle Peter. Now I'm thinking it would feel good to help people and maybe I would be good at it since I know how hard it is to live with all this sickness and dying. But it also terrifies me. Who wants to be around sickness and death all the time? I wonder why Dr. Rothstein chose to be a cancer doctor. Maybe she had someone die in her family.

It's been three weeks since we got back from California, and now Dad is sick. He's trying not to ask for too much, but I feel sorry for him and I am staying busy getting him tea and Tylenol, Kleenex and water. Deborah drops off some chicken soup. When I meet her at the door, I tell her, "I don't want you to catch his germs," and quickly begin to say thank you and good-bye. He sounds happy when I tell him who brought the soup he's sipping.

After all those days acting like an adult nurse, I decide I deserve a reward. I hope my birthday money from Gigi and Pop Pop will be enough to make my secret plan a reality. I call Clare to ask if she'll help.

As soon as we figure out that both of our soccer practices are canceled because of wet fields, we hatch our plan to go to the mall. Clare's mom drives us and announces that she's going to do her own shopping. She asks us to check in by cell phone a few times. We smile at each other and nod, being careful not to nod too enthusiastically.

After saying good-bye to Clare's mom, I put on my brave face and walk us over to the accessories store called Etcetera. They sell all kinds of jewelry and hair accessories. In the back, behind a black velvet curtain, they have an ear piercing section. I go into research mode and ask how much it costs. Then I ask if I can watch someone else do it first, which Clare and I do. The lady "patient" doesn't scream, so I get right up on the purple plastic stool as soon as she's done. Clare holds my hand and I close my eyes. Two loud gun shots later, I have gold studs in my ears. They didn't even make me have a parent sign anything! I guess it's kind of a sketchy situation, even though it costs forty dollars. Maybe that's why they have you go behind a curtain. Clare said she felt nauseated watching me, so I'm glad I couldn't see it happening to my own ears.

Joci notices my earrings as soon as she sees me on Monday morning. "Check it out, Corinna! Nice studs."

"Thanks. I finally got them."

"I thought your parents were totally against them. How'd you convince them?"

I wince before answering. "For my birthday."

"They look great. Now we're twins."

Four whole days pass before Dad notices my ears. I kept waiting for his outburst, but it never came. When he finally sees them, he just shakes his head. I'm not sure which is worse, the silent head shaking or the explosion I had been expecting. But what could he do? I guess he could make me take them out and let them close up. I know I have to be careful not to let them get infected because the last thing I want is to develop puss bubbles like Mom described to me in gory detail. The salesgirl who pierced them told me how to keep them clean and take care of them, so I'm pretty sure they'll be fine. I avoid Mom's urn for a few days, though.

There's this girl in my gym class named Nicole, who also got her ears pierced recently. I noticed because she asked our teacher if she could tape them when we were playing basketball. Nicole isn't in the "popular" group or even in one of the other "regular" or "normal" groups. I guess she's kind of a loner at school. I don't know her very well and she's never been in any of my other classes. She's kind of overweight and most of her clothes are too small, which leads to her getting teased almost every day in gym. Some kids call her Shamu, like Shamu the whale. I would hate to be in that situation. A lot of my clothes are getting small, too, but I don't think I'm what you would call overweight. I keep waiting for her to fight back in some way, but she just seems to ignore it.

What makes kids think they can say stuff like that to a person? They treat her like an alien or a freak. I know how that feels, for different reasons. I feel sorry for her, but I don't really know what I can do to make it better. It's been bothering me more and more.

Actually, there's a lot of name calling in my school. Two weeks ago, we had a substitute named Ms. Higgenbotham. Jake and Dylan, those mean boys who are such jerks, kept calling her Ms. Hineybottom. She had on the most unbelievable outfit. Very un-teacherlike. She wore a regular gray suit with shocking pink and red patent leather boots. We're talking *shiny*! I was so busy looking at her boots, I barely heard a word she said. At least Nicole's last name isn't Higgenbotham. It's Varney. Shamu Varney is a lot better than Shamu Higgenbotham or Shamu Hineybottom. I would hate it if I had some awful nickname that I couldn't get rid of.

I need to get brave.

Another Ending

This may sound strange, but I'm not sure I want the "death" group to end. The sessions have gone by pretty quickly, except for that first one. In our last meeting, we share our e-mail addresses and sign our names with a Sharpie marker on a smooth gray rock Ms. DuBoise gives to each of us. We take turns saying something that we wish for one another as we pass around that person's rock. Here are the wishes they give to me:

> *I wish you could have a whole day or a whole week*
> *without feeling sad about your mom.*
> *I wish you never have to feel this bad again no*
> *matter what happens in the future.*
> *I wish you could have less trouble sleeping.*
> *I wish you can learn to cook better than your mom could.*

It's hard to think of wishes for each of them. For Max, I say, "I wish you could have less suffering."

Right after the words come out of my mouth, I wish I hadn't said them. His eyes get big and teary, and I tell myself it was a stupid thing to say. I can't stop thinking about it, and about the Tweety Bird look he has in his eyes, so I miss some of the other things people are saying. I wonder if he will still have that look in high school. I hope not, because he looks kind of freaky, and it would be terrible if his eyes got stuck like that. I tried to say a nice thing, but it came out wrong. I hate it when I do that.

Then Ms. D. passes out a poem to each of us by a poet named Molly Fumia.

> *The paradox of healing*
> *is that it is both*
> *holding on and letting go.*
>
> *We hold onto memories,*
> *and we let them go;*
> *we hold onto feelings,*
> *and we let them go.*
>
> *We hold onto an old way*
> *of being, because the self*
> *we still are resides there,*
> *and we let go to a new*
> *way of being, so that*
> *the self can live on.*

Ms. D. gives us all a wish, too.

"My wish is that each one of you has someone to talk to when you need to or want to."

Then she asks us about who in our lives we *can* talk to about this stuff. I say I can talk to Dad, Clare, Aunt Jennifer, and my journal. I don't mention that my journal has a name, though, because I don't want them to make fun of me. I don't mention Ms. Beatty, either. Chris announces that he doesn't have anyone, so we tell him he can talk to us. Poor Chris. I don't want him to think I have a crush on him, but I should talk to him sometimes. Feeling alone is the worst.

Smells

I'm walking Joci down to the nurse's office because she got another bloody nose in the middle of math. I never have understood why bloody noses just start with no reason, and Joci said she doesn't, either. She's been getting them since she was little, and I've gone with her to the nurse many times. As soon as we walk into the office, the smell hits me. That yucky medical smell. I get a weird feeling, like I'm being transported back to one of those times with my mom in the hospital. While we are waiting, I decide to send a text message to Chris from the group. I know he spent a lot of time at hospitals, too, because his dad's diabetes made him really sick for a long time. On my way to lunch, I stop in the bathroom to text.

Do certain smells make u feel weird?

Yup. I try 2 avoid medical stuff big time.

I wouldn't feel comfortable asking Max stuff like that, because I'm afraid I'll upset him, and anyway, I don't think his dad spent time in a hospital, at least not connected with his suicide.

In the middle of doing homework, I get a call from Aunt Jennifer.

"How's my favorite niece?"

Hearing her voice makes me smile.

"I'm your *only* niece," I point out.

"You're still my favorite. Just wanted to check if you need anything from me."

"Hmm. How 'bout a visit?"

"I'm working on that," she reassures me. "Anything else?"

"No, that's it." I'm not really in a talking mood, but I'm glad she called.

After dinner, I decide that Sophie's Quilt needs a piece of the flowered canvas bag where Mom's journal is hidden. I wait until Dad is busy grading papers at his desk, and then I tiptoe into Mom's closet with our sharpest pair of scissors. I can't see a thing, so I have to take the whole bag out of the closet and then cut a square from the side. The bag will be ruined, but I think the quilt is more important. Before I return it, I let myself read another page.

Last night was a professional nightmare, the kind that makes you want to crawl into a hole. In the middle of our chamber music concert at the Lisner Auditorium, a cell phone went off. I was in the middle of a really challenging passage. The obnoxious ringtone was distracting and annoying. The stage manager had reminded the audience to turn off their cell phones, but this one kept ringing. Then the alert telling you there's a message went off. It was awful. It really threw off my concentration for the rest of that piece, and I missed one of my entrances. Fortunately, I'm pretty good at faking it, and unless you knew the piece, you probably wouldn't have noticed. We were backstage at intermission and I went to use the bathroom. I got something out of my purse, and to my horror, I realized that I'd received a message. The offender was MY cell phone. I was mortified. When we were together waiting to go back on, Nadia said "Wasn't that ringing coming from backstage?" I couldn't bring myself to tell them that it was my phone. To top if off, the review of the concert that came out today was unfairly negative. It was written by the local crime reporter, Gretchen something-or-other, who has neither played a musical instrument nor studied music in her life. She didn't even notice my missed entrance. She went on and on about the poor choice of pieces and poor interpretation. Like she knows!

I remember Mom telling me the same story many times, usually prompted by someone else's phone ringing during a quiet event. Reading about it in her journal made me realize it hadn't been a funny story to *her*, at least not at the time.

When I get into bed, I start thinking about Alex. I need to get his cell number so I can text him. The question is: Should I be brave and ask him myself, or should I get it from one of his friends? Maybe I'll get an answer in my dreams tonight.

I wake up with no memory of any dreams, helpful or not. As

I brush my hair in front of the bathroom mirror, I notice that my hair is practically down to my waist. What soccer player has hair that long? I haven't cut it since before Mom got sick. We kind of stopped doing those types of thing — haircuts, dentist appointments. Neither Mom nor Dad had any extra time or energy, and I didn't want to be asking for things or making it any harder for them. I don't think they could have really handled anything else on top of Mom's illness. And now Dad seems so tired most of the time. Well, not all of the time, but a lot of the time, dragging around like a wounded otter. But guess what? I need him to start taking care of some stuff for me.

Mom would be mad that I haven't been to the dentist or the pediatrician in a long time. And my hair is looking all scraggly and twiglike on the ends. Scraggly hair and split ends are definitely the worst, and I don't think Alex would be too impressed if he saw them up close.

Dad's sitting in the kitchen eating his cereal.

"Dad, do you know how long it's been since I went to the dentist? Not like I want to go, but I'm pretty sure it's time for me to get my teeth cleaned, and maybe even a checkup with my pediatrician. Oh, and I could really use a haircut."

He looks surprised. Maybe he feels bad that he hadn't thought of those things himself. He gives me a big hug and says, "I'll get right on it."

It's weird how a grown-up can forget about appointments that are supposedly so important. Mom was the one who kept track of those things. She always took me to Rodman's drugstore before my dentist appointment, let me pick out some chocolate treat in their huge candy section, and then after the thirty minutes you have to wait after your fluoride treatment, I would get to have the chocolate. By picking it out before I went in, it made the dentist appointments less of a dreaded event. Brilliant, right?

Two weeks later, Dad and I are late for my appointment, so I don't even ask about picking out a treat beforehand. When it's over, I ask Dad if we can stop at Rodman's the way I always did with Mom, and he replies, "That's crazy, to eat candy right after you get your teeth cleaned."

Well, too bad. I'm definitely going to take my kids to Rodman's, or whatever store is near their dentist, because I think it's a great idea, and so did Mom. My dad has a lot to learn!

Bad News

I'm out walking Maki after school, and my neighbor comes over to say hi. She's one of our *nice* neighbors, the one who organizes our block party every year. She tells me the incredibly sad news that a boy my age who used to go to our neighborhood preschool "lost his mother."

Well, he didn't *lose* her. She died. That is very different from losing her in a mall or on a crowded sidewalk. (Although I bet he'll keep looking for her, like I do when I'm in any crowded place. If I see the back of a head with hair just like Mom's, I want to follow the person until I can see their face, just to be *sure* it's not her. Needless to say, I always end up disappointed.)

This boy's name is David DiGenoa. He goes to private school, so I haven't seen him in a long time. Not only did his mother just die of cancer, but his father was *already* dead. He died a few years ago from some other kind of cancer. Now this kid has no parents. Zero. Nada. None. Life is so unfair! His situation is way worse than mine. Where is he going to live?

Who will be there to talk with him, to give him hugs, to reassure him that he will have a family to live with and love him? It's unbelievable. I hope, hope, hope that he has *someone* to take care of him, like a grandparent or something.

Because David's mom died in the middle of the school year, his whole school is probably finding out on the same day. Maybe it's better if you're sure everyone *does* know, and they know you know they know. It wouldn't stop kids from getting freaked out. They would still get scared about their own moms and dads. Do they think that talking to you or being near you means they can "catch" having a parent die? Nothing like feeling that you're contagious when you already feel so alone.

At school, I'm listening to see how the other kids react to the news about David. Some kids are clueless, even though it was in the news since both of his parents were pretty well known around here. Eliana tells me she saw it on TV. The clueless kids are busy talking about the usual stupid stuff.

"My mom gave me Gummi Worms today."

"I'll trade you chocolate pudding for Gummi Worms."

"I did three kick flips in a row yesterday at the skate park."

"Whose sandwich smells? I can't believe you brought tuna fish."

Other kids are gossiping in kind of a mean way, making up stories about horrible places where David will have to go to live.

"He's like Lemony Snicket in the Series of Unfortunate Events books."

Clare and I talk about how awful and alone poor David must be feeling. Joci agrees with us, which is a relief. I think that most kids, at some time or another, wonder and worry about what would happen to them if their parents both died.

After my neighbor told me about David, I decided I really had to ask my dad what would happen to me if he died.

He started shaking his head from side to side.

"Wow, I can't even imagine that and I don't want you to worry about it."

"But I am, Dad," I said, pushing.

"I have a plan just in case, but I don't want to talk about it. I'm sure we won't need it."

He was trying to reassure me, but it wasn't working.

"Well, I really want to know. What would I do?"

I could see how much it hurt him to think about it, much less to talk about it. I think he was about to cry. But I *needed* to know. He told me that I would go live with my aunt Jennifer. She's the aunt I feel closest to, so I guess that's a relief. I sure hope David has someone like Aunt Jennifer in his family.

After thinking more about David and his disastrous life, I decide to reread some of the letters I got from friends. I keep them in my Mom Box, along with the other things I've collected. I also picked out some good ones from the basket of cards and letters from my parents' friends. They do have good stories about my mom, like the one about her going to the movies with her high school friend. They brought in some sushi to eat during the movie. It was bad enough to bring fish into the theater, but then, thinking that the "green stuff" was guacamole instead of super-spicy wasabi paste, she popped the whole thing in her mouth, and she was going crazy with the hot, burning, spicy, eye-and-nose-watering stuff. That was before she got so into Japan and Japanese food.

Some of the letters are really sappy. One musician friend wrote, *"I shall never forget the beauty of when your mother and I made music together. She lives deeply in our hearts."*

Another one from a parent of one of her viola students said, *"She had a special gift of working with children and getting them to give their best and feel good about themselves."*

The letters from my friends are short and sweet. There aren't very many of them. I'm still disappointed that so few kids at school or my soccer team could find the time to write at least something. I read a few of the ones that I did receive:

Dear Corinna,

You poor thing. Having your mom die must be the hardest thing. Please know you are in my thoughts.

Your Friend,

Lena

Dear Corinna,

I am so sorry about your mom. She was a great lady. I will never forget the good times we had together with her. What a huge loss. I hope you are doin' ok.

Love,

Joci

Dear Corinna,

I am so sad for you about your mom. I am truly sorry for your loss.

Your friend,

Clare

Dear Corinna,

I just got back from camp and my mom told me your mom died. Sorry I missed the funeral. I'm very sorry about your mom. Maybe you can spend some time at our house.

Love,

Olivia

Dear Corinna,

Sorry to hear about your mom. Life sucks sometimes.

Doug

Yes, life does suck sometimes. I have to agree with Doug, a kid who I went to elementary school with but who I don't know very well. I was really surprised that he wrote me. That was really sweet of him. I still can't believe that Eliana and Juliette never wrote or called or even really said anything when I got back to school. I would totally say something to them if their moms died. At least Eliana came to the funeral.

It's confusing how I want people to acknowledge my mom's death, but I don't want to have to talk about it if I'm not in the right mood or place, which is a lot of the time. I think that my father would call that an oxymoron or a conundrum or some other fancy teacher word. Someone should invent a signaling system for awkward but important topics. Green for "It's a good time," and red for "It's not a good time; try again later." Maybe that's how I'll make my million bucks.

After all that letter reading, here's what I end up writing to David:

Dear David,

I am so, so sorry to hear about your mom. I know you must miss both her and your dad very much. My mom died, too, also from cancer. It has been the hardest thing in my life. You are a great guy, and I hope you have a lot of loving people to spend time with. I know I haven't seen you in a long time, but please know you are in my thoughts.

Your friend,

Corinna Burdette

I'm definitely going to write anyone else I know if their parent dies, even if they are not a close friend.

Aloha

While we're swabbing our flutes and packing them up after an early morning gotta-get-you-ready-for-the-concert band practice, Eliana whispers to me that she heard that her crush is going to be at the dance. The posters announcing the eighth-grade Aloha Dance have been plastered all over the hallways for weeks, and it's all the girls have been talking about.

"Cool," I say, placing my flute sections into the case's red velvet slots. Eliana goes back to get her music off the stand.

"Hey, Corinna . . ."

I turn around to see who said that. My eyes practically pop when I see that it's Alex.

"Do you know when that dance is?"

He's twirling his drum sticks, looking gorgeous with his unbelievably blue eyes. *OMG* is what goes through my head, not the date of the dance. I honestly don't know the exact numerical date or if it's Friday or Saturday night, which is good because otherwise I might seem too interested.

"No, do you?"

I can't twirl my flute case, so I twirl my hair instead.

"No." His voice cracks a little, which makes me want to smile, but I resist.

It's an awkward moment, like maybe he wants to say or ask something else. I almost ask him about kick flips or some other skateboard lingo to try to put him (and me) at ease. Luckily, I *don't* ask him a stupid question about grinding, because that certainly has two meanings!!!

"See you later," I manage to say, as I leave the room. I'm practically skipping down the hall, making my way to the girls' bathroom closest to my locker. Joci passes me and I signal her to come in for consultation.

"Guess what?" I tell her.

"What?" She looks at me with a mix of excitement and dread.

"Alex asked me if I knew when the dance was," I sing.

"No way!" She looks surprised and smiles.

"Yes way," my voice continues to sing.

"So are you going with him?"

"Do you think he likes me?"

"Well, duh."

"No, really?"

I can't believe my ears.

"Why else would he ask you such a stupid question?"

"He is sooooo cute. Don't you just love it when he plays the drums?"

"If you're into drums, yeah, I guess so," Joci answers.

Somehow I get myself to math. I hope that I can concentrate enough not to bomb the quiz. If Mrs. Giamatti introduces new material today, there's no way I'll be able to absorb it with these butterflies jumping around in my stomach.

Later, with my mind obsessing about Alex, I nearly sew my fingertip into a seam. I don't really want blood on my quilt.

Ms. Carey walks over when she hears my yelp and takes a look.

"You've done a great job on your quilt. It's not easy to keep all those seams so straight. Are you ready to put the backing on, or are you going to add more squares?"

"Well, I want it to be small enough that I can take it on trips, but big enough that it can hold a lot of memories. I think I'm done. Can you show me how to do the backing?"

"It's beautiful, Corinna."

Her eyes fill with water. So do mine.

The Trail

I'm glad that smells can trigger happy memories, too, not just sad ones. Dad and I are walking Maki on the Billy Goat Trail along the Potomac River after my soccer scrimmage. Maki is always smelling everything, but this time I'm the one smelling the pine trees and remembering when Mom, Dad, and I would walk here. Maybe Dad's affected by the smell, too, because he seems more talkative today than he's been in a long time. His face is looking more normal, too. Less pale and wrinkled, but still a lot older.

I've got my eye out for caterpillars. Hairy wanderers, Dad calls them. I haven't seen many yet this spring. Mom hated them. She used to make me and Dad spray the caterpillar tents in our trees with the hose before they could get out and drop on her head.

Dad brings up the idea of us taking the trip to Japan we had been planning to take with Mom this summer. They had wanted to wait until I was old enough, whatever that means, and apparently fourteen is the right age. I'm surprised that he still wants to go. I'm pretty sure I do. Mom got me so excited about it. Japan was a big part of her life, ever since that time in high school when she lived with her host family. I think she probably would have wanted us to go even without her.

When we get back from our walk, we decide to make maki rolls for dinner. We haven't done that in forever. We find all the ingredients at our usual grocery store, which is good because Mom used to go an hour away to the big Japanese grocery store. Making the rolls is so much fun. Kind of like old times, except Mom's not here. Actually, it's hilarious, in a crazy kind of way. We try to tightly roll the seaweed and rice around some cucumber slivers, but the rolls keep exploding.

"They don't look very much like the ones at the Japanese restaurants," Dad says.

"They don't look like the ones Mom used to make, either," I reply.

"We definitely need to work on our technique."

They taste just as good, though, even with their jagged edges. I keep thinking about Mom and the last time we made them together. She would be happy to know we were back to our sushi-making. Maki is begging for some maki, but it would probably make him sick. He has a delicate stomach sometimes. He does, however, get to lick the dishes in the dishwasher, and the drips from the top drawer make his head all sticky. It's like dog hair gel.

Joci and I spend our lunch period at the Kids for World Health bake sale table, which means we get to taste-test quite a few desserts. Miss Boppity Bop is one of our customers. She asks which things we made, but I didn't make anything, so she buys two of Joci's brownies.

By the time school ends, my stomach feels pretty gross. Olivia asks me to walk home with her today, and I agree to go with her. With Olivia, walking side by side is easier than face-to-face because she's one of those close talkers who gets in your personal space and makes you feel like backing away.

"March is supposed to go 'out like a lamb,' but it's more like a lion today," she points out as the leaves are blowing all around us.

Then I start telling her about Maki's dog hair gel situation. She doesn't seem to find it funny the way I do. She can be kind of nice sometimes, but she has this clothing obsession. Sure enough, she goes immediately from the topic of dog hair gel to Norah's shoes.

"Did you see Norah's cowboy boots today? Aren't they pukey? They're not even real leather."

"They're okay."

I've noticed that every time Olivia looks at things, she scrunches up her nose, like she's smelling them. This time, she's scrunching up as she looks at my new UGG boots that I bought with my saved-up allowance. I think she expects me to join in about Norah's fake boots, but I don't want to. It's not like it makes me feel better about myself or my own clothing mishaps. If I'm really being honest, I'm probably jealous of Olivia's clothes.

I try to come up with a safe topic.

"What are you doing this summer?"

"Camp," is all she says.

We keep walking, without talking, and at the corner, she sort of blurts out, "I feel sorry for you because you don't have a mom."

I don't know what to say, so I'm quiet for a while. Finally, I find some words.

"Yeah, it's really hard."

"You don't know how lucky you are to have *a mom"* is another thing that comes in to my brain, but my dry throat blocks it. One second later, she starts talking about this new girl's outfit.

"Can you believe she wore overalls in eighth grade? She looked like a baby."

"Whatever," I say.

Later, I call Clare to complain. Clare agrees that Olivia can be clueless sometimes. Then she invites me to a sleepover this weekend, and for the first time in a very long time, the idea actually appeals to me.

Anniversaries

The day after my fun sleepover at Clare's is April Fools' Day. April first is the one year anniversary of Mom's diagnosis. I remember Ms. DuBoise, the counselor, saying that anniversaries are important, but I can't remember what else she said about them. I text Yasmine to see if she remembers. She seems very good at remembering details.

My phone vibrates.

Something about finding a way to honor their memory and make them part of your day.

"So, Dad, what are we doing for April Fools' Day?"

"Well, it's not the same as it used to be, is it? Why don't we light a candle and play some of Mom's favorite viola music?"

"Okay."

Then he looks right at me and adds, "Maybe we should do something totally crazy, like eat green eggs and ham and drink Mango Tangos."

I'm glad April first is on a Sunday so I don't have to go to school and deal with the April Fools' stuff.

I decide I want to do something of my own for Mom, too, but I'm not sure what. By the afternoon, I get an idea. I examine my shell and rock collection, picking out my favorite ones. I use a Sharpie pen to write some words on three of the rocks — LOVE YOU, MISS YOU, MOM, and I arrange them together with some shells I collected with her on a pretty scarf that she wore a lot, and put them on top of the heater box thing in my room.

Dinner is hard. We light a memory candle, the kind that burns for 24 hours, and eat turkey chili from the deli, not green eggs and ham. We share a Mango Tango in two wine glasses. Dad plays some of her favorite viola music on the CD player, and then we listen to the Corrs, the Dixie Chicks, and U2, which she also loved. When the Sophie concert is over, I put on some of *my* music. We need something nice and upbeat. I end up choosing *Hairspray.*

As we're cleaning the table, Dad says, "I want to talk about doing something that will help us hold on to our memories of Mom. I know you've been going through all those old pictures, but maybe we could also make lists of memories and her favorite foods and songs and silly things about her or expressions she used."

"Yeah, okay. That sounds good," I tell him with a smile.

"Maybe we could even ask other people who knew her to write down a memory and include them, too. Friends from her high school and college, and people from her music world.

Deborah suggested it to me. Her mother did something like that for her after her father died."

I'm kind of shocked, because I think it's the most he's talked about Mom since she died. It's almost like he was waiting for the one year mark or something.

Up in my room, I start thinking about Deborah. I've been putting off having lunch with her since August, but now there are some things I want to ask her. I just have to get in a brave enough mood.

The next day, I'm walking home from school along the brook, thinking about how to tell Deborah I'm ready to have lunch together. It's a beautiful spring day, but super-windy. I zip my fleece jacket, trying to warm up. My heavy backpack is jammed full of the usual notebooks and my flute. Carefully tucked in the top is my newly finished quilt. The sewing isn't perfect, but I love it.

It's almost like Mom's spirit is swirling around me, along with the wind and leaves. Instead of being sad, though, it's comforting. I notice a duck with a bright green neck and head. He's all alone on the water, which is strange because I learned that ducks mate for life. Had his partner died over the winter? I keep walking, watching the duck. About ten minutes later, I see another duck, this one very plain brown, swimming around the bend, dunking down for food. As they get closer, they still act very uninterested, but when they are right next to each other, they start communicating in their duck way. I can tell they belong together and that makes me feel sad and glad at the same time.

I walk up to our house and notice that the first daffodil has opened in our front yard. Those daffodils come up each year, no matter what. They don't care if someone died. Mom and I planted those bulbs when I was in nursery school. She did the major digging, and then I put in each bulb. I wore my dad's huge work gloves and I could barely hold on to the bulbs because my hands were lost inside the giant gloves. Daffodils and spring flowers are nice, but spring is also the time when Mom was seriously sick. Sick plus sweet equals bittersweet, and bittersweet still equals sad. I wish I could find another way to solve that equation.

Invisible

I thought getting invited to a dance would be magical, but it turns out, it's a nightmare. Of all the disgusting boys I've ever met, Hank Greene could be the worst. He farts all the time in class and then announces that his daily breakfast consisted of a full can of baked beans. He actually thinks that makes him cool and works hard to keep his farting reputation. And, horror of horrors, he's who asks me to the Aloha Dance. Thank goodness Joci is with me and helps me think fast about our big plans with a group of girls for that night.

"We're going together with all our friends," Joci says quickly.

"Well, I hope you'll be dancing with me," Hank replies in his cocky voice.

"Umm. Maybe," I croak.

"Well, I'm down for that."

I walk as fast as I can down the hall toward the bathroom, with Joci close behind.

"Thank you, thank you, thank you for saving me from that disgusting boy."

"Did you hear what he said, 'I'm down for that'? Come on!"

The only problem is, if Alex *does* invite me, which I don't think he will, Hank will totally give me a hard time. But maybe it's for the best. I would be so nervous to go with Alex. I get butterflies just thinking about it. Besides, I'm used to dancing with my friends. I wonder if I would have talked to my mom about this boy stuff. I can't really imagine talking to Mom, much less Dad, about it in any detail. How could Dad know what it's like to be a girl? And it would be unbelievably embarrassing. I wonder what my mom's eighth-grade crushes were like . . . and whether she would have shared them with me if I had asked. I sure hope Dad wasn't like Hank Greene!

It's four nights before the dance, and my room looks like it got hit by a tornado. By the time Dad walks in to say good night, my rug is completely covered with rejected bottoms and tops.

"Joci invited me over to her house to have dinner before the eighth-grade dance on Friday night, but I have a *major* problem."

"What's that?"

"I have nothing to wear."

Dad points to the pink and brown dress still hanging in the closet.

"How about that?"

"Dad, are you kidding me? You actually think I'm going to wear that dress? No one wears dresses to these dances. It's not the graduation dance!"

"Calm down, Corinna."

"How can I calm down? Look at me! Just look."

"Corinna, it's going to be okay. Let's talk about this." He's moving his hands like a crossing guard telling a driver to slow down.

"I don't want to talk about it. You haven't even noticed that nothing fits me anymore. You don't even care what I look like."

"Of course I do," Dad says, trying to reassure me.

"Are you blind, Dad? I look like a fat sausage. I'm bursting out of everything!"

My eyes start burning.

"You do not look like a sausage. You look cute, like you always have."

"Dad, that is so lame. I do not look cute. Mom would never have been so stupid about all this. She would have taken me shopping a long time ago."

"Corinna, your insults aren't helping." He sits on my bed. "Can't we talk about this? Of course I'll take you shopping if you need something."

"But you haven't. Even when I asked you. I told you everything was getting small." My voice gets louder and more desperate. "Why didn't you notice? Why don't you notice anything? My hair, my clothes. You act like everything is frozen in time."

I'm breathing loudly, but neither of us says anything for what feels like a long time. Dad finally opens his mouth, then hesitates before quietly saying, "Yeah, I've been having a really hard time."

The skin on Dad's face looks all tight, with his mouth making new wrinkles, but that doesn't stop me from saying, "You think I haven't? I still have to go to school even on days when my body and my brain feel terrible and I can barely think and the kids whisper about me. You think it's easy for me?"

"Of course not. I know it's not easy. This is so hard for both of us, Corinna."

I'm looking at my desk as I tell him, "You never take me anywhere, except school and soccer, and swimming at the Y once in a while, and those don't even count."

"Corinna, I'm sorry. I know it's hard on you."

"I'm going for a walk with Maki," I announce and start walking to my door.

"Okay, do you —"

"I'm out of here."

"What about dinner?" he asks as I'm halfway down the stairs.

I grab the leash and rush out with Maki, slamming the door behind me.

"Maki, Maki, Maki. I'm so tired of Dad being so out of it. He has no clue. Why can't Mom be here to pay attention to me? It was so much easier when she was here to take care of these things. She actually knew what to do. Maki, what are we going to do?"

I can barely see where I'm going as the warm tears hit the cold skin on my face. After a few blocks, I calm down a little, but I'm not ready to go home. I've spent too much time at home lately. Maki loves the extra long walk, although he has no idea why I'm walking so fast and so far. Unlike me, he makes all kinds of interesting discoveries along the way. He actually runs out of pee because we walk so long. My nose won't stop running, so I decide it's time to head home. I'm beginning to feel a teensy-weensy bit bad about yelling at Dad. It's not like either one of us is a yeller; It just came out. But I don't really feel like apologizing. *He* should be the one to apologize.

Dad isn't downstairs when I walk in, so it takes me a minute to find him in the basement. Actually, Maki finds him. Dad is folding laundry. I hate the way he folds laundry. It always ends up wrinkled. Mom did it so much better.

"Hi, honey," Dad says, sounding awfully chipper. "Have a nice walk?"

"Yeah, I guess." I stay at the top of the basement steps. I don't like how he's trying to act like nothing happened.

"Feel better?"

"I don't know," I answer flatly and turn back into the kitchen. I'm not in the mood to talk.

Dad calls up the stairs, "It would be great if you could make your special salad dressing."

My special salad dressing is the balsamic vinaigrette dressing Mom taught me to make.

Everything coming out of his mouth tonight is annoying. Just looking at him and his same old khakis is annoying. He keeps calling me "honey." For some reason, it's really bugging me. It's going to be a long night.

"Dad, you just don't get it. You may be happy wearing the same clothes year after year, but I'm still growing, and things don't fit, and it's embarrassing to be bursting out of them. I can't wear pants that are too short to school. I have enough things to worry about without worrying about looking like a superdork. You should hear how mean they are to this girl named Nicole. They call her Shamu!"

"That's terrible," he stammers.

A little while later, we're sitting quietly at the kitchen table. Yesterday, I had put a vase of daffodils from our garden in the middle, the one made out of green glass, just like Mom used to. It sits between his side of the table and mine. I finally take a bite of my cheese ravioli, which tastes like paste. At least it's warm. Dad says he had no idea I was suffering so much about my clothes and he's really sorry he hasn't paid more attention to them having gotten too small and that he hasn't listened when I told him I needed things. I hope he's not just saying what he thinks I want to hear. I want him to *understand* it.

"So when can we go to the mall?"

"Well, it's too late to go tonight, but how about this weekend?"

"This weekend?! The dance is Friday night! This weekend is too late," I shriek.

"Well, I wish I'd known sooner that we had to fit this in. I have a faculty meeting after school tomorrow and you have indoor soccer at seven. I guess we could squeeze it in as long as you don't take too long."

"Can't you skip your stupid meeting? Or I could skip soccer. I really, really need to do this. I need pants, tops, a dress, shoes, I even need underwear stuff. It could take hours!"

"Well, let's start with the most urgent thing for the dance and hope we find it. We don't have to get it all at once. We can go back to the mall on the weekend for the other things. I hate to say it, but I really can't miss my meeting. I get the sense that my boss actually notices who's missing, and I need to show that I'm doing okay at work. She's going to be choosing the new department chair soon."

"Then can I miss soccer?"

"I don't know. Your coach won't be happy."

"Just tell him I'm sick."

"I'm not comfortable lying about that. I'll have to think of something, but I won't lie."

"Tell him I have an urgent situation that needs immediate attention."

"Something like that, yeah."

By the time I go to bed, I'm feeling a little more hopeful, a little less weighed down by feeling invisible in my own house. I hope my eighth-grade "fashion-don't" days are almost over.

Dance

The day before the dance, Joci asks me if I want her to invite Clare for dinner, too.

"That would be great. We can paint each other's nails."

"Does Clare use nail polish?"

"No, but maybe we can convince her to go wild."

I bring three different outfits to try and get their advice on, including the things Dad and I bought on our shopping trip. It had been the shortest mall trip ever. One store and no more. Dad spent the whole time pacing and looking uncomfortable and bored. I think he really hates malls and shopping.

Joci and Clare both agree that my new Gap shirt and jeans that I bought with Dad look the best. I had put on some of Mom's perfume before I left home. Just a little, on my wrists. It's kind of a grown-up lady smell compared to the berry and cocoa lip glosses and glitters my friends and I usually wear. I keep sniffing my wrists, worrying that people will actually think I smell like an old lady.

"What's with the wrist sniffing?" Clare asks.

I go to the bathroom, wash it off, and borrow Joci's body spray. The three of us now have matching smelly wrists. My nose is so full of perfume that my taco salad tastes like soap. Thankfully, my taste buds are back to normal by the time we eat our ice-cream sandwiches.

Getting dressed together is fun, even though my hair is totally not cooperating, but being around Joci's mom is kind of painful. I love her and she has been incredibly sweet to me, but I can't help thinking about *my* mom and how I'll never get to hear her funny dating stories like the ones Joci's mom has been telling us, or never, ever, hear her laugh again. I drift from their stories and laughter and get really quiet. I'm not going to try to explain to them what's wrong because I don't want to ruin the dance for them, but really, I want to skip the dance and go home. They're in a great mood, ready to have fun, but I'm feeling trapped and lonely, even though I'm with my two best friends.

The dance is basically a blur. There are some Hawaiian decorations and cardboard palm trees and one of those mirror balls, but it's still your basic stinky gym, with old sweat stuck in the air. The Black Eyed Peas are blaring, telling us to "get the party started." Everyone's singing along.

I see a boy I've never noticed before standing against the far wall. He's wearing a white T-shirt with math equations written on it in black Sharpie marker, and he is playing with his cell phone. I guess that's what people do when they need something to do with their hands. Maybe he's feeling as out of it as I do, only I keep my phone in my jeans, and I am certainly not advertising my relationship to math. I'm not so out of it that I don't notice Alex's late arrival, though. He's wearing a different orange shirt and his brown hair's still wet. He looks totally cute, but the last thing I feel like doing is dancing, so I sit on the hard blue bleachers, looking pathetic, watching Clare and Joci have fun dancing with a bunch of our friends.

Five minutes later, Alex actually comes over and stands near me for a few seconds.

"Hey."

"Hey."

"Aren't you going to dance?"

"I don't feel well."

"Oh."

"Yeah," I say with a shrug.

"Well, feel better."

"Thanks." I try to smile, to find a spark of energy, but I fail miserably.

"Yeah. Sure."

I feel totally stupid and can't think of anything else to say. He goes off to the corner where a lot of boys are playing Ping-Pong and foosball. I'm thrilled he talked to me, but I'm mad at myself for being such a drip. Then Hank starts walking over for some kind of showdown. Ick. I quickly turn around to talk to someone in back of me, but no one's there. I stand up and practically run to the other end of the bleachers, hopping down to get a drink. Finally, Joci and Clare come over.

"Corinna, come dance with us," Joci pleads.

"Did you see Hank trying to get your attention? Yuck," chimes in Clare.

Then Joci moves on to the next major news flash. "What were you and Alex talking about?"

"He asked what was wrong."

"What did you tell him?"

Just then, our principal, Mr. Maroni, walks over to us and starts talking to Joci about the school newspaper article about her being a rising tennis star in Montgomery County.

I think about escaping to the girls' bathroom, but I'm sure it will be full of girls and major dramas and gossip, so I go over to the concession stand to buy a bottle of water instead.

It's one sad evening and I can't wait for it to end. You really have to be in the right mood for a dance. Thank goodness I didn't make plans to spend the night at anyone's house, because this is one of those nights when you want to sleep in your own bed, in your own room, with your own pillow, under your own soft comforter.

When I get home, I call *Mom* on my cell phone, but Mom's voice doesn't answer. Instead, I get: "The number you have reached is no longer in service. Please check the number and try again."

I call out, "No! No, no, no!"

I pound down the stairs to find Dad sitting at his desk, paying bills.

"Dad, how could you?"

"What?"

I'm sobbing but manage to say, "You turned off Mom's cell phone. How could you do that?"

"Corinna, I had to."

"What do you mean, you had to?"

Dad's eyes get teary as he tells me, "I waited a long time because it felt so hard, but I couldn't keep paying fifty dollars a month forever."

"Dad, her voice. Now her voice is gone."

"I'm really sorry, Corinna."

He reaches out to hug me, but I push him away. I'm furious. I stomp up the stairs into my room, slam the door, and bury myself under my covers for a long, long sleep.

When I wake up, I can't bring myself to delete *Mom* on my cell phone. I'm in desperate need of distraction, so I decide to e-mail Aunt Jennifer to ask for more details about Mom's teenage love life.

A few hours later, Aunt Jennifer sends a great e-mail back.

Dear Corinna,

I'm so glad you asked for more stories about your mom. I have plenty of them. She was a character! I remember she had a crush on Aaron in sixth grade, but when he called to invite her to a movie, she was so nervous that she ended up calling him back a few hours later to cancel. That was the end of Aaron. Then in seventh grade, she had a few crushes. There were probably some she didn't tell me, but I heard a lot about Ethan, Will, and Sam. They might have been at some parties together, and I think there were a few school dances. I remember she had a different colored hair ribbon for each one. I think it was Sam who wore navy pants all the time, so his color was navy. She wore her hair in a ponytail with the navy ribbon a lot in those days! In eighth grade, I think she and Ethan were going together for part of the year, so they went together to the graduation dance. He was really cute, but she thought his legs were too hairy. Isn't that ridiculous? Let me know when you're ready for the next installment of stories about Sophie!

Love,

Aunt Jennifer

I'm lucky I can ask Aunt Jennifer, but what I really wish is that Mom could tell me *herself* about those boys and how nervous she was, how she figured out what to do, and things like that.

The Lunch

The day arrives for my lunch with Deborah, a Saturday when soccer doesn't interfere. She calls to say she's going to be ten minutes late to pick me up, so I have six hundred more seconds to get nervous. It could be awful. Is she going to ask me a million questions? I hope not. I want to be the one to ask the questions.

The doorbell rings and my heart starts thumping faster. I don't know why I'm so nervous. I've known her forever.

The first thing she says to me on the porch is, "Can I have a hug?"

"Sure."

She's a good hugger.

We get into her cute yellow VW Beetle car.

"How do you fit your cello in here?"

"I don't! My ex-husband usually drives this car. He needed the big one today to get his lawn mower repaired."

We arrive at Così café and both order the Signature Salad. The tables are really close together, so when she asks me, "How have you been, Corinna?" I look around to see if I recognize anyone before answering.

"Well, better than before, I guess. I mean, I still miss her a ton," I say, fiddling with my hair.

"Of course, and so do I, but she was even more important in *your* life."

She's looking right at me. I don't know what to say to that, so I take a few sips from my water glass.

"When do you miss her the most?"

I hesitate before answering, looking at the framed coffee-cup paintings on the wall.

"When I see other kids with their moms."

"I'll bet." She's quiet for a minute, and then asks, "How do you think your dad is doing?"

I move my water glass around in a slippery wet circle while I think about what to say.

"He's okay. He's getting better at grocery shopping and stuff. The fridge is a mess, though."

"Well, speaking of shopping, I'd love to take you clothes shopping sometime. Remember, I'm surrounded by boys in my family, so it would be a treat for me."

"Yeah, maybe sometime."

Her cappuccino arrives, along with my Tableside S'mores. I get busy toasting my first marshmallow, waiting for her to bring up her story-collecting idea that Dad told me about. Or should I go ahead and ask her directly? While I'm trying to decide, she leans in and says, "So, I don't know if your dad told you, but I've been in touch with one of your mom's college friends, Sue. I asked her if she and some of your mom's other college friends would write down some memories or stories about your mom for you. I thought you might like to have them."

"Yeah, he told me. Has anyone sent one in yet?"

I shove another graham cracker and marshmallow into my mouth, crumbs flying everywhere.

"Not yet, but Sue seemed enthusiastic."

"Okay, good," I say, still chewing on the last mouthful. "Thank you . . . I'm getting full. Do you want one?"

I'm exhausted from sitting with her, worrying about what she's gong to say, worrying about what I should or shouldn't ask her. It's a relief when she signs the credit card receipt and stands up to go. Luckily, she encourages me to choose the radio station for our drive home and all I have to do is thank her and say good-bye.

Over the past few weeks, we've had a long-term substitute in math. Our regular teacher is out for all of April for some major hush-hush family situation. The sub is lousy, and I'm getting more and more lost, and more and more frustrated. I actually miss Hawk Lady.

Eliana, Joci, Clare, and Olivia are all talking about Joci's upcoming birthday party at lunch. I interrupt the happy conversation and blurt out, "Long-term subs are the worst. She's terrible! I can't follow her explanations at all."

"Well, if those kids would shut up, maybe she could teach us something," says Clare.

Clare is probably right, and that makes it annoying.

"It's a total waste of time. She can't explain how to solve quadratic equations or the quadratic formula and all that other quad garbage." I'm just getting started on my rant. "She's pathetic and should never have gotten a teaching degree or license or whatever it is that teachers need," I add.

"Well, I feel sorry for her," Clare says a little defensively.

"Yeah, but what am I supposed to do? I'm already totally lost in math. She's the last thing I need."

Then Joci piles on. "You're being kind of harsh, Corinna. What's up with you?"

"Whatever."

I sound like a jerk, but I'm mad about math, and I'm mad that Clare and Joci are making me feel bad about being mad. Joci's in the advanced section of math, and Clare loves math, so they don't have to worry. But I do. And besides, at the dance when they were busy having fun and I wasn't, they didn't even seem to notice.

After school, I go to the band room to get my flute. My heart stops. My favorite "orange boy" is talking to Mr. Morgan about ordering new drumsticks.

"Hey, Alex. Hey, Mr. Morgan."

"Hey, Corinna."

I grab my flute and music folder and hurry out so Mr. Morgan can't force me into another heavy-duty conversation. Alex must have finished his fascinating drumstick conversation, because he starts walking out a few steps behind me.

"Wait up," I hear him say.

I turn around and wait for him. He doesn't say anything, so I ask him, "So . . . what do you think of the math sub?"

He laughs and says, "She sucks."

"Can you follow what she's saying?"

"No, she mumbles and I don't think she knows what she's doing."

"That's what *I* think. Joci and Clare think she's fine. I don't get it."

"Maybe they're math geniuses."

"Yeah, well . . . anyhow. I'm glad to hear you agree. See ya."

"Yeah."

I did it! I started a conversation with him. Check that off my list of New Year's resolutions! So what if it was a few months late. I sure hope this gets easier.

Secrets

On Saturday, I have a whole day with nothing to do but my outline for a five-page research paper on the internment of Japanese Americans. I'm looking online at photos by Ansel Adams and Dorothea Lange of the kids and parents who had to wear luggage tags with their camp destinations, and the signs that said Go home Japs. I'm pretty horrified to read about the treatment our country gave them even though most of them were U.S. citizens. I wonder if Mom knew about that.

Even though I chose the topic and it's pretty interesting, I'm not exactly thrilled to spend this beautiful spring day doing research. As soon as Dad tells me he'll be gone for an hour to get his hair cut, I head back into my parents' room, once again locking the door. I burrow through the hanging clothes and find the duffel bag with Mom's journal. Dad hasn't moved it. Maybe he doesn't know about it. I feel like a spy, but I can't resist reading more. I'm not prepared for what comes next.

The page is dated a year after the one before, so she must have been twenty-eight when she wrote it.

Well, so much for my attempt at writing about my feelings. My parents were terrible at the whole expressing-your-feelings thing, too. How did Jennifer get to be so good at it? At least compared to me, that is. I tried to explain to Daniel that my parents kept secrets from me, big secrets, and how betrayed I'd felt. I wanted him to understand how awful it was when I found out about my father. I'm not sure he gets it, that having my parents lie to me by NOT telling me that my dad wasn't my biological dad was a huge deal. If I hadn't overheard them arguing after they read some article about genetic testing, I'd probably never have found out. My dad was completely silent when I asked them about what they were fighting about. Mom said Dad and Jennifer might be at risk for Huntington's disease and should get tested to see if they carried the same gene as my father's brother, who had just been diagnosed with it.

I can't stop after one page. I have to get to the most important part.

Then I asked the obvious question of what about me, shouldn't I get tested. They both just looked at me. Finally, after what felt like a century, Mom told me that my genes were a different mix than theirs because they used someone else's sperm to help them conceive me. I was shocked and demanded to know why they hadn't told me. Mom tried to explain that the doctor had advised them not to tell me, that there was no reason for me to know because my father was truly my father, regardless of the whole sperm thing. But frankly, it was my information to know. And when you consider the whole genetic component of various diseases, it can be very important. Now that I'm pregnant, I've been thinking a lot about genetics and what I'm passing on to my baby. What if my donor father or his blood relatives developed or carried a genetic disease? I didn't talk to my parents for two weeks after I forced them into telling me. I could barely look at them. They were crushed, but I was outraged.

There is no way to stop before I get to the end of this, so I keep going.

After I told Jennifer, she tried to play the role of peacekeeper, but she couldn't really understand. She really was my parents' kid, 100 percent. That hurt, too, that we weren't 100 percent sisters.

It's super-weird to be reading this stuff about Mom, about my grandparents, and about my aunt. Why hadn't Mom burned it or asked my dad to do something with it? Did she *want* me to find it? Had she forgotten about it when she was getting more and more out of it at the end? What other secrets did she keep from me? I'm excited to read more about her, but I'm also kind of scared. I should probably talk to Dad or Aunt Jennifer about this shocking stuff, but it's totally weird and gigantically confusing, and I don't know how to even begin that conversation.

All this new information in Mom's journal has started me

thinking about who I am and who my mother was, and it makes me so mad that she's not here to help me figure that out. If only my parents had had me earlier, I would have had my mother longer. Is there also a secret about why they waited so long to have me? They were married five years before I was born. I feel cheated out of time with my mom, of having her be a part of my life while I go through high school.

Sometimes I wonder if there's anything I could have done that would have made things turn out differently. In my group at school, we talked about guilt, and it seems like everyone has something they feel guilty about. Some of the things seemed ridiculous, like if Chris had visited his dad on the day he died then he wouldn't have died at all, but maybe *my* guilty feelings sounded ridiculous to *them*.

My biggest guilt is that I didn't tell Mom I loved her on the day she died. Even though I knew it was probably her last day, I felt uncomfortable talking to her because she was so out of it. Maybe if there hadn't been other people in the room so much of the time, I would have found a way. At the end, it was kind of scary to see her lying there, barely breathing. I couldn't tell for sure if she was alive or not. I wanted to hold her hand, but I didn't know what I was and wasn't supposed to do. I wish someone had told me it was okay to talk to her and hold her hand. And I wish I knew what to expect when she died. I didn't know if there would be some dramatic, awful, scary event or if it would be peaceful. I wasn't even there when she died. It happened in the middle of the night, when I was asleep. The next morning, Dad came into my room and told me.

"Is her body still here?" I whispered.

"Yes, she'll be here until nine, when the undertaker comes," he whispered back. "Do you want to see her?"

I didn't want to, but that felt like an awful thing to say, so I told him I didn't want to go downstairs.

"That's okay. You don't have to."

But now I wish I had. I wish I'd said good-bye.

Speaking Up

When I get back from Joci's birthday party, I find a letter on my bed. I don't recognize the handwriting. Even though I love getting mail, this envelope is a mystery, and I'm worried it will be something I don't want to know. I can barely read the handwriting, but when I see it's signed by David, I go back to the beginning to see if I can decipher it. It's been two months since I sent my letter, and I really want to know what David DiGenoa has to say.

Dear Corinna,

Thank you for your letter. Sorry about your mom. I'm living with my grandparents now. Good luck.

David

Boys aren't exactly chatty in their letters, but it's nice he wrote back. I hope things go okay with his grandparents. It doesn't sound like he wants to become pen pals or anything, so I don't think I'll write back. Too bad he doesn't go to our school.

We could use more nice guys around here, guys who could be antidotes to boys like Hank and Dylan. At least Hank isn't in any of my classes, unlike Dylan, who is in almost all of them, including PE.

We're starting kickboxing this week. Dylan is bouncing a Super Ball up and down, trying to act cool while the rest of us are just standing around in our PE clothes, waiting for the teacher to show up and teach us some fancy kicks and punches. Then Dylan opens his big fat mouth. I can see the bright green elastics on his braces stretch, and I just know he's going to say something obnoxious. I hope they snap in his mouth.

"Hey, Shamu," Dylan teases.

Nicole looks like she's about to cry.

My face gets hot, my back starts to sweat, and I jump into action.

"You are such a jerk, Dylan. How would you like it if you got teased about your parents' being divorced or being a short shrimp or your crooked teeth? Huh?"

Then I turn to Nicole.

"Nicole, come stand with us. Just ignore him. He's nothing but a poser."

Nicole's face transforms from blank to a big, wide smile. I'm shocked at myself and how good it feels to stand up for Nicole. It's just too bad it took me so many months to get up my nerve to tell that loser to shove it.

Dylan tries a lame, "Oh, come on, I was only joking. Can't you take a joke?"

"You've got to be kidding," I practically spit out.

The girls in our class all nod in agreement, making a sea of bobbing heads.

"You go, girl," someone shouts.

"You rock!" cheers Eliana.

Soon the teacher arrives, puts on some rowdy music, and begins demonstrating roundhouse kicks, jabs, uppercuts, and hooks. I'm pretending Dylan is my target when I do my jabs. Jab, jab, jab. My jabs and hooks are flying. One time, I do a right hook up into my own chin, which kind of hurts, but luckily no one notices.

After our showdown with Dylan in PE, Nicole begins to hang out with Joci, Clare, Eliana, Lena, Olivia, and me. She's really fun, and when she doesn't have that blank look on her face, she's really pretty. I feel sorry for her, though. It must be so painful to be teased over and over about your body. It's hard enough to feel confident about how you look without other people being super-critical. But no matter what I say to her about the teasers being jerks, I can't undo the fact that she is a little heavy.

There are definitely times when I don't feel good about what *I* see in the mirror. I don't like my nose at all. It is way too big for my face. And my ears stick out, just like my dad's. I used to ask my mom if I could get them stitched closer to my head.

She always said, "Oh, Corinna, you're beautiful just the way you are."

But moms have to say that, even if it's not true.

Just when I'm feeling unsure about how I can help Nicole, she surprises me.

"Hey, Shamu," Jake taunts in a mean singsong tone in the cafeteria.

"Shamu? I'm sick and tired of being called Shamu. Screw Shamu. I am no whale, and I am no animal. I am Nicole, and I have feelings, and don't you ever call me Shamu again. Do you want me to call you skeleton because you are so thin you look like you could blow away? You pathetic wimp. Give me a break!"

"Yeah, Shamu, you tell him," says Dylan. The very same Dylan who just last week also called her Shamu.

"I'm talking to you, too, Dylan. Don't be calling me Shamu anymore."

"Okay, sorry. My bad."

Nicole continues, "What's with everyone? What's wrong with you that you have to go around insulting other people? That is so twisted."

Silence. No one knows what to say. I'm totally proud of her but scared, too. I'm scared one of those boys will hit her or something. Or that she'll hit one of them.

"Ow! Ow!" cheers Eliana.

"What *she* said," pipes up Olivia.

The whole cafeteria feels likes it's ready to explode and I don't want to hang around waiting for flying objects.

"Let's get this girl-power show on the road!" I announce with a mix of excitement and fear.

As we walk out of the hot, noisy cafeteria, I tell Nicole, "That was so brave of you," and wait for my heart to slow down.

After lunch, we have social studies. I'm half asleep and the minutes feel like centuries. Mr. Spinolli gives us five minutes at the end of class to start our homework while he meets with a group of kids about their final project. I look up from my notebook and notice Joci's face. She looks really sad, which is not normal for her.

The bell rings, and everyone is pushing out of the door at once, eager to get out of Mr. Spinolli's classroom. Joci is one of the last ones out the door, and I wait for her in the hallway, so we can walk to our lockers together after the stampede. We greet each other with the usual, "Hey," and then walk slowly down the hall. Not sure what to say, I ask if she's mad at me.

"No, just kind of bummed out."

"What's wrong?"

"My sister has mono, and my mom's all paranoid that I'm going to get it. On top of that, we had to cancel our trip to New York this coming weekend because she's so sick."

"That's awful. Do you think you're getting mono?"

"Every time I yawn or feel tired, I get worried, but so far, I don't have any of the other symptoms. I hate that feeling, like you're waiting to get sick."

"I know what you mean."

Hidden

Much to my relief, Dad has recently started playing tennis again with his friend Mike, the guy who got the facial. I can't see any improvement in his face when he shows up at our door, but he does smell like vanilla. Maybe he's using some new cream or something.

As soon as they leave, it's time for my routine. I run up the stairs into my parents' room and begin reading in Mom's notebook, starting at the place where I'd stopped the last time after that megashock of a secret about my mother's family.

I'm so worried because Corinna has a high fever. It is so scary when neither she nor her pediatrician can tell me what's wrong. I can't wait until her sweet little face is smiling again.

I must have gotten better, because the next entry is three years later. How could she have waited that long before writing again? I can barely go three *days* before I have too many things I have to get off my chest by writing in mine.

Deborah, Daniel, and Jennifer are all doing their best, trying to help me with the sorrow and pain I feel about losing my baby boy. I can't stop imagining what he would look like if he'd been born a few months later. It kills me when Corinna keeps asking me why she can't have a baby brother or sister. We almost told her about Mommy being pregnant, but I had read that a toddler's sense of time would make it feel like forever before the baby was born. So we waited. Then, after the miscarriage, I couldn't bring myself to tell her. What would I say? You had a baby brother who we were going to name Zachary, but he died before any of us got to see him? How would she be able to understand that? How can anyone understand that? But I do know that someday I will have to tell her. I want to tell her. I don't want to keep secrets the way my parents did.

Wow. Mom really had a lot of sad things going on that I didn't know about. This gets me thinking about how quiet she was whenever I begged her for a baby brother or sister. Mom's usual response was to tell me how lucky they were to have me. I got so frustrated that they never really gave me an answer no matter how I asked. Now that I've read about Zachary, I can't believe she had been pregnant while I was toddling around. I read her words over a few times. "It kills me when Corinna keeps asking me why she can't have a baby brother or sister." Those are almost the same words I got so mad at Joci for using, when she said it would kill her if her mom died. I hate to think that my words were so hurtful to Mom. I had no idea.

Speaking of words that hurt, could there be any more radio ads and TV commercials about Mother's Day?

"It's not too early to order flowers for Mother's Day."

"Don't forget to wish your mom a happy Mother's Day."

"Just in time for Mother's Day."

"Celebrate Mom."

When I'm not hearing the ads, I'm seeing them. Hallmark card signs fill the CVS pharmacy windows. *Talk about in your face.*

Sunday morning is Mother's Day, and it's one of those sad days. As soon as I wake up, I spread out my quilt — her quilt — on my bed and spend some time thinking about Mom, each square reminding me of different memories of her. The center square has a piece of the nightgown she was wearing when she died. It's really soft and delicate, with pale blue flowers on a white background. I think they are forget-me-nots. The piece from her blue flannel bathrobe reminds me of all those breakfasts together and of when she got up at night with me when I was sick or having a bad dream. She loved that bathrobe. Another square is from her purple silk scarf. It's shiny and smooth. One of the squares on the top row is from the blue swirly batik dress she wore all the time. Then there's the blue-and-white Japanese cotton I used from the napkins that her host family sent her as a gift one year. Each square is connected to a memory of her. During the day, I keep the quilt in my Mom Box, but at night, I spread it out under my pillow.

Dad hasn't suggested that we go on our annual Mother's Day bike ride and picnic at Lake Needwood, and neither have I. We used to decorate our three bicycles with ribbons on that day, but this year, our three bicycles stay parked in our garage, completely *undecorated.*

Later in the day, after neither of us has even mentioned Mother's Day, I ask him, "Dad, how come you and Mom never talked about the baby?"

He looks up and smiles.

"The baby. How did you find out about the baby?"

"I have my ways."

He seems a little nervous but keeps smiling.

"Baby Zachary. Well, it was really sad, a sad thing to go through, and we didn't want to be stuck in the sadness. I suppose we thought that if we kept busy with the rest of our lives, you know — teaching and music, and especially with our Corinna, that we'd be okay. And we were. But there's still a sadness. I'm not sure that ever totally goes away."

"Like with Mom, that sadness will always be there. She'll always be missing."

"Yeah. And . . . well . . . thank goodness we have each other. And we have Maki and lots of other people who love us and care about us."

Lying in bed at the end of what feels like the longest Mother's Day ever, I say to myself over and over, "A year ago today, she was alive."

Clothes

Mrs. Simmons seems to have stopped coming by, but she's often outside her house trying to start a conversation with me when I'm walking Maki. She hasn't brought up Mom's clothes again, which is lucky for her because I would really blow up at her if she did.

When Dad and I finally get around to sorting Mom's clothes, we agree to do just a little bit, to see how it feels. We make a pile to keep, a pile to give away to charity, a pile for particular people we know, and a throwaway pile.

When we come across something I'd cut up for my quilt, Dad doesn't even notice. His mind is somewhere else. I move the cut things to the throwaway pile — they're no use to anyone — but whoa, does it feel bad and kind of nauseating to throw them away. I put them in a separate garbage bag and move it to my closet.

We wait a week to make sure neither of us changes our minds before Dad calls the Salvation Army and women's shelter to schedule a pickup.

I don't have any bad dreams about the clothes that night, so I decide to carry the trash bag of cut-up clothes out of my closet and into the garage. I stand in front of the stinky gray trash can, pausing for a moment before I put the bag inside. *Okay, today's the day. Good-bye, clothes.*

I hold my breath, turn, and walk away. I wonder if anyone else in my group did that or if I'm weird. That would have been a good question to ask.

The garbage truck is making its usual loud, crushing noises down the street, reminding me that the clothing bag is going to be taken away and mashed together with garbage juices. It's not a pretty image, and I need to do something quick to distract myself from that horrifying, smelly thought. I decide to spend some time looking through my baby book.

Inside the book, I see Mom's writing and the cute things she wrote down. There are funny pictures of me pretending to read the newspaper, of me with underwear on my head, and one of me chomping on a bagel practically as big as my head. She also saved hair from my first haircut and pressed my tiny footprints onto the page. My favorite part is where she wrote down things I said when I was learning to talk. Apparently, I loved macaroni (still do) and had a few names for that: happironi and wacanoni. Maybe I should name my future dogs Happironi and Wacanoni. Then there were my bossy demands: "Do self." "Need it hug." "Need it kiss." I do need a hug and a kiss, but I'm tired of doing things "by self" or almost "by self."

Another of my favorites happened when we were eating chicken. (We sure have eaten a lot of chicken in my life!) Mom wrote down a whole conversation:

"Do chickens have feelings?"
"No, the chicken is dead."
"But how do they get the feelings out? What do feelings look like?"

Not bad questions for a two-year-old. Or even a fourteen-year-old. I wish Mom had written down her answers to those questions. What *does* happen to the dead chicken's feelings? I guess they just stop.

A few hours later, Joci calls to tell me she's upset about the grade she got on her *To Kill a Mockingbird* essay. She starts saying she feels like she's a terrible writer and she doesn't know how she is ever going to do the writing in high school. Her older sister has been scaring her about the much harder workload.

"That's so mean of your sister. You'll be fine. I know you can do it. If you need help, my dad can help you. He's good at that stuff."

Dad, the teacher, is still playing that Beatles song "Julia" all the time. And when I go up to get ready for bed, sure enough, it's playing. Maki is asleep on my bed. I pick up my pajamas off the floor and see something that doesn't belong there. I don't know if I should scream at Maki or laugh, but on closer inspection, I call out, "Daaaad!"

It's a Tootsie Roll poop. Not a Maki poop, but the good old Tootsie Roll trick.

Maki opens his eyes and looks guilty. I hear Dad on the stairs, laughing. The next thing he does shocks me. He actually asks me if I want to go clothes shopping together.

"Oh, yeah," I cheer, imitating the way my coach says, "Oh, yeah," when someone on our team scores.

Ghosts

Ever since I can remember, I've held my breath when we drive past a graveyard. Some kid told me a long time ago that you're supposed to do that. Why? To prevent death? To protect yourself from ghosts? I don't even believe in ghosts.

Olivia and I are walking to the library after school because we were assigned to be partners for our research project on the Korean War. She's wearing her stylish capris and layered T-shirts, along with her brand-new Reef flip-flops. They match perfectly, of course. I'm wearing a soccer T-shirt and pants that look more like capris because I've grown a few inches, but my navy Reefs just happen to match the blue shirt. I hate how I think more about clothes when I'm around her. We're walking right past the graveyard on Walnut Avenue. Out of habit, I start holding my breath.

"My uncle told me that the dead get really active when there's a full moon," Olivia announces. "He said that if they're still angry at someone from when they were alive, they seek revenge during the full moon, so you have to try not to do or say anything to make them even madder or they'll come back to get you."

I interrupt my breath-holding to get her to stop her stupid ghost stories.

"Yeah, right," I say, with as much sarcasm as I can.

"We can prove we aren't scared of them by taking this path. Otherwise, they might come back more often."

"No, Olivia. I don't want to. I'm staying on the sidewalk."

"We have to show we aren't afraid, Corinna."

I see something white on the ground and think how terrible it is that people would litter in a cemetery, but when we get close enough, I can see that it's a pair of white gloves. I have to admit, it creeps me out.

Olivia's nose scrunches up as she inspects the gloves.

"See what I mean. Look at these, Corinna. Last night was the full moon, and one of the ghosts must have been trying to get even with someone. She left her gloves behind as a warning."

"Olivia, cut it out."

"I'm serious. My uncle said it's true. He totally believes in ghosts, and he knows everything about that stuff because he works for the CIA."

I start holding my breath again and walking faster, but then I realize there's no way I can hold my breath all the way to the end of the sidewalk. Even the shorter path through the graves is too far for one breath. Plus, Olivia's not holding hers, and she's the one who believes in ghosts.

"This is stupid. There are so many stupid rumors and stories about ghosts and curses and death. And if you're trying to scare me about my mom, she's not even here, for your information."

"Where is she?"

"Not here."

"She's not buried yet?"

"She was cremated, and we have her ashes at our house."

"That's gross!"

"No, it's not. It doesn't smell or anything."

"Well, if I were her, I'd be mad you hadn't buried me, and you know what happens when the dead are angry."

"Well, if she's a ghost, then she'll be a good ghost."

I stay silent the rest of the way to the library, tuning out Olivia. I am so mad at her and can't believe how insensitive she's being with her "spooky" ghost stories.

I try to block out everything she said and start thinking about Mom's random dinner creations and the way she folded my socks in a ball and all the fun projects we did together and . . . how I will never, ever forget her. And even though her brain doesn't work anymore, I know in my heart that she won't forget me, either.

Something about surviving Olivia and the graveyard makes me feel ready to show Dad the quilt. After I finish my homework, I come downstairs with the quilt all rolled up in a ball in my hands.

"Dad, I have something to show you."

"Yeah, sure . . . Just a sec."

Dad finishes writing on the paper he's correcting and turns around in his swivel desk chair.

"What's that?" His chair squeaks as he leans back.

I hold it out for him to see.

"I've been working on this for a long time at school. Do you recognize anything?"

"Hmm, let's see. Is that . . . Mom's nightgown?"

"Yeah." I smile, and then ask, "What else?"

"Well, that must be the bathrobe she wore all the time, right?"

"Yup." I nod.

"All those pieces are from Mom's clothes?"

"Yeah." I pass it to him. "It's a memory quilt."

"Wow."

He shakes his head and his eyes tear up. That makes *me* tear up. We both have a "need it hug" moment, like I did as a toddler. I had been a little worried he would be mad that I cut up some of her things, so it's a relief when he doesn't seem to mind at all and gives me a great big hug.

"Mom would have loved it. Great idea. I see you chose not to use that brown-and-green dress of hers you used to tease her about!"

"Yeah, I hated that dress, didn't you?"

We both start laughing.

"Hey, guess what the history department head asked me to do?"

"I have no idea, Dad. What?"

"He asked me to start a Model UN chapter at the high school."

I guess that's really exciting for a history teacher. It's nice to see him happy about work. I've been so worried about him.

Words and Letters

I'm riding with Nicole to her house on the incredibly loud and wild yellow bus and I can't imagine how she's been surviving it, especially during the whole "Shamu" phase.

When we get to Nicole's house, her babysitter, Rosa, is there with her little brother, Luke, who is apparently obsessed with fire trucks. He's really cute and tries to get us to play with him. Nicole tells him to go fight some more big fires with Rosa in the basement.

As we munch on carrots and ranch dressing at her kitchen table, Nicole explains that Rosa lives with them because their parents travel so much for work. Luke runs back in, shouting, "My bottom is stuck together!"

"Luke!"

"Look," he says, turning around so we can get a better look.

"Luke, that's called a wedgie. Can you say wedgie?"

I laugh so hard I almost wet my pants. Rosa doesn't seem to get the humor in that. She tells Luke to sit down for snack time and starts asking about my family. I have to make that hard decision about how much to explain.

"Well," I say, "it's just me and my dad. My mom died last summer."

"Oh, I'm sorry."

She looks like she regrets asking. So does Nicole. I'll bet Nicole wishes she had explained that to her before my visit.

"Thanks," I reply.

I wonder if that whole thing with people asking about my parents will ever get easier.

Nicole and I head up to her room and make necklaces with beads. Her seed-bead collection is much bigger than mine, and she keeps it neatly organized in an elaborate red-and-gold box.

"I'm making mine for my cousin. What about you?" Nicole asks me.

I have to stop and think. When I was younger, I would have made it for my mom. Now, I might give it to Aunt Jennifer.

Dad's not home when Rosa drops me off, so I take the opportunity to go read another page of Mom's journal. It's the last page before a hundred blank ones.

Maybe someday I'll get better at this journal thing. My music comes so much more easily. Music is my outlet. Music IS my journal.

The end. I flip through, hoping to find more. Nothing was written in the last seven years of her life, not even after she got diagnosed with cancer. Nothing. Nothing more about me, either. How could it end here? Didn't she have lots of feelings to express during all of that?

Maki starts barking. It must be Dad coming home. Instead of Dad, though, it's the mailman. I rescue our mail from Maki's teeth as it comes through the slot. We still get the dreaded Sophie Burdette mail. I notice an interesting envelope with an Allentown, Pennsylvania, return address, and since Dad's not here, I go ahead and open it.

Dear Sophie,

I got your address from the Allentown High School reunion committee. I hope you're coming to our 25th reunion on June 20th. It would be great to see you.

Cheers,

Hugh

I don't think there are many Hughs in the world, so I'm figuring he just might be the Hugh who gave her the necklace. Obviously, Mom won't be making it to the reunion to slap hands or exchange kisses with Hugh. I wonder if they'll even know she died. That reminds me: I wonder if Deborah has received any of those letters she said she was going to ask Mom's friends for. I dial her number.

"Hi, Deborah, this is Corinna. I was wondering if you ever got those letters from my mom's college friends."

"I was just getting ready to call you. I got the last one yesterday."

"Really? So you have some?"

"Really. Shall I bring them over tonight?"

"Yeah . . . I guess that would be good." I'm trying to sound calm and nonchalant, but my voice is a little shaky.

"What time?"

"How about seven?"

At 7:10 P.M., Deborah rings the bell. I'm excited to be getting some blasts from my mom's past. At least I hope they'll be good blasts and not more bombshells.

"Hi, Deborah," I say cheerfully as my hands go to my pockets.

"Hi, Corinna. Here are the letters."

"Have you read them?" I quickly ask.

"I was tempted, but they're really for you, so no, I haven't."

"Thank you," I say, reaching out to receive them.

"Do you want me to stay while you read them?"

"That's okay, but my dad's in the kitchen . . . if you want to see him."

I head up to my room with Maki, prop up my pillows, and spread the five envelopes around me, trying to decide which to open first. It's a bit like opening up a picnic lunch packed by someone else and you have no idea if you're going to like what's in each of the little packages.

I open the first envelope, from Sue.

Dear Corinna,

My most memorable story about your mom happened on a beautiful spring day during our sophomore year in college. We were taking a study break to get freshly made cherry pie from the well-known bakery in the next town. We borrowed a car from an older student so we could get there and back before our next class.

We learned an important lesson in life that day: Eating hot pie (or anything hot) is dangerous while you're driving a car. I spilled the delicious, gooey, steamy pie filling on my lap, and it burned me, which distracted me at a critical moment. The car slammed into a stone fence and my teeth slammed into the steering wheel. Your mom also hit her head, but she kept her teeth. Needless to say, we didn't make it to class. We had to go by ambulance to the hospital, but luckily, we weren't too seriously hurt. Now, whenever I even smell cherry pie, I think of her. I think of her lots of other times, too. She was a dear, dear friend, and I shall miss her.

Love,
Sue Farley

I open Patty's story next. Her envelope has flower stickers on the back that smell like roses.

My Dear Corinna,

Your mom was the most thoughtful person I knew in college. She was always helping others in their moments of need. She patiently helped me study for tests and helped me to stay calm when I was sure

I was going to fail. She helped me with roommate problems freshman year, and then we became roommates for our final two years. I got appendicitis during senior fall, and she stayed all night with me at the hospital and into the next day. Ever since I first met her, I have been thankful to have her as a friend.

Sincerely,
Patty Steinitz

I'm expecting there to be a musical memory, and Michelle's letter covers that part of my mom's life, complete with a few music notes drawn under her signature.

Dear Corinna,

Sue asked me to write out a memory about your wonderful mom, Sophie. When she heard that the local animal shelter was going to have to shut down for lack of funds, your mom organized a huge fund-raiser. She got all the different musical groups on campus to perform on a Saturday night. Chamber music ensembles, jazz bands, the gospel singers, a cappella groups, drum groups, and a flute choir. She went around town putting up posters and getting the radio station to advertise, and they made thousands of dollars in ticket sales. We were so proud of her. She was passionate about animals and passionate about music. I am truly saddened that she died so young.

Sending love,
Michelle

Betsy's is written in fancy calligraphy, like it's an official document.

Dear Corinna,

I don't know if you remember, but I was in your mom and dad's wedding. They have been such wonderful friends to my husband and me over the years. Sue suggested I write a story about your mom so that you will have some nice things to read now and over the years. The funniest story I remember is from when she was staying at her professor's house. He and his wife were away, and your mom was there, house-sitting and taking care of their two daughters. Well, a squirrel got into the house and was wreaking havoc. It was chewing on the window frames and pooping all over the place. The girls were panicked, and your mom was trying to keep them safe and herself calm. She had to chase that squirrel out of the house, not once, but three times. The squirrel had gotten in through the chimney again and again. It was an epic battle.

Please give me a call if you are ever in Cleveland. I'd love to take you to lunch.

Love,
Betsy

The final story is from Abby.

Dear Corinna,

Greetings from Norway. I am on a new posting to the U.S. Embassy. Did you know that your mom is responsible for my joining the Foreign Service? When she told me about her exciting experiences living in Japan during her high school semester, I decided that I wanted to study abroad. I went to graduate school and learned Japanese, and that started me on this very interesting path. I have your mother to thank for opening that door in my life. She was an amazing person. I'm sure you are, too.

With warm regards,
Abby Liffland

Summer

Dates

It's the second day of June, Mom's birthday. Dad and I both have extra busy days at school, and I have to stay after for a math review session, but on the way home, we stop to get some yellow roses so we can put them next to Mom's ashes in the ginger jar. White doesn't seem right since that's what we had at the funeral.

She would have been forty-two today. She loved chocolate cake, so we make another stop to buy one at Patisserie Poupon, her favorite place for delicious treats. It's strange celebrating a birthday of someone who is dead, because she's not actually turning that age, and she's not having a happy birthday at all. But I guess it wouldn't feel right not to do *something*.

I cut us each a huge slice. As I stuff my mouth with a huge forkful, Dad says, "Did Mom love chocolate or what? You know it was because of chocolate that we met."

After swallowing most of that huge mouthful, I ask him to tell me that story again.

"It was at a friend's wedding. We were both in the kitchen

eating leftovers after most of the guests had left. She'd missed the food because she was playing music for the wedding, and I just wanted more because it was so good. There we were, diving into the chocolate wedding cake. I don't remember if we used forks or fingers."

"So how long was it before you fell in love?"

"I had noticed her before the cake eating, when she was playing a Beethoven trio. She was a beauty, and her music was amazing. But I didn't get the nerve to call her up for a full two days after the wedding."

"Two whole days?"

"Yeah, I was shy, but it was worth the risk."

"Don't you wish you had met sooner, so you would have had more time together?"

"There are lots of things I wish."

"Me, too."

After dinner and feeling very full of chocolate cake, I go into my room to try to figure out if this would be a good time to ask Dad about Mom's whole thing about her father. After all, it's her *birth*day. I've been wanting to ask him about it, to tell him I know, to tell him about her notebook, but I haven't known how to do it or how it would go. I've come close to bringing it up about ten different times but I just haven't been able to. I talk it through with Maki. Maki curls up next to me and falls asleep while I'm talking. So much for his advice.

I finally decide to just go for it, even though the thought of it makes my stomach feel tight. I go halfway down the stairs and sit on a step. Dad's sitting in his reading chair with the newspaper.

"Hey, Dad? I have something I've been meaning to ask you about."

"Yeah?"

He puts down the newspaper, and I can see his eyes look sleepy.

"Well, I kinda sorta know about Bapa not being Mom's biological father and about how Bapa and Grandma kept that a secret from Mom. What's up with all that?"

He sits up straight and looks like he's just touched something electric.

"Oh. Oh, wow. Uh . . . Well, what do you think about that?"

"Well, I'm mad at them for lying to her. And besides, the donor guy is my grandfather! How bizarro is that? And I have a right to know about my genes, too."

"Yeah, I hadn't really thought about it that way since I've always thought of Bapa as your grandfather, but you're right, it's your information, too."

"So when were you going to tell me?"

"It was one of those things that we knew we wanted to tell you, but we hadn't found what felt like the right time. There are some other things that I wish we'd shared with you, too."

Dad takes a big breath through his nostrils, letting it out slowly.

"Like *what*? That you're not my real dad?"

"Yes, yes, yes, I'm your dad, one hundred percent. This has nothing to do with that. I just wish we had had more family conversations about Mom dying before she died."

"Hmm. Well . . . You could at least have told me about this donor thing. What were you waiting for? Were you going to tell me on my wedding day or something?"

"No, of course not. But I'm curious how you found out. I mean, I'm glad you know, but how *did* you?"

"I'm quite the investigator. I found Mom's notebook in her closet, and she wrote about it in there. She wrote about a few other things, too. You might want to check it out."

Dad's eyebrows shoot up with a look of surprise.

"Did you know she had a diary?"

He shakes his head no.

"Well, it's in her closet, in the back behind the hanging clothes we saved, in a flowered duffel bag."

"I had no idea."

"Oh, and don't be surprised when you see a piece missing from the bag," I warn.

"Missing?"

"Yeah, I used it in my quilt."

I wait for him to react, but he just says, "Oh."

Even though *he's* not reacting, my insides are reacting big-time, telling me to skedaddle.

"Okay, so this is a lot to think about. I'm going to bed now."

I go up the stairs, two at a time, as he calls after me, "Okay. Just let me know if you want to talk some more. I may not be good at it, but I'll do my best. And I know Aunt Jennifer would be happy to talk to you, too."

Phew. I made it through that incredibly awkward conversation without totally freaking out. I'm glad there were no more surprises. I can't handle any more surprises.

Two days later, a bunch of us meet for ice cream at The Mix to celebrate Clare's birthday. I'm really glad she invited Nicole to come, but I start to feel bad when I see Nicole ordering the sugar-free, fat-free yogurt without any fun toppings. Maybe I should skip the toppings, too, but I've already started in on my Reese's Pieces and they are delicious.

"What were you and Eliana talking about in PE?" Olivia asks me.

I have no idea what we were talking about, but I find it annoying that Olivia is prying. Juliette changes the subject with her very serious announcement that she is going to have a crush on Nathan as soon as she's finished with Danny because Nathan is so much fun to flirt with. Joci and I make eye contact and try hard not to laugh. That's when shy Lena shocks us all with her suggestion that we try to start a trend by wearing hats every time we go to the movie theater. Everyone loves the idea and we discuss what kind of hat it should be.

On my way home from The Mix, I cross through the

parking lot on my bicycle and see a license plate that says JULY 22. I wonder what happened on July twenty-second. Did the driver win the lottery? Did he or she get married? Was it a good day or a bad day? Death is a different kind of anniversary than a birthday or a graduation day. You mark it, it marks you, but you don't celebrate. August fifth is the date I won't ever forget, but I don't exactly want it on our license plate.

I want to call Clare to ask her what her family does on her dad's anniversary so I can try to prepare myself for August fifth, but I decide I should wait until her birthday is officially over so I don't make her sad. When I see her the next day, she tells me, "We always light one of those twenty-four-hour burning candles, the kind they sell at the grocery store."

"We did that, too, on the anniversary of my mom's diagnosis. Did you do anything else besides that?"

"I think my mom goes to church every year on that day. And she takes us to the cemetery where my father's buried. My brother hates going. He always wants to stay in the car."

Later on when I see Dad, I ask him where we'll be on August fifth.

"Somewhere in Japan, but I'm not sure which town yet."

"Really? So we're going?" I ask, smiling a gigantic smile.

"Yup. Grandma and Bapa offered to pay for our tickets, and the more I thought about it, the more I realized that Mom would be mad if we *didn't* go. She really wanted her Japanese family to meet us."

That was so nice of Grandma and Bapa. We haven't seen them since Mom's funeral, but we've had some phone calls about the weather. I think we're all meeting at Aunt Jennifer's next Thanksgiving. That should be *interesting*. I mean, I'm glad we'll be with Aunt Jennifer, but now that I know this secret about my grandparents and my mom, it could be really awkward. Am I the only one with such a weird family?

Dreamer

All night I dream about Mom's notebook and secrets. I even dream that I'm telling Joci and Clare about it and they don't get why I'm upset.

"It's not a big deal," they both tell me. "Just chillax."

I wake up feeling super-frustrated with them. My mood gets even worse when I remember that I'm supposed to get to school early for another special band rehearsal. I have to rush, rush, rush, and then Dad drops me off extra early on his way to work.

I go through the side entrance by the lunchroom, having finally figured out that Alex sometimes hangs out there with the skateboarders before school. I'm not exactly a skater girl, but this morning, I'd rather see Alex than Joci and Clare, only Alex isn't at the side entrance. It seems that the laxbros have taken over that territory from the skaters. *Laxbros* is what the lacrosse boys are calling themselves now.

I'm the second person to arrive in the band room. Alex is already here, adjusting the drums. I guess drums need an awful lot of tightening. Or is it loosening? I try to think of something to say, but how many times can I ask about math subs?

"Hey, Alex, I heard you're running for class rep."

"Yeah," he says, looking up.

"Good luck."

"Thanks. Hey, did you hear that Connor is going to boarding school next year?" he asks.

"No. Really?"

"Yeah. And get *this*." Alex does a drum roll before making his big announcement. "He's running for class VP."

"You mean for boarding school?"

"No, for our high school, our ninth-grade VP." Alex's face gets even more adorable as he's telling me this. I can barely focus on what he's saying.

"That's ridiculous," I say a little too loudly. My voice squeaks on the word *ridiculous* and I cringe.

"Yeah, I don't know what's up with him. Guess he thinks it's funny," he says, his shoulders shrugging.

I tell my voice not to squeak again. "What a jerk."

"Yup, that's Connor." Alex smiles his adorable smile.

By then, the room is full and more kids are talking about the election. I enjoy being in a haze — or is it a daze? — for the rest of band.

After class, Alex walks with me and Eliana to our lockers and then continues past us. I'm in La La Land, thinking how sweet he is, while Eliana asks me if I am planning to come to her graduation party at her dad's bowling alley.

"Of course," I say distractedly.

Graduation announcements and invitations are everywhere. The big graduation dance is on Friday. I know that most of the kids in my grade will be going to the dance, so I assume Alex will be there, but I don't want to come right out and ask him. Olivia has to miss the dance because she has to go to her parents' college reunion. I wouldn't miss the dance for anything, even though the last one was so awful. This time I'm on a mission, and besides, graduation is supposed to be a time to celebrate. I still don't know what I'm going to wear, which is ridiculous since the dance is only five days away. Mom and I would never have left dress shopping to the last minute.

Fortunately, I've recovered from that weird dream and don't feel bad about asking Joci to ask her mom to squeeze in a mall trip to take care of this immediate and gigantic graduation-dance problem. I don't bother asking Dad. He obviously hates the mall, and teaching him to like it is hopeless.

Lucky for me, Joci's mother agrees to take us even though we're in the middle of exams. Looking at dresses is fun, and her mom is even more patient than my mom was while we try on a million dresses in four different stores. I buy a cool dress, turquoise with black lace over it, not too long, strapless. I'm thrilled and relieved to find one that fits me well. I show it to Dad when

I get home, although he wouldn't know if it was in style in the 1800s or now. He has major fashion disabilities.

It's hard to imagine having our predance prep at our house with only Dad there, so on the night of the dance, Joci, Clare, and I have dinner and get dressed at Clare's house. We pass around Joci's curling iron and I manage to burn the tip of my ear. Clare's lucky that her wavy hair looks good without a curling iron. I'm wearing my mom's black high-heeled sandals, even though they're too big. As we practice our dance moves, my feet are sliding around, which causes me to lurch and sends the three of us into hysterical laughter. The three of us have been getting along pretty well these days. Once in a while, Joci seems jealous of the special bond I have with Clare, but there's not much I can do about that.

When we arrive at the dance, Clare's mom has to sign us in at the desk. We hang out in the hall for a while before going into the gym, with all the girls checking out one another's dresses and makeup. Lots of ooh-la-lahs. Nicole looks especially beautiful in her dress.

It's completely dark inside the gym, except for some strobe lights. The organizers have tried extra hard to transform the gym into a ballroom with tons of shimmery fabric and balloons everywhere. Just like at the last Aloha Dance, there's not a lot of actual dancing going on. A few kids dance slow dances, the ones who are "going out," and there is a group of kids dancing dirty during some songs, but mostly it's groups of girls dancing and screaming and talking in the halls and bathroom, and boys either jumping up and down in front of the speakers or swarming the food tables. I sure hope they remembered to use their supersize deodorants for tonight. This gym is already maxed out on stinky sweat. Mr. Spinolli is guarding one door with his blue cheese breath, and Mr. Maroni, the principal, is at the other. I don't get close enough to him to diagnose his breath.

"Sorry, girls, the doors have to stay closed."

Even in our strapless dresses, we are boiling and desperate for fresh air. I'm sweating through the fabric on the back of my dress, hoping it doesn't show. Alex says hi to me a few times, every time we *happen* to be near each other. Shock of shocks, he is *not* wearing his orange shirt. He's looking hot in a blue-brown-and-white checked shirt and the same khakis as all of the other boys. I'll bet he wishes he was wearing shorts like he usually does.

Toward the end of the dance, when kids are actually dancing, we're next to each other in the sweaty crowd. He's doing some scuba dance move, with his nose plugged and his arm going up and down. He practically knocks me over with his scuba arm and then we both start laughing. I can't stop myself from looking over at him and he looks right at me and smiles. My heart is totally pounding. I don't want the dance to end even though my feet are killing me from sliding around in Mom's shoes.

I'm trying to send ESP vibes to the DJ to get him to play "You and Me" by Lifehouse, but instead he starts playing "Sweet

Caroline" by Neil Diamond and announces it will be the last song of the night. Which moron chose that song? Kids start jumping up and down in protest.

Alex moves a few feet closer and then looks behind him. Now what? What's he looking at? Should I move closer, too? As he turns back around, we make eye contact and I melt, moving forward until we're almost touching. Then he gently touches my bare shoulder with his hand. His hand is warm and sweaty, and he looks really nervous. I'm sure I do, too. Then he starts leaning over. His nose bumps my ear as he says, "What a lame song," and I realize that I'm taller than he is. While I'm telling myself how stupid it was to wear high heels, he's leaning over again, but not toward my ear. This time, he kisses me on the lips. I can't believe this is happening.

The kiss isn't exactly like the ones you see in the movies. It's more like an awkward move that you're trying to copy from some instructional video called *How to be a Great Kisser in Ten Days or Less*. But so what. It's pretty great and I am beyond happy. All I can do is smile. I smile for the rest of the night. When Joci, Clare, and I get back to Clare's house, our three cell phones are swamped with text messages asking about *the kiss*.

Ow owwwww, texts Nicole. Even quiet Lena texts, **Yea baby!**

Eliana, Juliette, Nicole, and Lena all want details, but I just want to talk about it with Clare and Joci, not the whole world. Even though I hate to have to wash the kiss off, my beauty consultants, Clare and Joci, tell me that pimple prevention means I have to wash my face thoroughly. I close my eyes and relive my first kiss before turning on the faucet.

My heart is swirling and twirling as I try to fall asleep. What a sweet kiss. What a sweet boy. Ahhh . . . I want to kiss him again! But when might the next time be? Will I have to wait until a high school dance? What will it be like when I see him at school? Am I supposed to text him or wait for him to text me? Joci and Clare both think I should text him if I haven't heard from him in twenty-four hours. Clare offers to get his cell number for me from her brother, who knows Alex's brother.

Neither of us texts the other the whole weekend, but when I see him at school on Monday, we smile at each other, and say, "Hey," at the same exact moment. Then he looks down, and I look past him to see if anyone is coming. His eyes go to my binders and he asks me what I'm doing this summer.

"My dad and I are going to Japan. What about you?"

"Going to camp in Vermont."

"Cool. I love Vermont."

"Well, Japan sounds more cool."

I can't think of anything to say. We stand there in silence. A happy, awkward silence.

The bell rings, and I reluctantly say, "Well, I have to get to class. See ya."

The electricity follows me down the hall all the way into the science room.

Graduation

Our last tests are finished, and all that's left is graduation. I can't help but wish that Mom could be in the audience. I know Dad will feel so alone in the sea of happy families.

The election results are posted in the front hall, and Alex won as one of the reps. I'm so happy for him. Connor won for VP, because most people, including the teacher who runs the student government elections, had no idea he wasn't going with the rest of us to our high school. Instead of having another election, they decide to bump up the runner up, and that person is . . . Nicole!

We spend most of the last day signing yearbooks. My crush signs: *"Have A Good Summer (HAGS) in Japan. Yours till submarines have screen doors, Alex."* The submarine thing is kind of random, and there's no reference to our amazing kiss, but I'm not going to mention it, either. Not that I don't think about it a million times a day. I write: *"HAGS. See you next year. XOXO, Corinna"* in his. I think long and hard about how many XOs to write, and I don't even notice when Ms. Carey stops in front of me to say hi. She has to call my name to get my attention.

After school, I clear out my binders, tossing huge piles of papers into my garbage can. I read over my English essay from last September, trying to decide what I should do with it, when Dad appears in the doorway to my room.

"Corinna, I was thinking you might like to pick out a piece of Mom's jewelry as a graduation present. Something from her. What do you think?"

"Um, yeah, sure. That sounds good."

I return to the essay I was reading, but he's still standing in the doorway.

"You mean *now*?"

"Why not?"

We walk into their room and I plop myself on their comfy bed. He brings over the oval jewelry box and puts it in front of me.

"You think there's a certain thing she would want me to have?"

"I think you should pick something. We didn't talk about it, but I know that it would make her happy to have you wear something of hers."

"Well, how about this hideous pin! Who gave her that? Or maybe this ancient-looking necklace?"

"Ever the clown, Miss Corinna."

"You really don't care which thing I pick?"

"No, it's your choice."

"This is hard."

I finally choose a silver chain with a round pendant that has characters on it. Maybe Chinese or Japanese? I don't know what it says, but I imagine it says something wise and good.

The Westhaven Middle School graduation ceremony is a mix of excitement and sadness. Something is missing, though. Duh. But Dad's here, all dressed up and holding pink roses for me. Gigi and Pop Pop couldn't come, and I didn't invite Grandma and Bapa. I'm still mad at them for lying to my mom.

We have to stand in alphabetical order, so I can't be with Joci and Clare during the ceremony. I'll have to get a picture with them afterward. The principal says something about the loved ones who aren't able to be here with us, which is nice of him, but it does make me choke up. I look up at the ceiling to keep the tears inside my eyes instead of on my cheeks, chin, and dress. The class speaker lists a bunch of memories from shows we put on, field trips, major weather events, the principal's broken arm, the mold growing on the library ceiling and walls after the huge leak, the successful book and used-clothing drives, and our Earth Day celebration. Yasmine is a few seats away, looking kind of watery-eyed, too. I wonder if she's listening to the class speaker or if her mind is on the Marines and her dad.

After the official ceremony, we move outside for the party. Miss Beatty, wearing a beautiful flowered dress and a warm smile, walks up to Dad and me.

"I'm so proud of you, Corinna. And I know your mom would be proud of you, too."

I swallow hard and smile at her. "Thanks, Miss Beatty," I say, feeling sad that she won't be my teacher anymore.

Everyone is taking pictures with their friends and families. I see Alex with his family and I wave to him. I sure hope his divorced parents don't fight on his special day. He nods and smiles and looks gorgeous. Dad turns to Nicole's mom and asks her to take our picture, which brings tears to my eyes. We hug each other after our photo shoot. Somehow, we get through it.

Preparations

It's time to focus on getting ready for our big trip. I'm excited, but kind of sad that we can't also go to Bethany Beach like we used to every other summer since I can remember. We didn't go last summer, either, because Mom was way too sick. Dad says we'll probably go back next summer. I hope we can rent the same house we rented with Mom. Maybe by next summer it won't feel so totally strange to go there without her. But maybe it will.

I hang out with Joci and Clare before they leave for their sleepaway camps. I've never been too interested in sleepaway camp even though my friends love it. Dad loved it, too. Mom and Aunt Jennifer also went to an all-girls camp in Maine where they sang all kinds of crazy songs about this moose. They used to sing the moose songs together at Thanksgiving and Christmas, which made it seem like fun, but I think I would get homesick.

Dad spends tons of time going through the old guidebooks Mom had on Japan. She had checked or underlined certain things or folded over pages, which gives him some ideas of where we should go. But those books are really old, so he ended up buying a new one. He tells me he chose hotels that, according to the guidebook, are ones where "tiny bit of English spoken."

Dad asks me if I think we should call or visit Mom's homestay family while we are in Tokyo. Both of us feel really shy about it since neither of us speaks any Japanese. We decide we should be brave and try to see them if they're in town. Mom would want us to. I'm going to let Dad do all the talking.

It's so strange to be going to Japan without Mom, but I pack the quilt, which means a little tiny part of her will be with us.

The day of our trip is busy with last-minute packing and measuring out scoops of dry dog food for every day we'll be gone. I dread dropping Maki off at the dog boarder's house because I always worry that he'll think we forgot him or don't love him. We're halfway to the dog boarding place when I realize I forgot his food and monthly heartworm medicine, and we have to turn around to go home to get them.

"We're going to miss the flight!"

Unlike me, Dad stays calm. And he doesn't forget our passports or tickets. Good thing I wasn't in charge of those.

The flight over lasts forever and ever. I have to stop looking at my watch because it's so discouraging. We are lucky that there are lots of movies to choose from. People are sleeping and watching movies at all different times, so that's kind of weird, and the lady next to us seems to be watching some comedy and is laughing way too loudly. She has no idea just how loud she is because she's wearing those clunky headphones. She's annoying because of her noise, but also because she's sitting in Mom's seat.

When we finally arrive at Narita Airport, it's the next day on the calendar because of the long flight and the time change. We take a fancy bus with lace headrests straight to our hotel, and although there might be cool things to see, I'm too tired to keep my eyes open. The hotel lobby is filled with flowering tree branches in a huge arrangement called ikebana, according to the hotel lady, but our room doesn't seem very Japanese. I guess I was expecting it to have colorful origami decorations or silk kimonos on the walls.

Because of our jet lag, we wake up really early, but we already have an early morning plan. We're going to the biggest fish market in the world, called Tsukiji. It's pronounced TSOO-KEY-JI, and it opens at four in the morning. The subway seems overwhelming with ticket machines to figure out, so we take a *takushi* (which means taxi). I reach out to open the taxi door. The driver wearing white gloves starts saying something very fast in Japanese. I'm confused. Then the door starts swinging open by itself. Mom never told us that the drivers get really mad if you try to open the door. Maybe it's a new invention since her time here.

When we get out at Tsukiji, we're surrounded by hundreds of stalls selling all kinds of stuff. Dried fish that looks like wood, tea in every size container, vegetables, some of which I recognize and some of which I don't, pots and bags of chopsticks and knives, and tons of seaweed. The seaweed makes me think of Maki at home, boarding, without us. Inside the big white building are stacks of Styrofoam boxes, and rows and rows of booths selling fish. Unlike the workers who are all wearing tall rubber boots, we're wearing sneakers. We try to avoid the puddles of fishy water on the floor, but you also have to be careful not to get hit by the guys whizzing by in mini motor-carts, yelling "*abunai*" or something like that (which must mean "look out" or "danger"). That's another thing Mom could have told us. I'm busy staring at a gazillion kinds of fish, crabs, eels, and other bizarre creatures, but these guys are working on a deadline and they're not going to slow down for tourists like us.

The whole place smells fishy. After a while, we head to the exit and find a row of noodle stalls. Men in blue overalls and blue boots are slurping their steaming bowls of soup and noodles, which look delicious. Dad points to a picture menu to help him order our food. We struggle to control the long noodles with our chopsticks. The noodles hang from our mouths and dangle into the large white bowls, the steam filling our nostrils and making our noses run. We are surrounded by noisy slurpers. Dad and I look at each other and burst out laughing at the sound effects. Then we pump up the volume of our own slurping to fit in.

Even with the guidebook, we don't know the Japanese customs, so it seems like we're doing things the wrong way almost all of the time; where to rest your chopsticks, how to pay at a restaurant, or what to say when you walk into a store. I quickly learn to wear socks and shoes, not sandals, because when you go into some restaurants, you have to take off your shoes. My feet get filthy from all the city walking and I can sense the hostess's disgust as I walk on the delicate straw mats with my grimy gray feet.

We get lost five to ten times a day in Tokyo, but we also find some of Mom's favorite places.

"*Sumimasen* (which means 'excuse me' and is our best phrase), can you help me find the Meiji Shrine?"

Trying to communicate is exhausting. Sometimes people pretend not to hear us or understand us, but other times they are incredibly helpful and we do a whole nodding routine with a mix of English and Japanese. We try all the foods we remember Mom talking about, including the things she didn't like, just to see if we agree. We do! Bean-paste ice cream is just not our cup of tea. We eat some things that contain various unknown substances, like an omelet-type thing with paste inside. The bright green-tea ice cream is surprisingly decent. There are also some pretty hilarious signs that are written in English for visitors like us. My favorite so far is: FOR RESTROOMS GO BACK TOWARD YOUR BEHIND. Excuse me!!

On August fifth, we find our way to the Asakusa Temple. It has a beautiful gate, but once we get inside the grounds, it's really crowded and filled with tacky souvenir stands. I pick out a few things for Joci and Clare, thinking they might like some of the silly stuff. Dad and I were both expecting a quiet, peaceful place where we might be able to light a candle or do something spiritual on the anniversary of Mom's death, but this isn't it.

"Do you think we should look for a garden or park, Corinna?"

"Sure, I guess."

"I brought some of Mom's ashes. I thought maybe we could scatter some here."

I'm surprised to hear that he brought them, and I start worrying about him spilling or losing them. After consulting our guidebook, we decide to go to Meiji Jingu. The shrine is really peaceful and the land around it is filled with beautiful trees and open spaces. We find a pond filled with bright orange and white fish, called koi. They're pretty and the pond is peaceful, but the idea of putting her ashes here doesn't feel right to me. I'm sure it doesn't feel right to the fish, either.

"Dad, how can we visit her if her ashes are here?"

"Well, I only brought a little bit in this Ziploc bag. The rest are still at home. I don't know. Maybe we should wait." He returns the ash bag to his pocket.

I tell myself to breathe slowly and deeply.

Are we ever going to feel ready?

Before we leave the little temple near the pond, I make a wish that next year will be easier. And I pray that Mom will stay a part of my life forever.

The Ishibashis

Dad was supposed to write to Mom's Japanese family before our trip, but he never got around to it, or maybe he dreaded it so much he "forgot." Luckily (or unluckily), they answer their phone. Dad's half of the conversation goes like this:

"Hello, this is Daniel Burdette."

"Daniel, Sophie's husband."

"Sophie, yes, Sophie."

"We are in Tokyo and would like to meet you."

"Yes, in Tokyo now."

"Yes, today, today we are in Tokyo."

"Can we see you?"

"Tuesday?"

"Okay, Tuesday at twelve o'clock."

"Where?"

"The Almond? What's the Almond?"

"I'll ask the hotel. Okay, the Almond at twelve on Tuesday. Thank you."

Dad puts the phone down slowly.

"I think we're supposed to meet them at something called the Almond on Tuesday. I hope the concierge knows what the heck that is."

The hotel concierge, whose English is pretty good and who has been super-helpful to us, explains that the Almond is a coffee shop with a huge pink sign in the middle of the big intersection in Roppongi, which is near our hotel. She also explains that because the addresses are so poorly marked in Tokyo, even the locals use landmarks like big pink signs instead of regular street addresses.

Miraculously, we find the pink sign and wait next to it for some Japanese people to come up to us. There are hundreds of people ignoring us, but eventually, a little Japanese couple comes up to us, holding our holiday card with the picture from two years ago, and they bow. Dad and I stick out our hands, they bow again, then we do both. After all the bowing and shaking, they both ask, "Where Sophie?"

All of a sudden, I realize that they have no idea. I feel a stab in my stomach. How are we going to explain? Their English is only a little better than our nonexistent Japanese. We do our best with charades, trying to show "death" in the middle of the sidewalk along the super-busy Roppongi Dori. The crowds are like the Fourth of July crowds on the Mall in Washington, DC, when you can barely move and you're sweaty, thirsty, and you just want to go home.

After using every hand signal for death we know — finger

across the throat, finger gun to the chest, sword to the stomach — and repeating the word "cancer" over and over, they seem to get it. Maybe they think she committed suicide. Their faces are like stone, with that gray look and everything. No one knows what to do or say. My mind starts thinking about who else doesn't know. What a weird thing to have people think she's still alive.

Once we get through the death part, we have to do more charades about what we're going to do. Go to a restaurant or to their apartment? Turn around and say good-bye? We end up following them to their apartment in near silence. We walk in and take off our shoes to join theirs at the step. Then I notice the low table with floor pillow "seats" is set for five. Mrs. Ishibashi tries to put away the fifth setting without us noticing. She serves *tonkatsu*, a deep fried pork thing, with rice, some kind of pickles that look like orange stones, and seaweed salad with mini-minnows. She keeps pushing the plate toward me and saying, "*Doozo, Doozo*" (which I've learned means "please"). What am I going to do with the pickles and minnow salad? Neither she nor Mr. Ishibashi turn their backs for a second, so I can't put it in my pocket or put it on my dad's plate. Dad's not making eye contact with me. I panic. Should I be rude and leave it on my plate or try to swallow it, gag, and risk vomiting? I decide I have to be rude and leave it on my plate.

We eat in almost complete silence. It couldn't be more awkward if we tried. I'm shifting around on my pillow, trying to get comfortable, hoping it will be over soon. It's hard to imagine Mom feeling comfortable here, but she always said she loved them and they took such good care of her. Dad has a fake smile frozen on his face. Mr. and Mrs. Ishibashi keep nodding and saying "*Doozo, doozo*" many more times. Mom should be here. If she were here, this wouldn't be so painful.

Eventually, Mrs. Ishibashi gracefully gets up and says, "Sad, sad . . . *ne*. Sorry . . . *ne*."

"Yes . . . sad," her husband says in agreement.

I'm desperate to pee and I can't hold it any longer, so I ask, "Bathroom?"

Dad tries to be helpful and adds, "Toilet?"

I find it down the short hall, and when it's time to flush, I'm faced with a bunch of buttons with Japanese characters on them. None of them have pictures that I can recognize. I take a guess. Two seconds after I press the middle one, water starts shooting straight up in the air and all over the little room. I press the same button, thinking it would turn it off. Then I press another, and that turns on some other noise. I quickly go out to get help. I wave to them to come, feeling totally embarrassed. Mrs. Ishibashi covers her mouth with her hand, and I can't tell what her expression is. She then goes in and pushes something to make it stop. No one is laughing. I probably ruined the walls and floor. I can't tell what they're saying to each other in Japanese.

We don't know any Japanese words other than "hello," "thank

you," "excuse me," and the names of some kinds of sushi, which obviously are not much help in this situation, so I say, "Sorry. Very sorry. *Sumimasen. Arigato*." (Which means "thank you.")

When Dad and I are finally out on the street by ourselves, we break down in giggles. What else can we do?

Aiko

At night, we get a call in our hotel room from Aiko, the Ishibashis' daughter. Dad is in the bathroom, so I answer. In very proper English, Aiko says, "Good evening. I am Ishibashis' daughter. My parents told me you are in Tokyo. They said Sophie did not come with you. They are worried about her, and please may I show you Kyoto."

"Sophie, my mom, she died from cancer."

Somehow, the words just come out of me. Then I put my dad on the phone.

Two days after Aiko surprises us with her call, we board the Shinkansen, also known as the Bullet Train. Arriving at Kyoto Station at 13:49 along with thousands of Japanese travelers, we look for the big Sony clock that Aiko had described. I'm worried we won't be able to find her, even with a meeting place, but I never would have guessed that we would stand out as if we were tall basketball players with red hair and blue skin.

"Hello, Burdette-san."

"Hello, you must be Aiko."

"Yes, welcome to Kyoto. I am so happy to meet you both."

She bows and shakes hands simultaneously, as do we.

"So, you must be hungry. Shall we drop off your luggage before lunch?"

Dad tells her, "We ate a lot of those sweet tofu rice things on the train."

"Oh, yes, the *inari*. They are tasty, *ne*? We call them 'food of the foxes.' "

"Foxes? Why?"

"*Inari* is the name of the rice god. The fox spirits guard the rice god. We offer *inari* to the foxes to honor them."

"Oh, wow. I never ate fox food before."

We take a *takushi*, again with white-gloved driver and automatic doors, to our miniature hotel. The Uemura Guest House is so delicate-looking, it looks like it's made out of paper-thin wood. A lady in a colorful silk kimono greets us at the doorway.

"*Irashimase*," she says in a high-pitched, singsongy voice. Aiko translates that into "welcome."

While bowing and saying "*Doozo*," she motions to the maroon plastic slippers lined up at the step just inside the door and we switch into them. Aiko comes in with us to translate, and she answers something complicated sounding in Japanese. The kimono lady keeps bowing and saying, "so, so."

She shows us to our room, which is practically empty. The

floor is covered with straw tatami mats, the kind I saw at the restaurant when I horrified the hostess with my dirty bare feet and at the Ishibashis'. I'm not sure if we're supposed to keep on the slippers or go barefoot this time. Dad and I both look at Aiko's feet for guidance.

The view from our window is of the most beautiful Japanese garden. In the center of the room is a low square table, with a tray containing tiny towels and blue-and-white robes. Next, the kimono lady shows us the bathing areas. There's a tiny toilet room that has its own pair of slippers just outside the door. Across the top of each toe is written TOILET. I sense another slipper rule, and I start worrying I'll cause a second flood.

Aiko points out the bath door signs, which each have a Japanese character on them. One is for woman; the other is for man. I try to memorize the shape of the woman character.

"First, you wash with soap in this area with the buckets. After you are clean, you get in the hot water and enjoy the *ofuro*."

"The what?"

"*Ofuro*, the hot bath."

It's hot and muggy, so I can't imagine wanting to get into the deep steaming bath.

"*Doozo*," says the kimono lady, who shuffles down the hall with quiet slippered steps.

"When you take the baths tonight, please bring the towel and enjoy the *yukata*."

"Say that again?"

"The blue-and-white robes. You close them left over right."

"Left over right? Why does that matter?"

"Right over left is only for the dead."

"Oh . . . great," I mumble. Dad and I look at each other.

We walk to the subway, and I get more and more sweaty. Aiko doesn't seem to be sweating at all. The Kitano Line is crowded with people going to the Ryoanji Garden. An English sign is posted at the gate: FINEST ZEN TEMPLE. It's refreshing to see a sign in English. Inside, there's another English sign: ROCK GARDEN MIGHT REPRESENT ISLANDS IN THE SEA OR A TIGRESS SWIMMING WITH HER CUBS. I can't see a tigress, but I do see perfectly geometric carved sand with some rocks arranged in it. Maybe those are the islands or cubs. It's really beautiful, and definitely mysterious. After walking around in silence, I ask Aiko, "Is it always crowded?"

"This is a famous temple, but it is more crowded this week because it is Obon."

"What is Obon?"

"Obon is the festival of dead ancestors."

"There's a festival for dead people?"

"Yes, we welcome back the dead during Obon every year. Families come to tend their graves."

"We don't have a grave yet for my mom."

"Oh, I see."

Dad explains to Aiko that we haven't felt ready to do that yet.

"Would you like to see a cemetery here, to see how we do Obon?"

Dad nods and I say, "Um . . . I guess so," wondering if Aiko is going to tell me ghost stories like Olivia or think we're weird for not having a grave yet.

The cemetery is filled with gravestones, people, and smoke. Men and women are sweeping and pouring water on graves and placing little drinks and flowers next to the headstones. Some of them have decorations made out of vegetables with chopsticks sticking out of them to look like animals. The smell of incense is so strong it makes me start coughing.

"The incense smoke helps the dead find their way to come back and visit," Aiko explains. "And the vegetable horses help the spirits travel home quickly. The vegetable cows help the spirits return feeling relaxed."

"Dad, do people pour water on graves in the U.S.?"

"I don't know, Corinna. I haven't spent any time in a grave-yard since my grandparents died when I was a little kid. Look at the little bundles of rice and fruit on that one . . ."

"Aiko, does everyone in Japan do this for their dead relatives?"

"Yes, but if they live far away, they might do it at a shrine in their apartment."

"People have shrines in apartments?" I ask.

"Yes, most people do. That way we can still talk to them and welcome them in our daily life."

"Do you have a shrine in your apartment?"

"Yes, for my grandparents. I have a little area with their photos, and I light incense and offer rice or flowers to them. When I need to ask them for advice, or if I want to tell them happy news, I light the incense, clap my hands, and then spend time with them."

"What does the clapping do?"

"It's another way to call them when you need them, along with the offerings," Aiko explains.

"Do you keep their ashes there, too?"

"Yes, some people do that," she replies, which I think is her way of saying she does.

"Dad, do you think we could bring some incense home with us?"

"Sure, that sounds good."

I don't know what I think of the clapping, but maybe I'll experiment with that part. I have a lot of things to tell Mom about our trip, not to mention that I now know her big secret. We get more and more drenched with sweat, and I am desperate for a drink. We pass a bunch of vending machines, and I search for something recognizable, or at least with a bit of English to guide me. I choose the Kirin Melon Cream Soda.

"Aiko, can you tell me a story from when my mom was living with you and your family?"

"Oh, yes, certainly. Sophie stayed with us in Tokyo when I was sixteen. She was my American big sister. I only knew a little bit of English then, but we laughed a lot. I asked her lots of questions about America and she asked me about growing up Japanese. We shared our dreams, too. I knew I wanted to be a teacher, but I wasn't sure about getting married and having kids. She was certain she wanted many children."

"Oh, wow, that's sad, then . . . that she only had me."

"But you are so wonderful and she was so happy and loved you so much. She wrote that in the holiday card every year. That she was so happy you were her daughter."

My throat tightens, and I don't say anything out loud.

Home

The days in Japan went fast, but the flight home seems even longer than the way over. At least this time we don't have someone getting drunk or laughing like a hyena next to us. It's interesting how sometimes time goes so slowly, like when you're in pain or in math class, or having lunch with people who are in shock because they just found out your mom is dead and you don't speak the same language. Other times, it goes fast or just regular. Even though Dad and I have endless hours trapped next to each other on the plane, I can't manage to find the right moment to ask him if he has more stuff to tell me about Mom. He hasn't brought it up even though he probably read Mom's notebook before we left. I'm exhausted and try to sleep.

Maki is so happy to see us when we pick him up. I can tell because he pees on my shoe while wagging his tail like crazy. We can barely get the front door open because the mail is piled up. Most of it is junk mail, but I am psyched to see that I got a ton of camp letters from Clare and Joci. There's also one from Aunt Jennifer.

Dear Corinna,

I hope you had a great trip with your dad. I can't wait to hear about it. I'm writing you a letter instead of an e-mail because what I want to say is extra important. Your dad told me that you now know about how Grandma and Bapa used a sperm donor to help them have a baby. Your mom was so mad at them for hiding that information from her, but I really think she finally forgave them. I honestly believe they did it because they felt it was best — best for the family, best for her. Bapa was and always will be her dad. They followed their doctor's advice and really thought they were doing the right thing. I also think that in this day and age, people share a lot more information with each other and they probably would have made a different decision if they were faced with it today. Talking about difficult, touchy subjects has never been easy in our family, and I know your mom had some of that difficulty, too. Maybe that's why she loved her music so much — it gave her a comfortable and beautiful way to express her feelings. I hope you will forgive Grandma and Bapa. I know they want to stay close and connected to you. They love you and your dad very much. Family connections are so important.

I hope this helps.

Love,

Aunt Jennifer

Biting my lip, I refold the letter. Then I fold it some more and keep on folding it until it fits into my palm. I'm glad she wrote, but I hadn't known that Dad told her that I knew, and I'm still not clear if he told Grandma and Bapa. As I walk upstairs to get out of my stinky airplane clothes, I start to smile a little. I'm really glad she wrote me that letter. I place it in my desk drawer under the pencil tray and hop into the shower. It feels great to get clean after all those hours of traveling and breathing airplane air. While I'm in the shower, I start thinking about what Mom would say about this. About me knowing, about Aunt Jennifer's letter, about me being mad at Grandma and Bapa. I think she would probably say something like:

"Corinna, they screwed up by not telling me, but so did I. I should have told you. I wish I'd told you. I hope you can forgive them and me. And more than anything, I want you to know how much I love you. You are my darling Cori, and I miss you."

I wake up at three A.M., just like I did when we first arrived in Japan, which gives me plenty of hours lying awake to start thinking about ninth grade — new school, new year, harder math, lots more kids. I worry about finding my way around the huge school and being late for classes. I wonder if I'll see Alex at orientation and if we'll kiss again when we say hello. *Dream on, Corinna.* I also wonder if Alex will still be wearing his orange shirt all the time, or will it be the year of the blue shirt? I brought back some cool Japanese notebooks with umbrella designs on the covers to remind me of our trip when I'm struggling in math. Maybe Alex will be in math with me again.

It's the day before school starts, and Dad's gone out to buy food for our school lunches, which is a good thing. I'm getting up my nerve to light some incense. I haven't developed the best match-lighting skills, because I've always been scared of getting burned, but here goes.

I drop the first match, managing to burn two fingers *and* the white paint on the mantel. The second match is more success-ful, and I place the incense on the metal toaster-oven tray so it won't burn the wood. I need to find one of those incense holders for next time. I'm not sure if I should talk to the incense or to the flowered ginger jar, but I decide the jar makes more sense. Then I remember to clap, like Aiko told me she does when she is talking to her ancestors.

"So, Mom, Japan was awesome. Thought you'd want to know. We got to meet your famous Japanese family. Aiko showed us some really cool stuff. She told us about Obon and welcoming the dead, so that's what I'm trying to do now. I hope you know you're welcome anytime. I also hope you know how much I miss you. . . . You know how you worried about not knowing your donor father's health stuff? Well, I'm worried about that, too. Like if he *and* you had cancer, what does that mean for me? I hate not being able to talk to you about stuff like that. . . . Dad's doing a good job, but it's not the same as when you were here. I hope you don't mind that we sometimes laugh and have fun. I don't think you would, but I don't want you to think we're not miss-ing you. Because we are. This last year has been really hard."

Then the phone rings and breaks my concentration. I don't know if I should answer it or ignore it. I decide to ignore it, but the loud irritating sound ruins the moment.

"Well, talk to you later, Mom. I love you."

Later in the afternoon, I go back to the mantel and continue the conversation.

"Hi, Mom. It's me again. Do you like the quilt I made? I'm putting it under your ginger jar while I talk to you. High school starts in three days and I'm already in the middle of soccer try-outs. I'm kind of looking forward to school and seeing my friends. But I'm scared, too. I guess that's normal. I hope you won't be too mad that I'm dropping band. I want to take ceramics instead. I'm definitely glad it's a new year, not more of last year. What a difficult year that was. Difficult is an understatement, right? It's still hard when the subject of mothers comes up. It's still a jab to my heart. But the jab is a little bit less painful. Even though I'll still be 'the girl whose mom died,' it's not quite so recent or so raw. It still hurts terribly and I miss you every day, but the hurt isn't such a bottomless pit. It's an invisible tattoo that's a part of me, but it's not all of me."

On the first Tuesday of September, Dad pulls into the staff parking lot on our first morning of going to the same school. I'm relieved to see Joci walking into the main entrance and I call out to her.

"Wait up, Joss."

Then I turn to Dad, who's trying to gather all his papers and stuff that exploded out of his briefcase onto the backseat during the drive.

"See ya, Dad."

His head is still inside the car, but I think he's smiling.

Even though the trip was great, it feels fantastic to be back and have time to hang out with Clare and Joci again. I'm so lucky to have them. Clare understands so much without my having to explain. And Joci's a great friend in so many other ways, even after all those hurts and misunderstandings. I really hope we have a better year together. Sometimes I worry that Joci and her mom will decide that they'd rather go shopping without me. What if Joci and I have another falling out? Then I wouldn't get to see her mom. I can't let that happen. What if Dad gets a girlfriend? What if it's Deborah? I'm definitely not ready to think about *that*.

Dad does seem more himself, but he continues to listen to the Beatles and he's still kind of quiet and sad. We've had some pretty good dinners. The chicken is moister than I'm used to. He might even be a better cook than Mom was. He hasn't tried to make any Japanese deep fried pork *tonkatsu* or minnow and seaweed salad. We're even having a few more laughs around here. I think the trip was really good for him. For us. I hope we'll be okay. I think we will.

ACKNOWLEDGMENTS

I have many people to thank for their support and wisdom on this project: My faithful agent, Cathy Hemming, who believed in the power of Corinna's story; my extraordinarily wise and talented editor, Jen Rees; my inspiring teachers, Jimin Han and Pat Dunn; my fellow writers, especially Tess McGovern, Lisa Cader, Sara Taber, and Michele Myers; my bereavement work colleagues, Mindy Farkus, Patty Donovan Duff, and Jane Cameron; the many people whose stories I had the honor of listening to as their counselor; my graduate school buddies, Barry Rosenberg and Alex Hartz, who were there for me when I needed to know I wasn't alone with my grief; my readers and supportive friends, especially Merna Guttentag, Sue Ringler Pet, Nordeen Morello, Linda Marrow, Linda Spock, Lauren Vinciguerra, Pat Discenza, Naomi Pollock, Liz Miller, Robin Rue, Cynthia Eyster, Sherry Kahn, Deborah DeMille-Wagman, and Josh Steiner; my young readers Susannah, Kathryn, Julia, Abby, Eve, Amanda, Caroline, Clare, and Kaiya; and my family, whose encouragement meant the world to me.

ABOUT THE AUTHOR

Carole Geithner has more than twenty years of experience as a clinical social worker, working in schools, hospitals, and counseling agencies with scores of children who have had a parent die, as well as adults whose childhoods were shaped by parent loss. She is Assistant Clinical Professor of Psychiatry and Behavioral Sciences at George Washington University School of Medicine.

She lives in Maryland with her family. This is her first novel. You can visit her online at www.carolegeithner.com.